BONE BOX

BONE BOX

JAY AMBERG

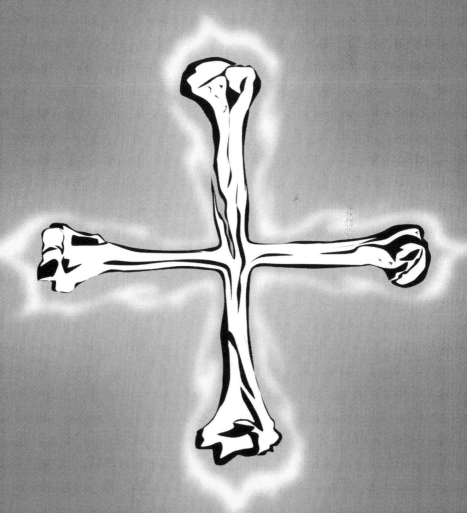

*Thanks to John Manos, Sarah Koz, Mark Larson, and Ann Wambach
for their advice and support.*
Discuss the book at bonebox.jayamberg.com.

BOOKS BY JAY AMBERG

Bone Box
Cycle
America's Fool
Whale Song
52 Poems for Men
AMIKA PRESS

Doubloon
Blackbird Singing
FORGE BOOKS

Deep Gold
WARNER BOOKS

School Smarts
The Study Skills Handbook
The Creative Writing Handbook
GOOD YEAR BOOKS

Verbal Review and Workbook for the SAT
HARCOURT BRACE JOVANOVICH

First Edition   ISBN 13: 978-1-937484-27-9
AMIKA PRESS   53 W Jackson BLVD 660 Chicago IL 60604   847 920 8084
info@amikapress.com   Available for purchase on amikapress.com
Edited by John Manos. Cover art by John Cowlin. Designed & typeset by Sarah Koz. Body in Dante MT, designed by Giovanni Mardersteig and Charles Malin in 1957, digitized by Ron Carpenter in 1993. Titles in Jessen Schrift, designed by Rudolf Koch, 1924–1930, digitized by Ralph M Unger in 2004. Thanks to Nathan Matteson.

For Ayasuluk Hill and Cappadocia and the world's other remarkable sites that have shaped civilization.

⚛ PROLOGUE
ASIA MINOR
FIRST CENTURY OF THE
COMMON ERA

At first light, the old man poured water from the amphora into the earthenware bowl. He slid his hands into the water, leaned over, and splashed sleep from his face. He then combed his fingers through his sparse hair and white beard, shook his hands above the bowl, and stepped from his stone hut into the morning. Though he limped, his gait was quick and deliberate as he followed a path uphill to the edge of a bluff. He stopped in an oval clearing, facing west toward the land and sea that were still dark. He knelt for a few moments in the matted grass and then moved to a low flat stone, where he sat with his legs crossed and his hands folded. His prayer was silent, pure homage to the Creator and His creation. The sun rose behind him, bathing him in light. The pain and stiffness seeped from his bones as he prayed.

When the land glowed and the distant city and harbor shone, he rose, stretched, and returned to his hut. He took a scroll that he had stowed between his mat and the wall and went back into the light. After unrolling the scroll, he reread his words. His hand, though contorted with age, had been constant enough that his lettering was neat. Given all that he had seen and done in his life, he had said finally what he needed to say—perhaps not eloquently, but in a way, he hoped, that others would understand.

He did not take the scroll back into the hut. This was, he knew, the morning, and his testament must outlive him. He walked back toward the bluff and then veered from the path into a stand of pines and scrabbled up through the scent and shade. When he tripped on a root, he grabbed a low branch to catch himself. By the time he reached the glade dappled with light, he was breathing hard. He fell to his knees at the mouth of a small hollow, laid the scroll at his side, brushed away the pine needles, and dug down through the dirt with his fingers until he reached the stone box that only he knew still existed. She had known, of course, but he had held the truth alone now for years.

He pried the box open and shifted the lid. As he gazed into the box, he began to tremble. Slow tremors ran from his shoulders. He had mourned and exalted hundreds of times before, and this was the last. Tears ran down his face, his shuddering quickened, and the pine-scented air filled his chest. Kneeling there, he took an older scroll from the box. His hands shook as he unraveled the document. Just as they had so many years before, the words rang him like a bell. His shuddering at first deepened and then slackened and finally ceased. His breathing slowed. Finally, his hands steady again, he slipped the document back into the box. He stared for a time at the bones she herself had placed there, but he did not touch any of them. He then lifted the scroll he had recently written and placed it in the box as well. His own words lay with the others—safe, he hoped, for a time.

He shut the box's lid, made sure it was tight, and passed his hand over the symbols and inscription. He continued to recall all that had happened until, when he heard voices in the distance, he buried the box with loose soil and pine needles. He crawled backward away from the hollow, brushing the dirt to cover his tracks, and then rested his hands on his knees and bowed his head. For a few moments, his world was pine, birdsong, and bright pools of light.

The old man made his way back to the path and the flat stone on the bluff. He sat facing west, breathing the beauty of the world, waiting for those who were coming. Although he did not welcome this moment, he was not frightened. He gazed past the city and harbor to the sea, a bright sash that bound heaven to earth. A rabbit crossed the clearing, butterflies fluttered above the grass, and gnats rose into the light. The voices were already near. The mob, which must have started from the city before dawn, was almost upon him. The distant sea sparked and flamed in the sunshine.

He rose slowly and turned to face the rabble. The sun blinded him for a second, but as he squinted he recognized the leaders, bearded men with flowing robes and clubs and whips, men he had known well, men with whom he had broken bread and prayed. Pharisees and Elders and Scribes. The younger men and boys who followed held stones in their hands. Three fat crones trailed behind.

He lifted his arms, his hands forward, palms out and fingers down. The horde halted a short distance from him. He looked each of the leaders in the eye, offering forgiveness he knew they could not accept. When the High Priest, a tall man with sharp features and thick lips, raised his whip, their eyes locked—a fleeting balance between love and hate, forgiveness and vengeance, life and death.

The High Priest's lips curled into a sneer. The whip cracked in the air. A guttural roar rose from the pack. The first stone struck the old man's chest, taking his breath and knocking him back almost to the edge of the bluff. He stayed standing even when the next stone shattered his nose. The first lash cut across his face and shoulder. His knees buckled, and he wobbled forward. A strand of spider webbing glowed in the grass. The pines swirled, and the sky quaked. The world reeled and faded through the flailing, the beating, and the tearing.

1

As the Boeing 737 shreds the clouds, the tankers and cargo ships spread out below on the Sea of Marmara. When the plane banks and turns, Joseph Travers peers down at Istanbul's red roofs and myriad minarets pointed like rockets ready to launch. A helicopter wheels above the terminal as the 737 approaches Atatürk International Airport. A lone black bird beats low across the scrub grass between the runways. War is simmering again in the Middle East—as it has been more often than not for thousands of years. But Travers' mission, he believes, is more mediatory than martial. Travers has come to Istanbul the day before his meetings partly to get a feel for the place and partly because there's not much to hold him in Chicago. On the flights over, he skimmed guidebooks about Turkey, particularly Istanbul, but this is his first visit to this part of the world—and he has only an outsider's understanding of the culture. As he passes through the terminal, a woman's voice on the loudspeaker seems to be repeating, "Buy bullets… Buy bullets…" He knows only a few Turkish phrases—*merhaba, lütfen,* and *teşekkür ederim*—"hello" and "please" and "thank you."

The taxi's route into the old city takes Travers along Kennedy Caddesi. The Byzantine wall, which withstood sieges for over a thousand years, rises on his left. On his right, the Sea of Marmara sparks in the late afternoon sunlight. In the narrow strip of park and breakwall between the road and water, men saunter in small groups and families picnic in the intermittent trees' scant shade. The majority of women are veiled, and none strolls alone—but the boys and girls run about playing like children anywhere.

When he checks into the Blue House Hotel, the clerk, a beautiful woman who looks like a young Audrey Hepburn, hands him a handwritten message that reads:

Joseph Travers, it is necessary that we meet today.
Contact me at 547 14 53.
Sophia Altay

Sophia Altay is Travers' reason for coming to Turkey, and he stares at the note as he rides with the bellhop in the narrow elevator. The penmanship is precise but with a flare for serifs. He tips the bellhop and gazes out his room's window at the Blue Mosque's domes and minarets. Neither Altay nor anyone else involved in the Ephesus Project knows he was coming in a day early. His initial meeting is scheduled for seven the next evening at the Pera Palas Hotel. And, though his mission matters to the future funding of her archeological dig, the insistence, even urgency, in Altay's note seems strange. He looks over at the painted ceramic tile hanging on the back of the room's door. Designed to protect against the evil eye, the nazar boncuğu has a black center with concentric outer circles of light blue, white, and dark blue.

He unpacks and washes his face before making the call. A woman's voice with a slight French accent answers on the first ring.

"Sophia Altay?" he asks as he sits down on the bed facing the window.

"Joseph Travers?" Her accent gives his name a subtle lilt.

"Joe," he says, gazing again at the minarets.

"We need to meet this evening, Joseph." Her tone is cool, if not exactly cold, and her statement sounds more like a fact than an idea. Apparently they aren't going to exchange pleasantries about his trip.

"Okay, Ms. Altay," he says. "How about dinner?"

"Yes. The terrace restaurant at your hotel. At twenty-thirty. Eight-thirty. That will give you time to get settled."

His phone, which reset to Istanbul time as the 737 landed, says 5:40. He left O'Hare the afternoon before and had only a ninety-minute lay-over at Heathrow, but he caught a couple of naps in flight and doesn't feel jet-lagged. "Sure," he says. "Good. Will anybody else be there?"

"No, Joseph," she answers. "Just the two of us." There's nothing romantic in her voice.

"Okay. Wear a gardenia in your hair so I recognize you."

"I will know who you are," she says before hanging up.

His breath catches as he listens to the dial tone, that particular sound once again striking him with loss and separation. The Blue Mosque's six minarets, barbed arrows, pierce the sky. His chest hollows, a void that spreads until his ribs feel as though they will blanch and crumble. He turns the phone off, wipes his mouth with his hand, inhales deeply, stands, and crosses to the window.

2

The sky is cobalt, but the sun is already low—and little light reaches the trench in which the two men work. The evening air is hot and still as though it has hung there for centuries. Sweat soaks the stout man's sleeveless T-shirt and mats the gray and white hair on his arms and shoulders. His nose is bulbous above his mustache, the top of his head bald except for long strands of hair hanging limply over his left ear. He grunts as he pushes dirt aside with his trowel. The taller, younger man is more careful, but he, too, breathes hard as he whisks dirt with his brush. The discovery, far more than the exertion, is taking his breath. He is clean-shaven; his features are fine, his black hair thick. Neither man speaks until they have completely uncovered the ancient ossuary, the bone box.

When the stout man stands, his head is still well below the trench line. He stabs the trowel into a pile of dirt, wipes his grimy hands on his pants, pulls up the front of his shirt, and smears the sweat from his face. He picks up an empty plastic water bottle, glares at it, and tosses it next to the trowel. The younger man sets his hands on his hips, catches his breath, and stares at the ossuary. The bone box, a meter long and seventy centimeters wide, seems to glow even in the trench's shadows. Although he can't read the words etched into the stone, he recognizes them as Aramaic. The symbols—the equal-armed cross within the circle within the six-pointed star—are familiar, but their juxtaposition is not.

As the call to prayer begins, a cirrus horsetail swirls through the rectangle of sky. The voice barely carries into the trench, but the two men turn and stand still. The heavy man murmurs prayers, and the thin one bows his head in silence, his prayer of a different sort. A prayer of both gratitude and supplication. A prayer that this ossuary is what he yearns for it to be. The cloud's wispy tail snaps clear.

When the echo of prayer ceases, the stout man squats and digs his fingers under the corners of the bone box.

"Wait!" the young man says in Turkish. "She should be here. We *must* wait for her."

Glowering across the box, the stout man grabs the hand-pick he used earlier.

"No!" The young man stoops and presses his palms on the ossuary's lid. "She must open it." His face reddens, and his fingers burn as though the ossuary is too sacred, too hallowed, too inviolable, to be touched by humans.

The stout man swings the pick across the young man's knuckles.

The young man leaps back, his eyes wide. His mouth opens, but words don't form. Blood beads on the index and middle fingers of his right hand.

The stout man leans over and jams the pick's tip under the rim of the ossuary's lid. As he pushes the handle with both hands, getting his weight into it, the lid creaks open. Keeping the pick in place as a wedge, he kneels and runs his stubby fingers under the lid. Stale air rises as he lifts the lid, holds it to his sweating chest, and stares into the box.

Despite himself, despite his stinging fingers and welling tears, the young man steps forward and peers into the box. Making the sign of the cross repeatedly, he takes a series of deep breaths in an unsuccessful attempt to calm himself. Blood trickles down his hand and drops, bright splotches darkening into sandy soil. Blinding sacrosanct light rises from the ossuary, weaving around them and spiraling from the trench. He glances at the stout man who is unable to see the light, runs his hand through his hair, and gazes back into the box. He cannot draw his eyes from the contents, though his pupils might at any second be seared and his skin peel away. The moment is every bit as frightening as it is exhilarating. His blood boils—the Janissary blood, the blood of his lost ancestors, the wanderers and cave dwellers alike. There is much more to this even than he imagined, much more to it than she will at first believe.

⚰ 3

Needing to walk before meeting with Sophia Altay, Joseph Travers leaves his room key at the front desk and heads out into Istanbul's early evening. Over the three years since Jason's death, long walks have become necessary for him, as essential as breathing. He went out at all times, light and dark, and in all weather, external and internal. He walked sometimes for hours until, at least for a few moments, he trekked beyond the void. And often those walks were the only thing that allowed his head to clear and his thoughts to settle.

A skinny young man, probably in his late teens, attaches himself to Travers before he crosses the street. The boy falls into step, says hello, and asks in passable English where he's going.

Travers doesn't think *walking through sadness* would work as an answer so he says, "The Blue Mosque."

"I will show you the way," the boy says, pointing along the Cavalry Bazaar.

Shaking his head, Travers says, "Thanks anyway, but it's not really necessary."

"It's no problem," the boy answers without missing a step. His smile is wide, his teeth crooked.

The bazaar's carpet and handicraft shops encroach on the mosque's property, and Travers has a fleeting thought that someone with a stronger sense of the sacred might well wind cord into whip. While they climb the steps and cross to the mosque's visitors' entrance, the boy asks where in America Travers is from. When he tells him, the boy says that his brother visited Chicago and that his cousin lives in LA. As an older man with packets of postcards approaches, the boy snarls something in Turkish that must mean, "Get away from my goddamned pigeon." After reminding Travers to remove his shoes and carry them in one of the plastic bags provided, he mentions that his family owns a carpet shop at the other end of the bazaar and that he'll be waiting for Travers at the mosque's exit.

Travers wasn't really able to focus on the mosque's exterior while he was being steered toward the entrance, but the interior takes his breath. It's enormous—and empty, with no pews and no altar. Small lights, fastened to circular bars hanging from hundreds of wires, illuminate the elaborate blue tilework. Men prostrate themselves on the prayer rugs facing the ornate mihrab, which marks the direction of Mecca. The minbar, a high elegant pulpit used by the imam to preach, stands to the right of the mihrab. Half a dozen children run about on the carpets in the vast space under the central dome. Women pray in an isolated niche on the periphery. They all have their heads covered, something that reminds Travers of the uniformed girls kneeling in Prescott's Saint Joseph's Academy chapel when he was very young. His mother was the school nurse, and she would sometimes bring him with her to work when he was himself too young for school. He liked her small white office with its neat stacks of medical supplies. And, as he sat in the back of the chapel with his mother at the weekly masses, the girls' high voices ascended in song, their Latin chants rising through the soft, stained-glass light and sweet candle scent.

Now, he stands on the periphery as well. He hasn't prayed in recent years, hasn't really been able to, but the mosque seems a good spot for it. He leans against a pillar for twenty minutes, waiting, but no chant wells up through the emptiness. Incapable of even an Our Father or a Hail Mary, he's struck instead by how isolated he feels. He hasn't yet seen another American, mostly because after the wars in Iraq and Afghanistan many of his countrymen aren't traveling to any Islamic nation, even a secular one. And Turkey's role as America's ally is becoming increasingly ambiguous as the anti-Americanism in the region becomes more rabid. A young man is lurking outside the mosque's exit and a woman is meeting him for dinner, but he still feels ostracized by language and religion and culture.

Before Travers has time to tie the laces on his walking shoes, the skinny boy is on him again. Travers sits on a ledge in the mosque's courtyard, looks over at the ablutions fountain, and tells the boy, repeatedly, that he's just arrived in the country and isn't going to look at, much less buy, any carpets. He came to Istanbul, at least in part, because in a world gone awry he needs to be taken by something magical, even perhaps a carpet ride, but he isn't buying anything just yet.

The boy is gone less than two minutes before another rug peddler hits on Travers. He is short and swarthy, and his English is halting—but he's still able to promise a better deal than whatever the young man offered. Travers retreats through the courtyard's exit into what's left of the Hippodrome. The Brazen Column, the Egyptian Obelisk plundered from Luxor, and the Serpentine Column taken from Delphi are all that remain of the huge stadium that was Constantinople's hub. He walks through the park thinking about the layers of fallen empires here—Egyptian, Macedonian, Roman, Byzantine, and Ottoman. He sits, finally, on a park bench by a fountain in a garden halfway between the Blue Mosque and Hagia Sophia, the 1,500-year-old Byzantine church. As the sun slips behind the stone wall, the light holds on the golden tips of the domes of both the mosque and the former church.

Travers watches the young men with their cell phones, the families with their veiled women, and the children racing to and from the fountain. Two boys, dressed in matching blue shorts and shirts, squabble near him, their words unclear but their tones unmistakable. For a moment, he is watching his own sons, Tom and Jason. He misses that squabbling, in a sense longs for it, though he knows he'll never again be referee or arbiter—or father. So much attention was given to Jason, the prodigal son, that Tom, as the dutiful firstborn, finally came to feel estranged. That and Tom's current need to keep peace with his mother still require a certain distance from Travers that neither of them ever mentions in their biweekly calls.

⌖ 4

The call to prayer begins as Travers steps out of the elevator onto the Blue House Hotel's rooftop. He finds himself up among the trees with the Blue Mosque looming on his right and the Sea of Marmara, darkly silver in the fading light, shimmering on his left. Her back to the mosque, Sophia Altay sits reading a sheaf of papers at a corner table. There's no gardenia, but he knows who she is because only two other tables are occupied, one by two young men and the other by a middle-aged couple. The amplified chant reverberates around the terrace. Travers stands for a moment listening to the plaintive, almost mournful prayer coming from the loudspeakers fixed to the mosque's minarets. Distant voices call from other parts of the city.

When a waiter approaches, Travers points to Altay. The waiter nods and waves Travers toward her. She is a petite woman in her late thirties, perhaps ten years younger than he is, with a narrow face and black hair that flows down her back in a loose braid. Her pale green blouse is buttoned up to her gold rope necklace. Her head is tilted, and her concentration is so complete that she doesn't notice him until he stands by her table. She glances up, quickly closes the folder over the printed sheets she was reading, and looks up again. Her eyes are almond-shaped, hazel, and so bright that he takes half a step back.

"Joseph Travers," she says, her accent again making his name sound exotic.

"Hello, Ms. Altay," he says, not taking his eyes from hers. They are more green than brown, perhaps because of the color of her blouse, and they shine in a stunning feline way. *Cat Woman*, he thinks. *I'm having dinner with the Cat Woman.*

She gestures toward the chair across from her, and he sits down. He can see the mosque's central dome and minarets over her shoulder. The sea glimmers off to the side. And her eyes don't blink. He sucks in his breath, picks up the cloth napkin, and wads it in his lap.

She slides her folder into a red and gold woven cloth bag, sets the bag on the floor next to her, and says, "Welcome to Turkey, Joseph."

"Joe," he answers. "Thanks."

They sit there in silence for a minute before the waiter comes over and asks him if he wants something to drink.

"Yes," he says. "Red wine. Turkish." He looks at her half-empty tea cup. "Can I... Would you like something?"

"Perhaps with dinner," she answers.

"A bottle of the house red," he says to the waiter. "Thank you."

They sit silently again for another minute. Her face tapers toward her chin. Her nose is thin, and her mouth is full, giving her an unconventional but striking beauty. Finally, he says, "So, Ms. Altay, how did you find me?"

She makes a steeple of her fingers and almost smiles. "Your sister," she says.

He laughs. His sister, three years his senior and his travel agent, has, for close to half a century, been a little bossy and, conversely, lax with the details of his personal life. "You talked with her?"

"Email," she says. "She seems quite nice."

Figuring she must have gotten the name and address of his travel agency through the Glavine Foundation, he asks, "What else did she tell you?"

"Nothing relevant."

Her answer seems more curt than it needs to be, and they lapse again into silence. She sips her tea, and he looks out to sea where a tugboat is nudging the bow of a massive tanker. The two men seated near them take out a digital camera and giggle as they compose photos of each other in the candlelight. The older man and woman smoke cigarettes and speak in exhausted voices with British accents. The waiter brings the wine, has Travers taste it, and pours two glasses. Travers raises his wine glass to propose a toast—to Turkey, to the Ephesus Project, to good food, to life, to anything—but he can't tell yet if he and Altay have any common ground at all.

They order dinner. He drinks his wine, and she finishes her tea. A cell phone in her bag rings, but she doesn't answer it. Travers' own phone, an old Motorola model he thinks of as his Amish phone, is down in his room. After Jason's death, he got rid of all of his advanced devices—the technology was too constant a reminder. And when he laid himself off from Motorola, he took only the Amish, which makes calls, sends text messages, and tells time, but has no frills at all.

Altay dabs her lips with her napkin and then locks on him with those feline eyes. "Why did you arrive a day early?" she asks.

He shrugs. "I wanted to see the city."

"Why are you here?"

He has numerous answers to that question but says only, "To check on the Selçuk sites. Make a status report for the Glavine Foundation."

She folds her hands and leans forward. "Why?"

"I sit on the Glavine Foundation board."

She stares at him. "But why *now?*"

He leans back and brushes his hand across his mouth. The Cat Woman's eyes are spectacular, but he doesn't like the way she's looking at him. "Bill Glavine asked me to. He's an old friend. A college buddy."

"And you've kept in touch all these years?"

"Not exactly. But our lives crossed pretty regularly in business. And he invited me to join the board last year."

She nods, and then her eyes fix on his. "And your role is..." She waves, her hand a quick specter in the candlelight. "As a corporate executive you recently fired scores of people..." Her smile is cross. "...including yourself. And now you've leapt at the chance to come here."

"Maybe, Ms. Altay," he says, "we should chat a little. Get to know each other a bit. Maybe talk about this with the others tomorrow night."

The waiter brings a long flat loaf of bread on a wooden plank, but she doesn't even look at it. Shaking her head, she asks, "*Why* are you really here?"

Ripping the end off the loaf, which smells wonderful, he meets her gaze. "I told you I'm here to visit the sites, get to know the operation, make an evaluation."

She puts her hands flat on the table as though she's about to pounce. "An evaluation? Come on," she hisses, "you know nothing about archeology. What is your *actual* agenda?" Her English, fired up, sounds British.

Anger rises in his belly. His real agenda is complex, but it has little to do with her or the Ephesus Project or archeology or the current state of international relations or, for that matter, anything geopolitical. His life is bounded by personal loss, not financial or political gain. It's not that he doesn't care, but his concerns are private, not public, his outposts and checkpoints internal. He tosses his napkin onto the table and says, "Ms. Altay, *why* did you want to meet this evening."

Half standing, she leans across the table. Her eyes are William Blake's tiger's. "If you think you can come here and ax me, you're wrong. I'll fight you tooth and nail."

"What?" he blurts.

"Saint John's is my site, and neither you nor any of those other..." She pauses. "...*gentlemen*...are going to terminate me. My work...the work...is important. More important than any of you can comprehend. I know what I'm doing. And I'll run the site as I see fit."

"What are you talking about?" He had a few meetings blow up on him over the years, but he generally knew beforehand both the odds and the causes—corporate intrigue or antithetical goals or personal vendettas among the participants.

She reaches for her bag, stands, and glares at him.

"What the heck are you talking about?" he repeats.

She twists the bag's strap around her hand, but the glint in her eyes softens. "You really don't know what's going on, do you?" she says, more incredulous than furious.

"I know this..." He passes his hand over the bread. "...I know that dinner...this meeting's...a mess. That you assume I'm here to do something I'm not. That whatever's happening makes you...angry." He picks up the piece of bread and drops it again. "But, no, I don't know anything about what you're saying."

She stands there, one arm extended, one hand holding the bag's strap against her hip, her head cocked—a girl making like a little teapot. She's a head shorter than he is, maybe five-foot-three, and her waist and hips are svelte in her long khaki skirt.

"Sophia," he says, "let's start over." He rises and offers her his hand. "Hi. I'm Joe."

She looks at his hand, gazes into his eyes one more time as if checking to make sure he really isn't her executioner, slides her bag to the floor, and shakes his hand. "Hello, Joe," she says.

"Would you like to have dinner?"

Glancing at the darkening sea, she says, "No… Yes…yes, I would." When they're seated again, she adds, "You really don't know what's happening here, do you?"

"Apparently not." In his career, he made sure he was always prepared for meetings. He'd always done his homework, and thorough preparation was often his edge. Though he knew he hadn't gotten up to speed here, he didn't think he would be so completely out of step. He picks up the piece of bread again, breaks it, and finally takes a bite. He then pours himself another glass of wine and raises his glass—but not in a toast. "I'm here for a lot of reasons having to do with my own life," he says, "but I promise I'm not here to fire you. Or to close your site." He sips the wine. "Maybe you can tell me why you think I am."

Her phone rings again, and she leans over, reaches into her bag, and mutes it. She raises her glass, swirls the wine, bites her lip, and begins to talk about her work as the director of the Ephesus Project in Selçuk. As she speaks, other customers arrive. The waiter brings tomato and cucumber salad to the table. Across the terrace, two young women in long green skirts play music on traditional Turkish instruments. The oud player looks Arabic, and the flute player appears European— and their songs are sad and beautiful. A single star gleams between the mosque's minarets. Altay's sea bass arrives with its head and tail before the waiter prepares it for her tableside. The vegetables in Travers' shish kebab taste as though they were picked that afternoon. The German narration from the Blue Mosque's light show sounds like a distant diatribe.

When Altay mentions for the second time that Leopold Kirchburg has summoned her to Istanbul so that her employment can be terminated, Travers asks, "But does he actually have the power to fire you?"

She finishes her wine and puts down her glass. "Yes. And no. The Herr Professor has organized and consolidated the archeological

sites around İzmir under his directorship of the Aegean Association."
Shadows from the candle play across her face. "He has developed...
cultivated a mutually beneficial relationship with the Turkish Ministry of Culture whereby he receives all of the credit for the finds and Turkish museums receive the artifacts."

Travers pours each of them another glass of wine. "But...," he says as he finishes.

"My...Saint John's is an Aegean Association site but is funded by the Glavine Foundation. American philanthropics fund a number of the Aegean sites."

"So he's the association's director, but he's not the money."

"Exactly." She takes a sip of her wine and looks into his eyes. "He's a brilliant academician. The heir of Austrian aristocrats. A thorough organizer and an ambitious director." The sea bass and the wine and the music and the conversation about her work have tempered her antagonism, but an edge is returning to her voice. "However, he abhors the heat and sun and dust of the sites in summer."

"Prefers Vienna's clime and culture?" Travers asks. "A director in absentia?"

"Exactly. He'll condescend to meet here in Istanbul, but he hasn't visited Saint John's in a year." She sips her wine and cocks her head. "Too much grit for him."

"But from what you've told me," he says, "it sounds like the site is running smoothly."

Her eyes fire. "It is. I've followed his directives to the letter. All year. Everything *exactly* to his specifications."

Travers drinks his wine, feeling its warmth seep through him. "Then, what's the problem?"

"Leopold is..." She stops herself, takes a breath, and banks the fire in her eyes. "I and some of my staff have begun a supplementary dig that we work *only* after all of our Ephesus Project tasks have been completed each day." She takes another sip of wine and glares across the table. "We are digging without Leopold's explicit permission. He loathes that I am taking initiative."

Looking in her eyes, Travers sees both how deeply compelling and absolutely defiant she can be. "But that doesn't sound actionable," he says, "at least not enough to terminate you. It sounds more personal."

Her eyes spark again for an instant, and then she looks away for the first time. "The problem," she says to her wine glass, "is professional."

⟊ 5

The young man sits in the last seat in the back of the first Kent coach out of İzmir in the morning. The sun is well up, the passing fields bright. Though his backpack is stowed in the luggage compartment, his second bag stands on the floor between his legs. He is cramped in the seat, but he needs to touch the bag…to be in constant contact with it. He leans his head against the window away from the fat man next to him who farts garlic and snores.

When the young man failed to reach the director by phone the evening before, he did what he had to do and fled into town on the local bus. He hunched in an alley doorway, praying all night for an ephemeral peace, but he did not sleep. The cold mortar scraped him, and every noise spooked him. Rodents with gleaming eyes skittered around him, but he remained vigilant, his anxiety over what he did and what he possessed keeping him awake then and keeping him alert now.

Once he boarded the coach at dawn, he noted the arrival of each of the other passengers, even the women and children. No one was familiar except for one man who sat up front with his family…a man from his past, but not a digger or a preservationist. A man whose middle-aged paunch and receding hair reminded him all too much of his debasement. The man pretended not to notice him, and no else has spoken to him. Though fear keeps stirring his bowels, he should be safe, at least while he is on the bus. When the ubermeister realizes what has happened, he will loose the hellhounds on him, but they should not be hunting him yet. They will pursue him to the ends of the earth and wreak vengeance upon him. He has done the right thing, he is sure, but that won't stop the hellhounds.

He gazes at the scabs forming on the knuckles of his right hand. The cuts still sting, especially when he closes his hand. He should have waited for the director, should have talked with her as usual, should have let her make the decision. But she was away, and there was no time. The fires of betrayal burned white, and he had to act decisively. He had to save the ossuary's contents, preserve the holy relics, at any cost. Though the artifacts are inscrutable, he *knows* in his bones that they are more important than his life. What he has done is a sin, but necessary, the lesser evil to prevent the greater iniquity.

His right elbow rests on the narrow track at the base of the window. His arm vibrates as the wheels roll across the pavement. His reflection in the window jiggles, but his eyes still meet his eyes, noting the contradictions that have always been there—the face of both continents, the mixed heritage that others sense despite his attempts to conform, the features that attract women, especially older women, to whom he is not attracted. His name, Abrahim, must somehow give him away. Or, more likely, his eyes. They are brown—but not dark like his countrymen's—rather the color of sand.

He stares at his reflection. He thought conservation would enable him to bridge the chasm he felt. And it did for a time. Preservation crosses cultures. Working with people from Europe and the States as well as his countrymen, he has unearthed Islamic and Christian artifacts. He has pieced together Roman tiles and Greek amphoras. Shards don't care whose blood flows through him. And the director, at least, accepted that he is who he is. But will she understand why he has snatched the ossuary's contents from her as well as from the ubermeister and the hellhounds? Will she forgive him?

Passing out tea and wafers, the coach's steward has twice tried to make eye contact, but Abrahim will look only at his own reflection in the glass. He has done what he has done. But for all his depravity, he never would have sold out the relics. Not for any amount of money.

Not even to save his life. He would never sell his soul to save his life. And now he must continue to flee the site, the town, the area. He cannot go home. They will look for him there. He knows where he must go instead. When he reaches Kayseri, he will find a café and email her. He will explain what he has left for her, what he has hidden, and what he has taken. From Kayseri, he will vanish into the heart of Anatolia.

ⵟ 6

Joseph Travers walks Istanbul the next day. He starts with Topkapi Palace's grounds—the gardens and pavilions but not the harem or treasury. He needs to be outside and moving, in the sun and heat. When he called the Glavine International office the night before, William Glavine, Jr., admitted there were staffing issues with the Selçuk-Saint John's Cathedral dig that they hadn't discussed, but he told Travers it was a matter of ego and turf not life and death—and nothing, given Travers' business background and mediation skills, he couldn't handle. In fact, Glavine had asked him to represent the Foundation's interests in Turkey *because* the site evaluation was essentially a personnel matter rather than an archeological problem.

As Travers walks among the pavilions in the palace gardens, his mind shifts, as it inevitably does early in his treks, to the losses in his life. In an attempt to root himself in the present, Travers stops at a lily pond by the Baghdad Pavilion. He breathes the sweet blossoms and watches the carp ripple the water, but he still can't help remembering the exact moment his ex-wife, Mary, called his office, hysterical and incoherent, screaming about Jason and the BMW. It took Travers a moment to comprehend that there had been no accident. Fire burst in Travers' belly and flamed through him producing, paradoxically, an icy sweat that froze his breathing. Choked, he gaped at the pen in his hand, the notes scrawled on the legal pad, and the sheaf of contracts—all objects suddenly and utterly alien. Mary ranted on, but he was already bound by fire and ice. And when she hung up, the buzzing began. The long walks ensued through every season and locale. Here at the lily pond, a carp's tail breaks the water's surface, a quick pop followed by concentric circles spreading outward.

Leaving Topkapi's grounds, Travers passes the Executioner's Fountain where the sultan's minion washed off the blood after public beheadings. He then circles Hagia Sophia without going in to see the church's famous mosaics of the Savior and Virgin. Instead, he heads deeper into the city toward the Grand Bazaar. When he pauses at Constantine's Column, the last flame-darkened remnant of the emperor's forum, he notices a man in a pale yellow shirt also stop forty feet behind him on the sidewalk. The man was lurking earlier by Topkapi's Gate of Salutations, and with his light skin, closely cropped brown hair, and thick neck, he looks to Travers more European than Turkish.

When Travers begins to walk again, his yellow-shirted shadow crosses Divanyolu Caddesi and trails along the other side of the street pretending to window-shop. The road rises gradually, and Travers quickens his pace on the steeper grades and slows on the flatter stretches. He's not imagining his shadow keeping a regular interval behind him, but he can't understand *why*. He's carrying nothing of value, has no information anyone would want, and isn't meeting anybody.

More confused than frightened, he keeps altering his pace. He expected a sense of mystery, of adventure, something emanating from Istanbul itself. The Islamic overlay on the Byzantine city, though, diminishes any sense of the exotic. A man is tailing him, but no dark-eyed beauty beckons from an alleyway. And all his trekking the last three years has put him at ease on foot—if not in mind—almost anywhere. The Grand Bazaar itself is merely a huge shopping mall with thousands of small stalls and stores including hundreds selling gold jewelry. He serpentines through the throng and leaves the bazaar through the rear exit—but doesn't shake the shadow.

The warren of narrow streets beyond the bazaar is crowded. Vendors pushing carts peddle all manner of stuff from incense sticks to plastic scuba diver dolls. The veiled women shop in groups, and the men smoke and chat. The national government in Ankara may be rattling swords, but in Istanbul's streets none of the words or gestures seems political. People are simply leading their lives, buying and selling, eating, drinking tea, and talking endlessly. The Spice Bazaar at least smells marvelous, and there are scores of herbal aphrodisiacs among the spices and seeds and sweets sold in the stalls. The shadow, not the city, is causing the muscles in Travers' neck and shoulders to tighten.

Travers stops on the steps of the New Mosque, finished in 1633. The shadow keeps his distance, loitering at the souvenir booths on the side street. As Travers sits on the twenty-third step and drinks a bottle of water, he looks across the Golden Horn at Galata Tower where the Ephesus Project dinner is scheduled that evening. Tour boats dock along the shoreline, and traffic streams across the bridge. Sophia Altay talked a lot about her work and explained at least some of what caused her to believe he had come to Istanbul to fire her, but she did not say why she was undertaking the supplemental dig or what specifically she was looking for. She was certainly passionate about archeology, but she remained guarded about what she actually sought. She expected him to believe her version of the power struggle occurring at Saint John's and to trust her, something that wasn't all that easy at this point in his life. But she wasn't herself offering trust, or anything else, in return. If there was any quid pro quo, he missed it.

Near the bottom of the New Mosque's steps, the shadow reaches for postcards with his left hand. Even at that distance his nose looks crooked, as though it has been broken more than once. Holding the bottle of water to his temple, Travers notices a second man, neither peddler nor tourist, standing at a nearby kiosk holding a plastic replica of a mosque. The man is older than the shadow, darker and heavier and more nondescript in black pants and a plain blue shirt—but he's every bit as out of place.

Travers' breath catches; his skin prickles. Are they some surveillance tag team? Or is the older guy shadowing the younger? His mind, Travers thinks, is playing tricks—delayed jet lag or some deeper disorientation. But it's not in his head. The two men are standing down there, thirty feet apart, each pretending to scrutinize some mundane trinket. The younger is keeping a furtive eye on Travers, and the older is waiting for someone to make a move. Something is happening here. What it is isn't exactly clear, but Travers is already involved.

Travers gulps the rest of the water and bolts through the crowd. He climbs quickly through the steep streets and alleys toward Suleyman's Mosque. He rounds a corner, clambers up the street, and rounds another corner. Panting, he looks over his shoulder but doesn't see either shadow. A sour odor permeates the narrow lane, but it might only be his agitation. It's not the place or the crowd but the sense of being sucked into something unfamiliar that's causing sweat to roll down his face and chest.

He doesn't slow until he reaches Suleyman's Mosque. The mosque's courtyard provides shade and a stunning vista of Istanbul's sprawl across the Golden Horn, but Travers is too uneasy to settle there under the flowering trees. As he paces the path along the mosque's wall, a young couple strolls by, but no one else is around. He circles the mosque past the Muvakkithane Gateway where the mosque's astronomer determined the times for prayer. The four minarets rise into the azure sky, and the graveyard spreads below a canopy of trees. The tomb of Suleyman the Magnificent, the Ottomans' greatest ruler, gleams in the mottled sunlight.

Finally, Travers is able to sit on a bench by the mosque's exterior wall overlooking the Golden Horn. His breathing slows, and the sweat on his chest and back cools. The young man and woman are seated on the lawn in a patch of shade. She is thin and dark; he has black hair and sharp facial features. The cars and trucks and boats and pedestrians—the Golden Horn's bustling commercial traffic—suggest that nothing out of the ordinary could possibly be occurring. But it is, within Travers and around him. He gazes over at the couple under the tree. They are hardly speaking, a soft word now and then, and barely touching, her left hand grazing his right. Four months before, when Christine said good-bye and walked out of his condo for the last time, Travers felt a pure and vast emptiness. She is still very much on his mind, and he longs for her touch, even the simple quotidian contact they shared for six years.

Now, seated in spotted shade surrounded by incandescent light, he feels more estranged than empty—disconnected from everyone and everything. And yet, he's being followed by *two* men. Or not. Shaking his head, he smiles. Here he is, utterly alone in Istanbul at Turkey's most sacred Islamic site overlooking the juncture between Europe and Asia, and he's imagining he's being stalked. Laughter starts choking out through the tension, lopsided chunks from deep within him. The couple glances at him, the woman smiling demurely.

Three minutes later, when the laughter finally subsides, Travers gathers himself and goes back around the mosque past Suleyman's tomb, out the gate, and toward the cabstand behind the mosque. Heat rises in waves from the hood of the first taxi. And Travers is not imagining any of whatever is happening. The second shadow, the heavyset man in the blue shirt, leans against the back of the taxi. His arms are folded across his chest, and he's scowling at exactly nothing. Up close, he looks like the second rug peddler's brother at the Blue Mosque. Travers no longer feels jangled, but he wants no confrontation either. He cuts into a narrow lane, and on the hot, hurried walk back toward his hotel, he feels haunted by history he doesn't understand.

⟟⧂⟟ 7

Nihat Monuglu meets Travers in the Blue House Hotel lobby at 6:45. Pushing fifty, he's short and stocky—heavily muscled and bald and ruddy and round-faced with a thick mustache going gray. His Mercedes sedan, though clean, smells of smoke. He talks constantly, inquiring about Travers' trip and welcoming him to the country on behalf of the Ministry of Culture. He offers Travers a Yenidje Régie Turque from his gold-plated cigarette case, telling him that it is the finest Turkish tobacco. When Travers declines, he doesn't himself smoke.

As Monuglu snakes through traffic with aggressive nonchalance, Travers glances out the window at the sideview mirror. If there are any shadows following, they are likely catching exhaust fumes and little else—but he's still uneasy. When he returned to his hotel, the bright-eyed clerk seemed to have glanced at him differently than she had the day before. And his room had been searched, his papers riffled and his clothes rummaged. Everything had been gone through and then too carefully rearranged, as though somebody wanted him to know his room and his belongings were fair game. Three briefing folders he had left on the desk were now alphabetized. And it wasn't a maid: a masculine odor permeated the room.

Monuglu and Travers cross the Galata Bridge and circle up a hill away from the Golden Horn. A valet takes the Mercedes at the entrance to the Pera Palace Hotel, and, as Monuglu ushers Travers through the lobby, he chants a litany of the hotel's famous and powerful patrons, including Mata Hari, Jackie Onassis, and Atatürk himself. The first of their group to arrive at the Grand Orient Bar, Monuglu and Travers sit at a round table in the center of the room. Fewer than a dozen other customers are there, and it occurs to Travers that maybe none of Istanbul's establishments catering to a foreign clientele is busy. Wars flaring in the region and continuing monetary troubles have, among other side effects, made Istanbul less international—a fact Monuglu assiduously ignores as he continues to extol the city's virtues. Travers listens and nods, but he's wary as well; Monuglu's manic friendliness is almost as disconcerting as the shadows' silent presence earlier.

"Raki," Monuglu says. "You must try the raki." He glances at the bartender, stands, and swings a fifth chair around to the table. He then lumbers to the bar, where he greets the bartender as though they are old friends.

The bar has a large mirror behind it, in which Travers can see Monuglu laughing and chatting with the bartender. Ornate chandeliers hang from the high gold and white ceiling. Rugs spread across the inlaid wood floor, and the armchair Travers sits in is lumpy. In fact, the whole place sports trappings of a British Victorian bar a century past its prime. Only the jackhammer outside obliterating the bar's piped-in Turkish music rivets Travers to the present.

Monuglu leads the bartender back with a tray of five short glasses of clear liquid and five tall glasses of ice water. When Monuglu pours the syrupy liquid into Travers' water glass, the concoction turns cloudy and white. As he mixes his own drink, a tall thin man appears in the bar's doorway below the antique rifle hanging on the wall. He surveys the area, says something to the bartender, and struts toward the table with long strides and thrown-back shoulders.

Looking up from his task, Monuglu says, "Herr Professor Kirchburg, mein alt Freunde."

The man waves his hand over the raki and says, "Nihat, old man, I see that, as per usual, you're conjuring white lightning for a visitor." His accent is German, his English British.

Monuglu stands, shakes the man's hand, and turns to Travers. "Joseph," he says, "I would like you to meet Professor Leopold Kirchburg, the founder and director of the Aegean Association."

"Herr Travers," Kirchburg says, "we have been awaiting your arrival. Welcome to the cradle of civilization."

"Thanks," Travers says, nodding. "I'm glad to be here." The man is in his late fifties, fair-skinned, and at least six-foot-six. His blond hair, specked with white, reaches the collar of his maroon sport-shirt, and his neatly trimmed beard swirls with gray and white as well as blond and brown. His pale blue eyes take Travers in and size him up.

"Please," Monuglu says, gesturing to the chair between them. "Have a raki."

"I've ordered a Tanqueray and tonic," Kirchburg says, wrapping himself into the chair opposite Monuglu. He crosses his leg and, swiveling toward Travers, points at the raki. "Poison," he says. "Pure Ottoman poison." He glances quickly over his shoulder at the bartender.

"You have found your accommodations satisfactory?"

"Yes, sure," Travers answers. As he sips the raki, which tastes too much like licorice, the jackhammer looses a particularly strident riff. "You've just arrived, too?"

"Ja," Kirchburg answers. "I'm staying at the Çırağan Palace Hotel, if you need to contact me."

Monuglu leans forward with his gold-plated case open and says, "Yenidje, Herr Professor?"

Kirchburg takes a cigarette without comment. Monuglu snaps the case shut, brings out an old-fashioned Zippo, and lights first Kirchburg's and then his own cigarette. Monuglu inhales deeply, sits back, and exhales over his shoulder.

"I trust that the Glavines are well," Kirchburg says, smoke escaping his nostrils.

The Aegean Association, existing only as an umbrella organization, depends on outside sources for much of its funding, and Glavine's father, William, Sr., has been footing bills for the Selçuk-Saint John's excavation site for the past seven years. "I haven't seen father or son since the April board meeting," Travers admits. "But Bill and I have talked half a dozen times." He smiles and shakes his head. "Between work and the new baby, he's a little busy." Eight months earlier, Travers was one of 425 guests at Bill Glavine's third wedding. He and Glavine had first met at Georgetown when as undergraduates they both tended bar at The Tombs, the campus hangout. After college, Glavine went to work for his father, eventually taking the family construction company international and making hundreds of millions of dollars. Travers and Glavine reconnected when during the technology boom Motorola was building additional factories worldwide. After Travers' departure from Motorola, he joined the Glavine Foundation board. And he accepted Glavine's offer to visit the excavation sites in Turkey, even though Glavine was more than a little vague on the details. After all, Glavine's new wife had just given birth to her first child, his fifth, a boy.

As he reaches for his raki, Travers adds, "Bill's father is convalescing well, but the second stroke has slowed him down a lot."

Kirchburg raises an eyebrow, rocks his foot, and nods to the bartender, who slips the gin and tonic onto the table. He lifts the glass, holding it with his fingertips as the cigarette dangles between his fingers. "To the history we unearth, gentlemen," he says.

"Here, here," Monuglu says before taking a long pull on his raki.

"Joseph," Kirchburg says, "you will, no doubt, immediately note what needs to be done at the Saint John's excavation site." He swirls the ice in his glass three times before sipping the drink. "I am to understand, am I not, that you are prepared to provide the Glavines' consent to my decisions?"

Travers shrugs. He has, in the last twenty-four hours, realized that he doesn't know exactly what's on Bill's mind, much less his father's. Thoughts of the shadows following him and his room's search make him hesitate. "What, Professor Kirchburg," he asks, "is the problem?"

Kirchburg sips his drink and licks his lips. "*She* will be here shortly." He glances at Monuglu, who blows smoke at the chandelier.

The jackhammer's thunder fails to drown the music which has taken a turn into Seventies British disco.

Travers looks at the grape motif in the stained glass of the arched upper windows of the bar. "And *she* is?"

Kirchburg mashes the half-smoked butt of his cigarette in the ashtray and strokes his beard. "Both Fräulein Altay and Herr Lee should have been here by now," he says, glancing at his gold Tag Heuer. "It's typical of her to be late, but Charles is usually punctual. Isn't that true, Nihat?"

"He is," Monuglu says. He takes out his cigarette case again, but Kirchburg shakes his head.

Yes, he is, Travers thinks, watching the man who has to be Charles Lee stride briskly into the bar. A fit, good-looking guy about Travers' height, with short brown hair and a square face, he has that American self-assurance that shows in his gait. His khaki suitcoat is unbuttoned, and his red and blue striped tie jounces as he moves. He carries a can of Coca-Cola in his right hand.

Monuglu rises to greet Lee.

"I apologize, Nihat," Lee says, shaking Monuglu's hand. "A necessary delay." His drawl makes the last word sound like *dahlay*. He nods to Kirchburg. "Leopold, mein Freunde."

Waving his cigarette case, Monuglu introduces Travers. Lee's handshake is firm. He is tan and well-built, with shoulders as broad as Monuglu's and a waist as thin as Kirchburg's. His suit is freshly pressed, his tie's windsor knot impeccable. A miniature gold eagle, wings spread in flight, is pinned to his lapel. His small eyes are blue, but a far deeper shade than the Austrian's. Although he's a few years younger than Travers, his age is starting to show in lines around his eyes.

A Glavine Foundation memo informed Travers that Lee, the new Associate Director of the Eagle Consortium, was a faux good ol' boy with lots of family money, political connections, a stint in the Air Force Reserve, and a law degree from Regent University. The Eagle Consortium itself is staggeringly well-endowed. The Glavines support the Saint John's dig; Eagle's funds underpin *all* of the Aegean Association's excavations. The Consortium's pockets are deep, but the donors, CEOs and politicians and Christian religious leaders, want to know the bottom line for the projects they support. The markets haven't fully rebounded, funding for Middle Eastern projects is down, and they want bang for their remaining philanthropic buck. And, the memo concluded, they also want to ensure that Association sites bolster American interests in the region.

Lee sits down, takes a deep drink of his Coke, and leans forward. "I was detained, gentlemen," he says, "because I got wind of the fact that our bird has flown the coop. Left Istanbul on the afternoon flight to İzmir."

A smile fleetingly passes Monuglu's face.

"Typisch," Kirchburg mutters. His eyes narrow, and color rises on his pale skin.

"She didn't contact you?" Lee asks.

"No," Kirchburg scoffs. "Of course not." He swigs the rest of his gin and tonic. "She understood the importance of this meeting."

"I do believe you've got a point, Leopold," Lee answers, looking at Travers. "Either she doesn't have a lick of sense or something's out of whack at Saint John's."

⟟⊕⊣ 8

At dusk, Sophia Altay shovels dirt back into the trench. Her boots and blue jeans are dusty. Her breathing is deep and steady; her whole body sweats. Everything from her socks to the scarf holding her hair is damp, but the strenuous work is helping her think. She was absent from her site one day, and her life is altered. A single day. The ossuary that she herself has covered again with dirt is authentic. She is certain of it, absolutely sure. The symbols and the inscription both indicate it, and the location is exactly where she finally understood it must be.

Gnats swirl about her head in the gathering darkness. A blister between her thumb and forefinger has torn open, but the stinging, like the shoveling, focuses her thoughts. Abrahim and Kenan are the two men she trusted most, the only two she would allow to do the work while she was gone. Normally, they worked well together despite their vast differences—age, appearance, upbringing, education, emotion, inclination, outlook, all of it. They shared the same goal, though, and they were both absolutely loyal to her, or so she thought. And so, despite what has happened, she still hopes. The weight of the discovery was simply too much for them, especially Abrahim. Kenan, too, in his own way.

She steps back, leans on her shovel, and catches her breath. The area looks like someone has hastily begun to backfill it, but it's all she can do under the circumstances. When Kenan showed her the ossuary, she knew that nothing would ever be the same. When he told her what happened after the discovery, she knew she was finished as Saint John's director. As she flung dirt into the trench, she realized that her career didn't matter. It's all she knows and all she cares about, but it's insignificant in light of the discovery. She must determine what to do based on the situation she finds—not on what she wishes it were. Whatever happens, this is *the* moment of her life. Of this, she is sure.

In spite of Kenan's tirade about his thievery, disloyalty, and disappearance, the boy, Abrahim, can't have deserted her. In fact, she knows that he will be in touch soon. Yes, the discovery would have overwhelmed him. The import astounds her, and she is far more inured to it than he. Kenan and Abrahim should never have opened the ossuary without her. Never. And, though Kenan insists Abrahim did it, she knows better. She sent Kenan away for the night as soon as he brought her to the ossuary not simply because she was angry at him—though she was, deeply—but because she needed to work and think, which she couldn't do with him hovering about her.

Her understanding of others, particularly males, has been both her blessing and her curse since she was a girl. She can read Kenan and Abrahim and all the other diggers. She knows Leopold Kirchburg's arrogance all too well. She's aware that Charles Lee's ideology and dogmatism prevent any real and deep effectiveness. Nihat Monuglu is, whatever else he might be, a Turk. Bill Glavine needs to impress others with his wealth and is himself impressed by power—and, therefore, neither impresses her nor wields power over her. William Glavine, the father, is the only one who truly understands archeology even though construction made him rich. But he is infirm and, she realizes, no longer making Foundation decisions alone. He could stay her execution, insist on sending an envoy first, but that is all. Finally, she at first misjudged the new American, Joseph Travers, because of her own anger. And she must not let her emotions negate his or anyone else's potential usefulness.

She pulls off her scarf and shakes loose her hair. Balancing the shovel across her shoulder, she gazes at the cairn they built with the stones that first told her that this must be the place. There *had* to have been a first century dwelling, set apart, a place removed from both the bustle of the city and the settlement atop the hill. A place with good light and a view of the sea, but separate—a place where prayer might be offered each day. For most of a year, she walked the area with Abrahim almost every evening, often in silence, noting the contours and the tableaux. And eventually, he or she or both felt their way back through the centuries. Digging only in the evening when the day's work was done, they took months to find the right stones—and then months more trenching along the periphery toward the bluff to discover this spot. Now she gazes at the cairn, a pyramid more than two meters high topped by a cut hexagonal rock that could well have been a capstone. The other stones are smooth, twice the size of bricks, and gray-brown. Though not uniform, they are similar enough that they must have served as sections of walls violently torn down but then left, as though they were too sacred or too accursed to be taken elsewhere.

The breeze tickles the damp strands of hair on her neck. It's a glorious evening, the canopy deepening and the stars blinking in the wind. Her life is utterly insignificant beneath this vast beauty. But her moment in time, this critical moment, is upon her.

 9

Nihat Monuglu leads the group on foot the seven blocks to Galata Tower. As they pass the restaurants with their café tables spilling out onto the street, Charles Lee and Leopold Kirchburg talk on their phones. Joseph Travers' Amish is back at his hotel, turned off. Lee's announcement cut an abrupt edge into Kirchburg's evening, and he's barking terse, imperious German. Lee quizzes someone, his words a mixture of good ol' boy amiability and legal jargon. And there are no followers, or at least none as blatant as those earlier in the day.

At one corner, a dervish in white robes and a brown cylindrical hat is performing on a makeshift stage. In the shadow of a nearby wall, a crippled old woman covered in black sits begging. A scrawny dog lies asleep at her side. Lee and Kirchburg hurry ahead to get away from the music blaring from an old casette tape player, but Monuglu, pausing with Travers, fires up a Yenidje and claps Travers on the shoulder. "Welcome to Turkey, Joseph," he chortles. "Welcome to Turkey! My country, the land and the people, will change your life." He then leans in closer and whispers, "I wonder, my friend, why you did not tell these gentlemen that you already met Sophia Altay." As he chuckles softly, Travers, smelling raki and cigarette smoke, stares at the whirling, sweeping dance. "But do not worry, Joseph. It will remain a secret. A secret between friends."

Built as a watchtower by the Genoese almost a hundred and fifty years before their favorite son made his famous voyage to the New World, Galata Tower has the look of an uncircumcised priapism. The restaurant on its ninth floor is circular. The ceiling is conical, and the large central chandelier is surrounded by smaller ones. The four men take a table by a window looking back across the Golden Horn toward the docks, New Mosque, Spice Bazaar, and Suleyman's Mosque. In the fading light, Travers can barely make out the spot along the wall where he broke into laughter that afternoon. Lee and Kirchburg, seated opposite Travers and Monuglu, finally pocket their phones. Monuglu orders more raki for Travers and himself. Kirchburg has another Tanqueray and tonic, and Lee a Coca-Cola straight from the can. He wipes the rim with his napkin before popping the top.

They share a meze plate heaped with meats, cheeses, vegetables, hardboiled eggs, peppers, shrimp, and yogurt. Monuglu tells them the story about how the first man to fly took off from Galata Tower and glided on mechanical wings across the Golden Horn, but the unspoken subtext is Sophia Altay's flight and what it means to each of the men. The background music features an over-orchestrated version of the Beatles' 'Blackbird.' And the raki doesn't taste to Travers any less like licorice.

Sunset at Galata Tower is an event, and tourists, mostly young women, mill on the balcony outside the window. The sun becomes a molten ball above Istanbul's roofs and minarets; the Golden Horn shines in the evening light. The tourists' laughter filters through the window. Travers came early to Istanbul in the hope of discovering magic, but instead he's found a web of human intrigue more byzantine than that in the corporate world he left. He looks over at a woodcut on the restaurant's wall depicting that first flight that Monuglu told them about. "Leopold," he asks, "before Charles arrived, you were about to explain the problem with Ms. Altay."

Kirchburg licks his lips, tilts his glass, and knocks back most of his drink. "Ja, Herr Travers," he says, "Fräulein Altay." He glances at Lee before looking directly at Travers. "The occasional noteworthy discoveries of archeology make it appear glamorous," he says, "but the work is actually difficult, even tedious. Discipline is, therefore, necessary to any successful site. As is a clear chain of command. Not unlike the military. Directives are not phrased as orders, but…" He shrugs, puts down his glass, and opens his palms. "There is room for initiative and even creativity." Disdain slips into his voice as he pronounces that last word. "But only within the context of the site goals."

Monuglu gazes out the window as though he has no interest whatever in this part of the conversation.

"With your background," Lee says to Travers, "think in organizational terms." He stabs half a hardboiled egg with his fork. "With this kind of work, y'all can have only one cock of the roost. And everybody's got to know who he is."

As Travers nods, he wonders exactly how much information Lee has about him.

Monuglu stares at one of the tourists on the balcony, a red-haired young woman in a tight orange dress who has her hip pressed against the railing and her head tilted as she speaks on her cell phone.

"And Ms. Altay doesn't run her site in an authoritative way?" If Kirchburg can tell Travers is baiting him, it doesn't register in his eyes.

"No," the Austrian says. "No. That's not the issue." He finishes his gin and tonic. "She expects a great deal from her workers, everyone from the conservators down to the laborers. And she inspires a certain loyalty, especially among the diggers."

"Then what's the problem?" Travers asks. To curb the taste of raki, he eats an olive from the meze plate, then slips the pit onto his plate.

"She's a maverick," Lee says, raising his fork. "Pays no never mind to Leopold's orders. And digs all over God's creation."

Kirchburg looks at Lee as if to remind the American to stop interrupting. "Do not misunderstand, Herr Travers," he says, his voice tight. "There is nothing personal in my decision. Fräulein Altay and I are not antagonistic. I retain the utmost respect for her abilities."

"But you've decided to fire her." Travers makes it more a statement than a question.

Having finished his raki, Monuglu holds up his empty glass so that the waiter can see it.

Kirchburg places his elbows on the table, raises his hands, and drums the tips of his long, thin fingers against each other. "The situation has become untenable. Her dismissal is necessary. She is, however, a Glavine Foundation employee."

"I see." Travers turns to Lee. "And the Eagle Consortium supports Herr Kirchburg's move?"

"Leopold," Lee says, "is the only one over here with the bona fides to determine what's what at the sites." His voice slips into its management mode as he taps his fork on the Coke can. "The reports my people have provided corroborate that Ms. Altay is diverting resources and energy from the central task to peripheral digs."

"Fraudulently?" Travers asks.

Lee shakes his head. "No. Not at all. But in violation of Herr Kirchburg's explicit directives."

Kirchburg inspects his manicured fingernails for a moment before asking, "Are you familiar with the Saint John's site, Herr Travers?"

Monuglu has taken out his cigarette case and is rolling an unlit Yenidje Régie between his thumb and index finger.

"No," Travers admits. He's already well aware that Bill Glavine neglected to provide even a site map for him.

Kirchburg exhales slowly. "The Saint John's site is located on Ayasuluk Hill outside Ephesus, adjacent to the present town of Selçuk. The site has been worked for decades, since 1921, to be exact. The Cathedral of Saint John has been excavated and partially restored. The current contract, agreed upon by all parties, including the Glavine Foundation, calls for work *only* on the citadel at Ayasuluk's highest point north of the cathedral."

Travers takes a drink of water to dampen the effects of the raki. "And Ms. Altay is focusing on the cathedral?"

"No." Kirchburg leans forward, looming over his side of the table. "That would be too logical." He scratches his beard for a moment. "She is digging holes around the periphery of the cathedral, unearthing stone huts and insignificant shards. Counterproductive in the extreme, *and* an eyesore for tourists."

"What Leopold is telling you," Lee says, "is that she's trashing the site and putting each of us—the Aegean Association, the Eagle Consortium, the Turkish Ministry of Culture, and the Glavine Foundation—between a rock and a hard place."

Travers turns to Lee. "But you said that something must have happened there for Ms. Altay to have left Istanbul so suddenly. Has she discovered something?"

Lee looks at Kirchburg, who waves his hand dismissively. "Potsherds," the Austrian says. "An intact amphora, at best."

"But then what was her rush?" Travers asks.

"Laborers and conservators have a tendency to exaggerate their discoveries," Kirchburg says. He shakes his head and exhales slowly, as though he is weary of dealing with an overly inquisitive child. "And Fräulein Altay is impertinent."

Travers glances out the window. The New Mosque is bathed in light, but only the minarets and porch of Suleyman's Mosque are lit. "Whose hire was she?" he asks.

Kirchburg sits back, picks up his empty glass, sets it back on the table, and strokes his beard again. "I did. And it was the correct decision. Absolutely. Her education is first rate, her vitae impeccable. Interviews, recommendations—on paper, there was no stronger candidate. And everyone was taken by her. Even the elder gentleman, William Glavine, interviewed her during his annual inspection of the Selçuk site."

"But...?" Travers asks, glancing at Lee.

"Before my time," he says. "Ancient history."

"She does not," Kirchburg says, "have the capacity to retain focus on difficult tasks." He picks up the glass again and holds it so that the light from the candle in the center of the table refracts through it. "This is her second year as Saint John's site director. Her work last year was acceptable—indeed, exemplary—but this year she has overstepped her authority." He turns the glass in his hand. "I assure you, Herr Travers, that it is only with much deliberation that I've made the decision to terminate her."

Travers eats another olive. "If Altay's firing is a done deal," he asks, "why am I here? Am I supposed to be the messenger?"

"No," Kirchburg answers, looking closely at him for a moment, maybe recalculating something. "As I told you, she is, contractually, a Glavine Foundation employee. The elder Herr Glavine insisted that his own representative conduct a site evaluation prior to my implementing any significant changes."

Or the old man will pull the plug on the funding, Travers thinks. He flattens his hands on the table, takes a breath, and smiles at the others. "Okay," he says. "Good enough. Then that's what I'll do. I'm scheduled to fly to İzmir tomorrow morning anyway." He cocks his head and, still smiling, looks into Kirchburg's eyes. "We'll see what Ms. Altay has found at Saint John's."

⚚ 10

Sophia Altay's eyes gleam as she scrolls through the text. Her fingers tremble, and her neck and breasts tingle. Her whole body feels electrified, as though a current is passing through her. Her experience, her whole life, has prepared her for this moment, but she's still utterly undone. The ossuary itself is a watershed, an epochal discovery in the history of archeology. But the contents, these documents…this letter will *change* history.

Wearing a burgundy silk bathrobe, she sits at her computer. Her hair, combed out, is still damp from the shower. Abrahim's email was waiting for her when she returned to the house after reburying the ossuary. She read the message twice, found the flash drive hidden for her in the restoration house, and then forced herself to shower before she perused the documents. This first letter has taken her breath—if she'd had any idea what it was, she'd never have showered. Abrahim's flight with the original documents was reckless, but his world is fraught with angels and demons. And his fear of betrayal was overpowering even before the discovery of the ossuary.

She stands, wipes her sweating palms on the silk of her hips, and brushes her fingers through her hair. She still can't quite breathe, can't quite imagine what Abrahim must feel holding the documents. Their existence…merely touching them must be galvanizing. Maybe it's good that he's unable to read Aramaic. If he fully understood what he possesses, he would melt…or immolate. He at least had the presence of mind to photograph the documents and the ossuary's other contents with the site's digital camera.

She pulls the bathrobe more snugly around herself and paces tight circles in her office—a clean, well-lit, and organized space in her home. The attached restoration house is a cluttered maze of equipment, records, and artifacts. Normally, she needs both for balance, but in this moment in which the earth is shifting beneath her and the stars are wheeling above, this office with this document on the computer screen is everything. These words glowing in this place are the only thing.

She sits and scans the Aramaic script again. Both the quality of the reproduction and the idiosyncrasies of the writing make it difficult to read, but the gist is unmistakable. Spinning her pen in her fingertips, she mulls the letter's provocative opening. *Hear, O Israel! Worship the Lord your God and serve Him only. Hear me, all of you, and understand. The Kingdom of God is at hand! The Day of God's vengeance is upon us.* She opens her leather-bound notebook and sets it in her lap. But when she starts to write, her hand shakes the words into runes. She must get control…must carefully transcribe the letter.

She taps the pen's tip on the notebook's page, pixillating a crucifix.

Is she in as much danger as Abrahim said? She's definitely vulnerable—in no small part because he pilfered the ossuary's contents. But she would be in harm's way even if he remained. The discovery itself is inflammatory, and possessing the contents is pure peril. Covering up the ossuary will only delay the flashpoint a day, perhaps two. She can't keep the find a secret for long, but every hour will help. Once the ossuary comes to light again, it will cause a religious, political, and media firestorm. And the moment in which Nihat and Leopold and Charles Lee realize that the contents are missing will be incendiary. In her return message to Abrahim, she left him clear instructions for contacting her at eight o'clock. But she can't wait for morning. She has to discover where he has gone and what he has done with the ossuary's contents. She must locate the originals at any cost to herself and, if necessary, others. And somehow…somehow…she must act, at least for a day or two, as though nothing extraordinary has been found at Saint John's.

⚐ 11

Clenching the Toyota sedan's steering wheel with his stubby fingers, Kenan Sirhan glowers at Joseph Travers in the rearview mirror. Outside of İzmir, the Toyota speeds on the two-lane roads past fields and stone buildings from another age. The car then winds along steep bluffs on the Aegean coast above coves and beaches in impossibly clear light.

Sirhan, Sophia Altay's driver who met Travers at İzmir's airport, looks like Nihat Monuglu's cousin—bald and barrel-chested with a bulbous veined nose and a white mustache. Unlike Monuglu, though, Sirhan is dour and surly and speaks only fragmented English. His dark eyes hold barely suppressed rage, and Travers was Motorola's

Vice President of Operations long enough to recognize the look of an employee harboring resentment. In a boom and bust business, he shut down too many factories and laid off or fired too many people to take it lightly.

Trying to ignore Sirhan's bile, he looks at the shimmering water and lets Homeric phrases roll out—*A favorable breeze, a fresh west wind, singing over the wine-dark sea.* Still, he can't wash away a sense that his visit to Istanbul provided none of the uplifting magic he sought. He remembers the second shadow slouching at the cabstand across from Suleyman's Mosque, Leopold Kirchburg's curt German and Charles Lee's Southern slang, and Monuglu's smoky breath as he suggested that nothing escapes his notice.

Sirhan takes Travers directly to the Saint John's Cathedral archeological site. They drive along Selçuk's main street and wind up a side street to the parking lot by the basilica's outer fortifications. The sky is clear, and the air shimmers in the noonday sun. Travers buys two bottles of water at the souvenir stand and offers one of them to Sirhan. He shakes his head vehemently and then leads Travers up the marble ramp to the basilica's main entrance, the Gate of Persecution, flanked by two square towers.

As Travers follows, Sirhan marches under the stone arch and past the old man at the ticket booth on the left. They file up through the ruins of the cathedral, moving too quickly for Travers to get a good look at any of the restored columns or red brick and white stone walls. Though mostly they cross packed red dirt, geometric floor tiles line the area near the tomb of Saint John the Apostle. A boy is trying to sell coins to an elderly couple in the apse, but no other tourists are around.

They cut through the octagonal baptistry and come out into a work area with a white railing and an orange sign that says:

GIRILMEZ

KEIN ZUTRITT

NO ACCESS

A single-story, white stucco building with a burnt-orange tile roof stands among the pine trees to the west. To the north, the stone citadel

with its massive jutting towers crowns the highest point of Ayasuluk Hill. Archeological flotsam rings the work area—piles of timber,
stacks of loose rocks, rows of pillar segments, a cement mixer, and
an old steel mining conveyor. A dog barks in the distance, and pale
blue smoke swirls from the stucco building's brick chimney. Near the
building, a thin young raven-haired woman sits under a tree on what
looks like an ice-cream-parlor chair. She leans over a wheelbarrow
full of murky water cleaning a ceramic shard. When she sees Sirhan
and Travers, she slips the shard onto a drying screen, leans back, and
shouts something in Turkish.

The door to the building beyond her opens, and Sophia Altay
steps out. She looks almost girlish in work boots, blue jeans, and an
old brown T-shirt. Her hair is pulled back under a red bandana. She
thanks the young woman and nods to Sirhan, who bows slightly and
backs into the shade of the nearby pine trees. As she comes forward,
Altay wipes her hands on her jeans. "Welcome to Saint John's, Joseph,"
she says. Her eyes, more brown than green against her T-shirt, show
a concern, even anxiety, that he didn't see during dinner at the Blue
House Hotel.

"Thanks," he answers. "I'm glad to be here…to be out in the light."

She takes a deep breath, brushes the back of her hand across her
mouth, and waves toward the top of the hill. "Well," she says, "would
you like to see the dig?" She glances at her watch. "Or, are you hungry?"

"The dig would be good," he says, holding out one of the water
bottles for her.

"No, thank you," she says, nodding to Sirhan. "But…"

Sirhan starts to lumber over, stops, glances first at her and then at
the ground, and shakes his head again. Altay offers the bottle to the
young conservationist, who looks at Travers with large brown eyes,
takes the bottle, and murmurs, "Teşekkür ederim."

Travers and Altay follow a dirt path toward a cyclone fence topped
with strands of barbed wire. Just before they turn by the old rubble-
stone outer fortification, she pulls a bunch of grapes from a vine
climbing the fence. Offering some to Travers, she asks, "How was
the meeting?"

He eats a couple of the small, tart green grapes. "You were missed."

Her step falters for a second, and she yanks two of the grapes from the bunch, pops them into her mouth, and chews hard. "Each of those *gentlemen*," she says, twisting the last word, "has an agenda that runs contrary to my work here."

"That may be true," Travers says as he looks up at the monolithic citadel. He doesn't add that Monuglu knew about their dinner and that Lee had information about which flight she took from Istanbul. Instead, he asks, "Against *you* or the work here?"

"Both," she says. "I know what's best here. And I won't bow to any of them."

The certainty in her voice doesn't surprise him. "Still," he begins, "you should…"

"Don't tell me what to do," she snaps. "None of those Pharisees understands…" Shaking her head, she takes a deep breath. "You were there," she says, the edge in her voice only a little less sharp. "Would it have mattered if I was at that meeting?"

He looks at her as they pass a line of bicycles leaning against the stone wall. "Maybe not," he says. "But it still would've been better if you and Professor Kirchburg talked…"

"Leopold…" She practically spits the name.

He stops, picks a grape from the vine next to him, and rolls it between his thumb and finger. "Nothing's a done deal, Ms. Altay," he says. "At least as far as I'm concerned."

She stares at him, her eyes narrowing in the sunlight, and says, "You have no idea, Joe. No idea."

He tosses the grape away. "I need some time to…"

"Time?" She lifts the bunch of grapes, begins to speak, and looks off toward the horizon. "*Time?*" she repeats, half coughing and half laughing.

Turning before he can say anything else, she climbs the hill away from him.

He glances in the direction she was gazing. Beyond the stand of pines, the sloping groves, and the fields, the Aegean is a thin blue ribbon binding land and sky.

⌖ 12

A tractor pulls a flat wooden wagon around the side of the citadel and down the path. Five men sit on the wagon with their legs dangling over the side. Travers has almost caught up to Altay when the tractor stops so she can speak to the driver, a wizened old man with white stubble and a black cap. They talk for a moment over the engine's racket, and then she greets each of the laborers on the wagon. Their boots are dusted with red dirt, their dark pants grimy, and their shirts soaked with sweat, but they all smile at her, crooked teeth gleaming under mustaches.

As she watches the tractor rumble down the hill, Travers says, "I really don't react well when someone I'm working with stalks off a second time. You should know that." He smiles. "And talking with me, will, I think, help."

She stares up at the citadel.

He's sweating through his shirt, too, the heat a little like it was during his childhood summer days in Prescott, Arizona, where the sun scorched rocks and stunted creeks. "How's the dig going?" he asks.

She tugs at her bandana, sucks in her breath, and scuffs her boot in the red dirt. Exhaling, she turns toward him. "Slow," she says. "Steady."

He opens the water bottle and takes a swig. "What drew you back here so quickly?"

She selects and eats half a dozen grapes one at a time. "I belong here." She wipes her mouth with the back of her hand. "I'm of more use here than there."

He waves at the citadel. "Have they found something?"

"Nothing there that would please Leopold." She shakes her head. "But come, I'll show you."

As they approach the summit, she says, "We've discovered mudbricks and potsherds proving that this hill was inhabited well before the Mycenaeans and the Hittites built their first forts. People have lived here for more than four thousand years. In fact, one of Ephesus's incarnations was likely founded at the peak of the hill."

Up close, the thick stone walls and fifteen towers make the citadel look like a medieval European fortress complete with battlements and crenellations.

"And," she adds, smiling dryly, "there remains a serious dispute over exactly where in the area Saint John died."

"The apostle?"

"Most scholars agree that John the Apostle brought the Christ's mother to Ephesus from Jerusalem after James, her second son, was murdered. There's a shrine, a reconstructed house, on a hill the other side of Ephesus." As she talks, her voice becomes more calm without losing any certainty. "No tomb or other physical evidence links the site to Mary, but successive popes during the last century declared it an official place of pilgrimage. At this time of year, thousands of Christians visit the House of the Virgin every day." She gazes down at the ruins of the cathedral. "John moved to this hill after she died."

"And he's said to have died here?"

She nods.

"Down by the cathedral or up at the citadel?"

She waves at a large cairn near the bluff about halfway up from the cathedral. "Or somewhere in between."

Travers looks toward the cathedral's excavated columns and walls. Two boys are running through the right transept, but the area is otherwise empty. "And you believe it?" he asks. "That John came here?"

"Absolutely." Her eyes glint. "I *know* that John lived and died on this hill."

She is almost smiling as she turns and waves toward the citadel. Though the conversation isn't really over, he follows her up the path. They enter the citadel through its eastern gate overlooking Selçuk. Because the diggers are down at the restoration house for lunch, they have the site to themselves. As soon as they're inside the walls, noise abates and light sparks around them. Dirt tracks lead to the small stone mosque with its truncated minaret and to the remains of the cistern. Worn paths cross among the archeological trenches. Grass sprinkled with yellow and purple wildflowers spreads to the walls.

He knows little about the everyday tasks of archeology, but even in his ignorance he can tell that there's a chaotic order to the work. Unused scaffolding pipes and fittings are stacked separately from two-by-fours and timbers. Trenches and quadrants are numbered, and even the piles of dirt are marked.

As Altay leads him down a wood plank ramp into the dig, she says, "We've been excavating the cistern this summer. I'll spare you the jargon, but if you have questions about how I'm running the site, please ask."

Her dealings with her staff have already answered his more basic questions, and it isn't time yet for the deeper ones—so he simply looks around. The cistern walls have regular stone and brick courses. Blue crates on the floor hold plastic bottles of chemical agents. Water jugs stand under the scaffolding, and tile fragments lie on a screen. Scanning the layout of the dig, he turns full circle. "This wasn't built as a cistern," he says.

Glancing at her watch, she answers, "No, it wasn't."

"We're standing in the apse."

Shaking her head again, she smiles. "Yes," she says, "we're in a Byzantine church. Much smaller than the cathedral down the hill—but probably also dedicated to Saint John. It's one thing that Leopold and I agree on."

A loose tarp strung on poles shades them, but the air is hot and heavy beneath it. Still, his breathing is more labored than the climb up the hill should warrant. Sweat beads on his forehead, and his mind begins to race…. After his parents' divorce, Travers, his mother, and his sister moved back East to Detroit where his mother had grown up. University of Detroit High was a good school, but greater Detroit was definitely not the Northern Arizona mountains. He did well in his classes, but, as the new kid from the small town out West, never quite fit in. His mother's eldest brother, a Jesuit who ran University of Detroit Press, took Travers under his wing. After his sister went off to college, his mother fought her increasing loneliness by spending long nights with old boyfriends. Travers didn't have the clear spiritual vocation that the Jesuits told him he had, but the seminary at Columberre seemed as though it might provide a community, a sense of belonging. It couldn't, of course—he lasted less than a year, but certainly long enough for him to recognize the cruciform shape of a church even after it has been desecrated and roofed over with a barrel vault.

The Jesuits did, though, take care of their own, and he arrived at Georgetown University the next fall without ever having applied. He bartended at The Tombs, as much for the camaraderie as the money, and he met, among others, Bill Glavine and Mary McDonald. Mary was attractive and artsy and wild-eyed enough to turn his head. Though he knew even then that she dwelled in a land of emotional peaks and valleys and he tramped in the foothills, he thought they could find common ground. And, in truth, he loved her. After graduation, he took a job with Sara Lee in Chicago. His college friends were getting married at a rate of one a month, and Mary was into decorating. Tom was born a year after the wedding, and Jason followed two years later. Travers felt useful, and, though he never loved it, he settled into corporate life.

At the same time he was withdrawing from the foothills onto some vast emotional plain, Mary's sojourns on the summits and in the gorges became more extreme. Medications helped her intermittently but did little for their marriage. He became adept at compartmentalizing his life. His career kept on track, but his home life derailed—and after fifteen years, he and Mary separated. And now, Jason, his relationship with Christine, his job, and his life in Chicago—all of them are gone...

He drains the rest of his water, measures his breath, and glances again around the site. The air is stifling. Sweat runs down his neck and spine. Altay takes the empty bottle from him and drops it into a steel drum used for garbage. She tucks loose strands of hair back under her bandana. He needs to move so he steps away and looks at the tile fragments arranged on the screen. The colors are faded, but he can make out an old man's bearded face encircled by a halo.

She comes over and stands beside him. "Archeology is always a puzzle," she says. "Sometimes the pieces fit together." She stoops and shifts one of the shards slightly. "And once in a while you find something that changes the way you see the world."

He looks into her eyes, which are beginning to veil. "Here?"

"Nothing here. You're seeing what we've found here."

He goes over to look more closely at eight amphoras lined against the wall. Five have tapering necks, and two have unbroken handles. Altay joins him again, but neither of them says anything more.

ⵕ 13

When Altay and Travers leave the citadel, Kenan Sirhan is using a shovel to tamp the ground near the cairn on the knoll. He wears a sleeveless t-shirt, and, even at a distance, his sweating shoulders and bald head glisten. Fresh dirt is piled in the trenches, but there's no equipment or other signs that the site is active.

Altay and Travers head much of the way down Ayasuluk Hill in silence. The path they're on winds down toward the area where the laborers are eating lunch. The building nestled among the pines at the edge of the worksite is connected by a courtyard to another house with stucco walls and an orange tiled roof. It stands atop the steep stone curtain wall that runs below the western end of the cathedral's atrium. Together, the buildings look to him like a Spanish hacienda perched on the edge of a mesa in Arizona. Farther to the west, a thin haze hangs over the Aegean.

"Seems like a good place to work," he says.

"It is," she answers. "And to live. The smaller house, the one with the view, is mine…" Her smile is ironic. "…as long as I'm Saint John's director."

"Have you worked in the area before?" he asks.

"I was born in Istanbul, but I was educated in France and England."

She gazes over at Kenan for a moment. "I worked on sites in Cappadocia, but I had only been to the Aegean on family holidays."

The thin, young Turkish woman is serving steaming tea to the laborers who sit on beds of pine needles in the shade of the trees. The small clear cups look dainty in their hands.

As Altay and Travers approach the restoration house, she says, "I have a good deal of office work this afternoon. You'd probably enjoy Ephesus and the House of the Virgin more than staying around here."

"More archeological tours?"

"Yes," she says, "but with a purpose. Those sites will put the work here in perspective."

He knows that hanging around Saint John's might help his evaluation in some way, but what he really needs to do is to get Altay talking—and that isn't going to happen in the afternoon. "How about dinner, then?" he asks.

She hesitates before nodding. "I'm very busy, Joe," she answers. "But, okay. Later. That would work."

"Do you have a favorite place in town?" he asks.

"Yes," she answers. *"Here."*

It's his turn to hesitate.

"I insist."

"May I…"

"No." She smiles. "You don't need to bring anything. Visit Ephesus, get settled at your hotel, and come back after nineteen-thirty. Kenan will drive you. He's at your service for the duration of your visit."

He looks back up the hill where Sirhan stands on the knoll, the shovel over his shoulder, staring to the west.

⚐ 14

Altay kneads the dough. Her kitchen is as neat as her office, and everything has its place. When she's finished with the dough, she'll cut the vegetables and dice the meat for the güveç. She doesn't really have the time to prepare dinner, but she realized early on that cooking would be less time consuming than going out to eat. She will also need Joe Travers to complete certain tasks for her. And in any case, cooking, like shoveling dirt, helps her think. The translation of the first scroll is going well. Even though some phrases, apparently dictated to a scribe, are unfamiliar, she has a draft pretty much completed. If she works through the night, she'll have a clean translation by dawn. The second document, written in a halting, less fluent hand, perhaps that of someone who learned to write later in life, is she believes, of less import. Still, she should, in another day, have that document completed as well. Thinking about the letters causes her skin to prickle, even now as she works. She can't wait to see the originals.

She's had two emails from Abrahim, the first in the morning from Kayseri and the second mid-afternoon from Göreme. If what he says is true—that he overheard Kenan speaking heated German on the phone to someone less than an hour after they found the bone box and that Kenan kept repeating the words *ossuary* and *euros*—then the danger is even more imminent than she thought. Early this morning, she had the diggers fill in all of the trenches around the knoll and remove all of the equipment from the area, but that won't likely throw Leopold off for long.

She covers the dough and puts it in the refrigerator. She then scrubs her hands and picks up her kitchen knife. Working deftly, she slices the potatoes. Neither Kenan nor Abrahim has been completely honest with her. Abrahim will, she believes, go where she has instructed him to go and do what she has told him to do. After all, he left the flash drive for her and is taking care of the originals. But she can't imagine that he's carrying around the ossuary's other contents. And in his emails he'll only refer to the documents, nothing else. His possession of them is burning him alive. It is as though they are white hot, and he must hold them until the flames consume him.

And, Kenan…he denies having a phone conversation with anyone. But she can see in his eyes that he is not telling her the truth—and that his lying to her is a blade that is already stuck deep in him and turning. He speaks German from his years as a laborer in Hamburg, but he insists he would tell no one, not even his own wife were she still alive, of their discovery of the ossuary. At least she is sure, given his pained and sullen silence, that he really doesn't know what happened to the ossuary's contents.

As she dices the onions, she strikes the cutting board hard and fast. The calls she received early that afternoon from Istanbul were antagonistic, but, given what's at stake, the threats are empty. Her job is history, her life here at Saint John's over. Her task is simple: obtain all of the ossuary's contents, protect them at any cost, and present them to the world. Joe Travers' ignorance of the situation may, ironically, be his greatest strength—and her best asset. He will likely do as she says not because of who she is but because she has begun to understand that he is someone who *needs* to feel useful.

⭥ 15

Just after five-thirty, Joseph Travers walks along the main road from the Hitit Hotel into Selçuk's town center. The citadel looms on Ayasuluk Hill to his right. An open truck carries slouching field hands, men and boys, back toward town. A separate truck transports women and girls wearing scarves on their heads. When he reaches the first of the cafés with old men drinking tea and smoking, a tractor pulling a wagon laden with watermelons turns the corner.

One melon rolls off the back and splatters on the pavement. Farther on, a man shoes a horse in a narrow courtyard.

Earlier in the afternoon, Kenan Sirhan took Travers to Ephesus and the House of the Virgin Mary. At Ephesus, the Roman capital of Asia Minor and the best preserved of all ancient cities, the sun started to cook Arizona style. The second-story windows of the Library of Celsus held patches of cobalt sky, but sunburnt Germans vying for camera angles kept the facade's statues of Knowledge, Virtue, Wisdom, and Destiny obscured. Then, Sirhan, scowling as always and smelling of earth and sweat even though he had changed his shirt, drove Travers up a winding mountain road through a pine forest that reminded him of Prescott National Forest and Granite Mountain. He thought about summers spent wandering around with buddies, following creeks, sliding down dry washes, and playing war games in which they died and lived again a thousand times. They roasted hot dogs over open fires and drank root beer from cans and crushed the empties with their heels. And they didn't head home until the pines impaled the sun.

When Sirhan dropped Travers in the parking lot of the House of the Virgin Mary, five tour buses were disgorging Spaniards. The scent of pine was in the air, but the throng of pilgrims was so large that he skirted the house and found a path that bent away from the Virgin's shrine and spring. A couple of hundred yards later, he came to a clearing. Ephesus spread out below him, the tourists like ants. The bay beyond the ancient city shone darkly.

Now, the first Roman-coin peddler hits on him the moment he turns onto the street leading up to Saint John's. The boy is no more than fourteen, with large, dark eyes that give no hint that he knows the cobs he holds in his palm are neither old nor valuable. His pals up the road offer the same fare—at reduced rates. Saint John's wooden gates are closed, but when Travers hammers on them, there's a scraping along the ground behind them. The coinmongers sidle away as the old ticket-taker opens one of the gates. When Travers mentions Altay's name to the man, he waves him in. He then closes the gate and pushes a brown stone, apparently the only lock, against it.

Still almost an hour early for dinner, Travers strolls through the ruins of the cathedral. Saint John's tomb, located at the intersection of the nave and the aisles, has four short columns rising at its corners. Patterned marble slabs cover the underground crypt, which isn't open to the public. A sign nearby states that an inscription carved in the marble over the tomb read, "This is my resting place forever, here will I dwell." But when archeologists first opened the tomb, it contained only a fine dust that quickly dissipated in the air.

Near the cathedral's atrium, another sign in Turkish, German, and English says, "The excavation and restoration of the Basilica of Saint John on the Ayasuluk Hill are sponsored by the Ministry of Culture of Turkey; The Aegean Association, Leopold Kirchburg, Director; and the Glavine Foundation, Dayton, Ohio." Among the stories about how Ayasuluk Hill got its name is one that asserts that, through the centuries, Saint John's tomb rose and fell as though he were still breathing inside. The locals, understandably mystified by these occurrences, coined the phrase, *holy breath,* and eventually associated it with the hill itself. Travers crosses to the curtain wall that drops vertically from the end of the atrium. It was added, long after the cathedral was built, to ward off marauding Arabs. The drop down to the rubble below is precipitous, but the view westward over paths and gardens and palm trees and the Asa Bey Mosque is spectacular.

Travers makes his way back through the ruins to the work area adjacent to the restoration house. Not wanting to bother Altay yet, he sits in dappled shade on a section of column laid out in the grass. The workers have all gone for the day, and the tractor and wagon are parked off to the side of the main path leading up to the citadel. Light plays among the pines, shadows dancing on the beds of needles, the red earth, and the grass. The rows of pillar segments lined near him gleam. Brown birds flit about, darting and swooping for midges. Wind rushes through the pines and willows. In the distance, dogs bark and trucks rumble. He takes a series of deep breaths and watches the patterns of sunshine and shade shift across the ceramic shards on the screen next to the wheelbarrow and on the red and yellow flowers planted in beds near the restoration house. The call to prayer rises from the mosque in the valley.

As he sits, the noise subsides. A flurry of birds, scores and scores of them, whirl and spin above him in the light. At one moment they are black, and at the next gold. Wind ebbs and flows. Time furls and then whisks away, black and gold as well. Energy swirls and spills, cascading around him. A coruscating surge rolls over him. And he feels a presence in the breeze and in the light. A presence that takes his breath, tosses time, and flicks light. There's no vision, no apparition, but there's something. He doesn't understand what's happening—everything, all of it, is at once in and out of time. He feels both full and empty, rooted and transcendent, himself and a witness, absolutely present and infinitely everywhere. The silence disquiets him.

Sound returns as the birds wheel away into the sun. Traffic and dogs and his own breathing amplify as he falls back into the stream of time, not at all sure what has happened. When he looks down, his hands are shaking. The nape of his neck tickles. He glances around, but no one else is there.

⚷ 16

After a time, Travers becomes aware of Kenan Sirhan moving slowly near the cairn on the knoll. He trudges with his head down, as though he's searching for something. Stooping, he examines clods of dirt. He then stands abruptly and hurls a chunk onto the ground. A puff of red dust rises like smoke from a small explosion. He shakes his head three times, hitches his pants farther up under his protruding belly, and starts down the narrow track. He's only fifty yards away when he notices Travers seated on the column. Though he misses a step, he pulls in his gut and raises his head. Not acknowledging Travers at all, he takes a key chain from his pocket, opens the door to the restoration house, and goes in.

Five minutes later, as Travers is trying unsuccessfully to comprehend that sense of presence he felt, Sophia Altay and the young woman who was earlier cleaning artifacts stroll around the side of the restoration house. Altay pats her on the forearm, waves as she walks down the path, and turns toward Travers. She wears a long denim skirt and a sleeveless blouse the color of cinnamon. Her hair is pulled back in a loose braid. "Joe," she says, "you should have let me know you were here."

Wondering if, as in their two earlier meetings, they'll have to work past her defensiveness, he says, "I was early. Didn't want to bother you."

She leads him along the walkway under the pines between the restoration house and the cathedral ruins. The breeze riffles white sheets and a pillowcase on the clothesline strung across the courtyard between the restoration house and her residence. A large open amphora lies on its side amid cactus growing at the courtyard's periphery. A smaller, more ornate amphora, cleaned but not yet restored, stands by the wall. Concentric rows of faded Jerusalem crosses decorate the jar.

They walk around to the porch without going through her house. The aroma of spiced stew is in the air. With an overhanging roof and a view of Ephesus and the Aegean, the porch has the feel of a veranda. Ceramic wind chimes hanging from one of the rafters jingle in the soft breeze. A low wooden table separates a pair of cushioned wooden armchairs.

"Would you like a drink?" she asks, waving him to the chair on the left.

"Anything but raki," he answers.

Placing a hand on her chest in mock distress, she says, "Please, I *am* half-French." From the Glavine Foundation background information, Travers already knows that her father was a Turkish diplomat in the early days of the Republic and that her mother was a French archeologist. Altay was educated at Sacred Heart and the Sorbonne in Paris and at Cambridge where she completed her DPhil in archeology. But she grew up an international child, and he really doesn't know how Turkish or French she is—or for that matter, if either culture defines her.

While she's in the house, he looks out over the valley to the thin line of sea. The hill falls sharply below the low stone wall just beyond the porch, and shades of green run in patterns to the horizon. The sun is low enough to be bright in his eyes, and the westerly breeze makes the evening comfortable.

Altay pushes the screen door open with her hip and steps out carrying an open bottle of red wine, a bowl of black olives, and two glasses. He takes the bowl and glasses from her and sets them on the table.

"How was Ephesus?" she asks as she pours the wine.

"The restoration was amazing," he says, "but I like the feel of it here at Saint John's better."

She looks at him for a moment before placing the bottle on the table and taking a seat in the other chair. "What do you mean?" she asks.

He picks up the glass and swirls the wine. The waves of refracting light bring Homer's wine-dark sea to mind. "It's a feeling," he says, knowing that's not an explanation. He can't tell her about the presence, even if he could articulate it.

"A feeling?" Her eyes, bright with the setting sun, still hold uneasiness. She's suppressing strong emotion, doing a good job, but her eyes suggest that she's not going to be able to hold it in through the evening. She raises her glass and tinks it against his.

He tastes the wine, thinks it's terrific, and drinks deeply.

When Altay catches him eyeing the label's appellation, she says, "The estate's a family secret."

He lifts the glass and turns it in the light. "This is your family's?"

She smiles, then does the Cat Woman thing with her eyes, anger supplanting the other emotions that are there. "Leopold and Charles Lee are in town," she says.

"In Selçuk?" The night before, neither of them mentioned anything about coming.

"Yes. Leopold wanted a meeting of all the principals tonight." She keeps her eyes on Travers. "But I told him that nine tomorrow was the earliest I could arrange it."

He realizes, among other things, that Kirchburg isn't keeping him in the loop. He's not sure if the Austrian has downgraded him to the

Glavines' messenger boy or upgraded him to Altay's co-conspirator and therefore an enemy. "When did they get in?" he asks.

"The afternoon flight. İzmir around seventeen-hundred. Lee is staying at your hotel, but Leopold went more upscale."

"Why are they here?"

She eats an olive. "Because they are Pharisees."

She keeps using that term. "Pharisees?" he asks.

She slips the olive's pit from her mouth and tosses it over the low wall and down the precipice. "Powerful, arrogant, deceitful, hypocritical, self-righteous men," she says.

That seems harsh, particularly for Lee, but Travers remembers how she bristled when she first met him. He drinks more of the wine. "But that doesn't explain why they've come now," he says.

"They think I'm holding out on them. Covering up a significant find."

He looks into her eyes. "And are you?"

She selects an olive and slides it into her mouth.

"Ms. Altay…Sophia," he says, "are you holding something out?"

She stares out toward the distant Aegean. "There is something. Something incredibly important."

Knowing better than to shout, *Well, what the hell is it?*, he eats an olive so fresh that it has to have been picked that afternoon.

She tosses the second pit over the wall and then gazes at the wine glowing in the light striking her glass. "They're…it's not something from the citadel. And not something I'm simply going to hand over to Leopold."

He spits the olive pit into his fingers and flings it over the precipice. Trying to keep his voice even, he asks, "Will you tell me about it?"

"Maybe. Probably."

Aware that she's playing him, he says, "You'll have to inform the Glavine Foundation."

"I know." She lifts her gaze from the wine to his eyes. "Le pére. William Glavine, Sr. But the Pharisees will…"

"You think Kirchburg will steal the credit?"

She glares at him for a moment before her eyes soften, the green

becoming even more vibrant. "No," she says. "That's not it at all."
She curls her right leg under her so that she faces him more. "He *will*
certainly steal the credit. That's what he does. But that's not it." She
leans toward him. "I *love* my work. My work *is* my life."

He nods, though he knows he doesn't really understand because
he never actually loved his work. He liked many aspects of it, had
good years, became proficient, even expert, and been well compen-
sated—but he never loved it.

"I told you earlier today," she says, "that archeology is a puzzle. And it
is. You find artifacts and piece them together until you understand…"
She gazes at her wine again. "You come to understand the people
who lived in that moment…in that time and place." Putting her glass
on the table, she adds, "And if you're lucky, that understanding leads
you to an understanding of yourself, of your moment in time."

He nods again, though he has never thought of archeology that way.

A phone in her house rings, but she ignores it. She traces the top
of her glass with her forefinger. Her hand is small but not soft. Her
nails are cut short, and her knuckles are chafed. She wears no ring,
no jewelry except a single gold rope bracelet. She looks up at him as
she begins to speak again. "Once a generation or so, someone finds
something that alters the puzzle itself…"

The intensity in her eyes startles him.

"…something that changes the way we all understand the world
and ourselves."

He has no idea what to say but wants to keep her talking. "You
mean, something so valuable?"

"Something beyond value."

"But something the Pharisees, as you call them, would take from you."

"Yes." The word sounds hissed. "Or despoil. Or destroy."

He watches her eyes harden again. "Is it here?" he asks.

She takes her glass and breathes the wine's bouquet, allowing her
anger to diffuse. "I need time to understand them…it. And to understand its impact, the effects it will have."

"But you suggested this afternoon that you have no time. Or only
a little time, anyway."

She bites her lip. "Hours. A day at most." She tilts her glass toward the setting sun and speaks more to herself than to him. "I must decide what needs to be done. Until then, I will not turn anything over to Leopold or anyone else."

Neither Altay nor Travers speaks for a minute. Birds call, and traffic rumbles. The fields are going gold, and the sky is at once deeper and brighter. When a gust of wind rings the chimes, she leans back and looks out toward the sea.

Pushing her at this point will, he thinks, do little good, and so he asks, "Did you always love your work?"

She turns her head slowly, as though she's hearing his voice echo from a distance. "Yes," she says. "When I was a child, I visited my mother on sites so I knew there was no glamour in the work. But I still loved everything about it, even the dirt and sweat." She smiles to herself. "Especially the dirt and the sweat." She stands, pours more wine into his glass, and adds, "I'll be right back."

⊞ 17

While Altay is in the house, Travers eats more olives and chucks the pits into the sunset. Wondering what she's discovered that might prove invaluable, he imagines a gold reliquary or a cache of precious jewels like the pile Heinrich Schliemann took from Troy. He gazes down the hill beyond the Isa Bey Mosque at the ruins of the Temple of Artemis, said to have been the most wondrous of the Seven Wonders of the World. Now it's little more than a pile of rubble on especially low ground between Ayasaluk Hill and Ephesus. The temple's marble pillars were used to build Hagia Sophia in Istanbul, and the remnants with any archeological significance were later carted off to the British Museum. Altay said that the artifact was not from the citadel, and so many layers of vanquished empires and cultures and wealth and grandeur lie within his sight now that he can't guess if the artifact is Hellenistic or Roman, Byzantine or Islamic. Or something even older. Even more curious is Altay's attitude. She seems more apprehensive than excited by her discovery, more burdened than uplifted.

Altay returns with a basket covered with a red cloth. "The evening's too nice to be indoors," she says. "And güveç is best eaten outside." As she unwraps the bread, steam rises from the oval loaf. "The güveç will be ready in a few minutes."

He nods. "You were telling me," he says, "that you visited your mother at the sites."

"Yes," she answers, "in Greece and in Turkey. She was tireless, very organized. Physically slight, but strong-willed." She tears a piece of bread from the loaf and holds it steaming above her glass of wine. "My father sometimes referred to her as his Bonaparte."

"Has she visited you here?" he asks.

"No. She died two years ago. Lung cancer. Only sixty-seven." She puts down her glass. "She had been an avid smoker since her school days." An ironic smile crosses her face. "She liked Turkish cigarettes as much as Turkish men."

He doesn't pursue the remark. "Did she ever see your work?"

"Yes. I spent two university summers in Cappadocia. Do you know the area?"

He shakes his head. The sky is fading and the breeze dying, a sort of nocturne playing as prelude to night itself. He holds his glass in both hands and breathes the wine.

"In Central Anatolia," she says. "It's unlike anything you've ever seen. Steep lava formations intercut with valleys. Soft volcanic spires and turrets for miles. For more than a thousand years, people hollowed caves in the cliffs, even entire underground cities. One summer, my job was to explore the cliffs, mapping undiscovered caves." She waves the piece of bread. "Please, have some."

He tears off a piece, but the bread is still too hot to eat so he slides the chunk back onto the cloth.

"The cave dwellers...the troglodytes..." She smiles again. "They were mostly Christians, so many of the caves were small churches carved in the tufa. Some around Göreme, the Dark Church and the Church of the Virgin Mary, are quite famous now. But I mapped some that had not been seen for centuries."

"Are you Christian?" he asks.

"I'm an archeologist," she says sharply, but then her voice softens. "My mother was Catholic, my father Muslim. I was an only child, and my parents had careers that took them away from home a great deal. I received strong doses of both religions from grandparents who thought the other religion anathema." She puts her piece of bread in her mouth, chews for a moment, and swallows. "For a time in my university days I became a Baha'i. But that attempt at mingling the religious traditions only angered relatives on both sides." She shakes her head. "So now I am unapologetically an archeologist."

For a second, he feels time coiling and energy sluicing again. "And those cave churches you discovered," he asks, "did they affect you?"

"Spiritually?" She takes a long sip of her wine. "Yes, they did. Exploring them was the best time of my life. Even now, if ever I needed to get away, to take time off from my work, I would go directly to Göreme. There's a cave church there that only I have visited in a millennium." She twists more bread from the loaf. "What about you?" she asks. "Where would you go if you needed to get away?"

He sips the wine and looks into her eyes. "Good question," he says. Right after he fired himself from Motorola, he went back to Prescott in search of the sense of belonging he remembered feeling as a child. His mother and father had met when she was a nursing student and he was premed at the University of Michigan. After a shotgun wedding in Grosse Pointe, Michigan, the week they graduated, the couple moved to Prescott where he worked the soda fountain at his family's Eagle Drug Store on the corner across from the Yavapai County Courthouse. Both mother and child barely survived a difficult pregnancy, and Travers' older sister, Margaret, was born six weeks prematurely. His mother's tubal ligation followed, and his father's dream of medical school began to fade. The small town, large sky, open spaces, and easy access to Whiskey Row a block from Eagle Drug beckoned him, but she had trouble appreciating the country music and cigar smoke spewing from the bars, the old miners in their coveralls hanging out in the courthouse square, and the cows straying from the dairy at the south end of town.

Travers' adoption three years later temporarily bridged the gap between his Eastern mother and Western father, but his father's one beer with old friends after work gradually slipped into shots and chasers spilling into the night. Travers' mother often sent him to fetch his father who sometimes rolled willingly home and sometimes tousled Travers' hair and slurred that *he'd be along soon enough, partner.* But what Travers recalled most about those years was looking out at Thumb Butte from his back bedroom window, turning on the swivel stools at the counter in his father's drug store, rearranging supplies in his mother's small offices first at Saint Joseph's Academy and then at Sacred Heart Grade School which he attended, going to Saturday matinees at the Studio Theater, and having everybody in town pretty much know who he was.

People liked his father—some of the women to whom he made regular deliveries, perhaps too much. And though people were friendly to his mother, she never forgave her husband's falls from the wagon or the talk she sometimes thought she heard. The split was inevitable, but Travers never saw it coming—and the move to Detroit wrenched him from the only world he knew.

Travers' visit to Prescott after leaving Motorola was anything but a homecoming. Jack Daniels and Lucky Strikes had done in his father twelve years before. He hadn't much spoken to any of his boyhood friends in decades, and the two who had attended his father's funeral had had little to say other than cursory courtesies. His birth mother, whom he had only known was a northern Arizona rancher's daughter, had never come forward. His house had been razed to build a larger, boxier home. The courthouse still stood and Whiskey Row still thrived, but the town's sprawl had scoured the old businesses. Eagle Drug was gone along with the dairy, Sears, Woolworths, and the Piggly Wiggly. A *paved* path wound up Thumb Butte.

Travers drove to Granite Dells, the swimming hole outside of town that had been the far end of the world for him and his buddies. They rode their Sting-Rays along the path next to the railroad bed, paid their nickels, swung from the tire on the tree's overhanging branch, and dove from the brown wooden platform. But when Travers returned, the Dells had become a dry gulch. The diving platform stood above ruptured concrete, rusted railings, and twisted ladders. The surrounding granite outcroppings were utterly silent, with no echoes of joyful screeches or splashing laughter. On the hills above, the layers of fallen pine needles were already altering the contours of the slopes. And Travers learned again what he already knew—that in America you can't go home because it's no longer there.

Now, Travers smiles at Altay, shakes his head, and repeats, "Good question." He tilts his glass so that light pools in the wine. "Göreme sounds great." Leaning forward, he adds, "Sophia, I need you to…"

Shoes scuff on the concrete as Kenan Sirhan leads Leopold Kirchburg around the corner of the veranda. The Turk looks even more swarthy and stumpy standing next to the pallid and lanky Austrian. Sirhan scowls; Kirchburg, arms folded across his chest, cocks his head, seemingly bemused. Sirhan speaks urgently in Turkish, and the only word Travers understands is *Kirchburg*.

By the time Travers stands, Altay is already on her feet, her fists balled at her sides. She says something curt and shakes her head. As she and Kenan exchange terse Turkish, Kirchburg begins to smirk.

Kenan turns toward Travers, raises his hand, jabs his forefinger violently in the air, and spits Turkish in a threatening tirade that ends with *Amerikan*. He smells of raki.

"Hayır, Kenan!" Altay shouts. "Dur!"

Sirhan wipes his head hard, almost scraping the baldness with his fingernails, and glares at Travers.

"Hosca kalm, Kenan!" Altay says, barely controlling her voice.

Sirhan yanks at his mustache and mutters, "Sons of Greeks!" in English. He glowers once more at Travers, turns on his heels, and slouches back around the corner.

"Gute Nacht, Fräulein Altay," Kirchburg says. He smiles down at her and then nods to Travers. His pleated slacks are unwrinkled, and his shirt is starched. His variegated beard looks freshly trimmed.

Altay purses her lips, takes a breath, and says, "Leopold." Her voice is flat, without a trace of the emotion it held when she was speaking of her summers spent exploring Cappadocia.

Travers takes a sip of wine and swirls it in his mouth.

His pale eyes glinting, Kirchburg says, "I trust that I am not interrupting anything…important."

"Sophia and I were about to have dinner," Travers says.

Kirchburg's smile narrows. "I would join you," he says, taking a step forward, "but I have already dined."

Altay reaches for her wine, stops her hand just above the glass, and balls her fist again.

"Sophia," Kirchburg says, crossing the porch, "there are matters we need to discuss." His smile thins to a pinched line.

Altay stiffens.

"I have critical concerns…"

"In the morning, Leopold," she interrupts. "I have already told you…"

"I have called repeatedly." Though Kirchburg's tone is almost gracious, he puffs his narrow chest and pulls himself to his full height. "You failed to answer."

Travers finishes his wine and slips his glass onto the table.

Altay stares up at Kirchburg's face. Her eyes fire with that feline antagonism Travers saw at their first dinner in Istanbul, but she says nothing.

Travers looks out at the darkening sea. A star glimmers well above the horizon, but there is no moonrise yet. The breeze barely stirs the silent chimes.

"Tomorrow, Leopold," Altay says.

Kirchburg strokes his beard with his index and middle fingers. His gold, opal studded university ring flickers. "I am here now," he says. "Your position requires…"

Travers squares his shoulders. "Herr Kirchburg,…." he begins.

"I am speaking to the Fräulein," Kitrchburg says without taking his eyes from Altay's face.

"Yes," Travers answers, watching Kirchburg. "And I'm talking to you."

His lips twisting, Kirchburg glances at him.

"Doctor Altay," Travers says, "has told you that whatever you need to talk about can wait until morning."

Kirchburg shifts his gaze to Travers. "You do not comprehend the situation."

Travers scratches the side of his nose. "That may be true…"

Kirchburg's face darkens with the fading light. "If you do not leave *now*, I will have you removed from your position with the Glavine Foundation."

Travers holds Kirchburg's gaze. "That," he says, "sounds like a threat."

"It is a fact, Herr…"

"Stop it, Leopold!" Her eyes gleaming, Altay looks from Travers to Kirchburg. "Leave!" She glares at Kirchburg. "Both of you!" Without looking away from Kirchburg, she touches Travers' forearm. "I apologize, Joe."

Travers brushes his hand along her shoulder. Still staring at Kirchburg, he says to her, "Another time. Thanks for the wine."

Altay steps away, crosses between the two men to the screen door, opens it, and enters the house, letting the screen door clap behind her. She then shuts the interior door without slamming it.

Travers takes the piece of bread he broke from the oval loaf. The aromas of the bread and the güveç hang in the air. Raising the bread, he says, "I'll see you out, Leopold."

Kirchburg shakes his head. He continues to scowl at the closed door for a moment before shifting his gaze to Travers. His thin smile is condescending, as though to suggest to Travers that this skirmish may be ending in a draw, but he, Travers, has no idea what the war is much less how to win it.

"The front gate, Herr Professor," Travers says.

⚰ 18

Travers wakes from a dream of tunnels, caverns, and subterranean cities. Lost in a labyrinth lit only by flickering votive candles, he makes his way along stone corridors lined with images of saints so faded that the red of their robes and the gold of their halos are barely visible. The passageways widen and narrow in a pattern he can't figure out. Intermittently, shadows sweep the periphery of his vision, but he remains alone. The ground beneath his bare feet is sometimes smooth flagstones and sometimes gritty cinders. The air blows hot, then becomes cool and still, then sultry, then dank. Behind the sweet odor of melting wax lurks a mustiness, as though he has stepped into an ancient vault recently opened. Broken wheelbarrows, discarded shovels, heaps of potsherds, and rows of dark plastic bottles line the walls. And piles of children's bones lie at each of the domed intersections.

Sweating and disoriented, he rolls over on the bed and stares at the ceiling. Birds are chirping over the rattle of the air conditioner, but he blinks only darkness. He sits up and squints at the digital alarm—4:47. He's at the Hitit Hotel on the main road at the outskirts of Selçuk in southern Turkey, not in some macabre underground maze. When he returned to the hotel from Sophia Altay's house, he saw Charles Lee swimming laps in the pool. Lee had an efficient, even mechanical, stroke, and he didn't notice Travers. Travers had a far greater need to walk than talk so he left the hotel. The road was busy at first, but none of the passing vehicles even slowed to check out the solitary rambler. An hour out of town, as the traffic subsided and the stars spread around a quarter moon, his mind traveled back along the path he had so often trod the last three years…

Were there signs along the way to Jason's suicide? In retrospect, of course there were. Tom handled the divorce better than Travers thought he would, but Jason, who had his mother's moods, did not. School was easy for Tom, and baseball provided both outlets and rewards. Nothing came easy for Jason, except electronics.

Over the next few years, Travers paid greater attention to his career and his relationship with Christine, who was markedly more subtle and stable than Mary. He continued to provide Jason with state of the art gadgetry, which wasn't what he needed. Though Travers called the boys every Sunday evening, his conversations with Jason were usually labored. Notre Dame proved a good fit for Tom, but Jason, home alone with Mary, seldom left the basement his last two years in high school. Father and son went out to dinner every second Wednesday of the month. Jason was often sullen, but sometimes, when he had a brainstorm about a movie he would make or a digital innovation he had in mind, he became exuberant. Mary complained to Travers about Jason screaming threats of suicide at her during their endless arguments, but the boy never used the word with Travers. Between confrontations with his mother, Jason got high, surfed the net, and tinkered with his inventions, never quite finishing any of them.

Two thirty-day stints in Chicago hospitals' "young adult programs" had little lasting effect on Jason. The Friday of what would have been the Thanksgiving vacation of his freshman year in college, he rigged a hose from the exhaust of his mother's BMW to its window. His use of foam and tape to seal the window was both clever and meticulous. And Travers has been walking through the nights ever since…

Now, Travers wobbles to his feet, teeters into the bathroom, and turns on the light, which buzzes before snapping brightness all about him. By the time he returned to the hotel around midnight, the bar was closed and the lobby empty. His Amish phone held no messages from Altay or Kirchburg or Lee or anyone else, and so he went to sleep only to wake at the subterranean labyrinth. Now, despite his nocturnal trek and his lack of sleep, he's wired. The face in the mirror looks haggard, but the eyes gleam. He douses himself with cold water in the shower and brushes his teeth. His fingers and toes tingle. He isn't exactly hyperventilating, but his breathing is quick. When he pulls on shorts and a T-shirt, his legs and arms quiver. His feet prickle in his walking shoes as he goes down the stairs and out into first light.

The moon is still well up. Cars and trucks pass him at intervals, slapping the cool air and splashing light across the pavement. A man on a black bicycle peddles by. A cock's crowing interrupts traditional Turkish music playing somewhere among the flat-roofed buildings at the base of Ayasuluk Hill. Though the sun isn't yet up, the citadel holds light. A tour bus with tinted windows blows past him. A single, large black-winged bird soars like a shadow.

The jangling in his hands and feet abates as he walks into town, but he still feels disjointed. Women with scarved heads huddle silently near a flatbed truck with its motor running and its exhaust pipe belching blue-gray fog. A block farther on, men slouch smoking on a wooden wagon hitched to a tractor. Travers' breathing doesn't calm until he makes the turn toward the cathedral's gate. A mangy black dog tracks him, wagging its tail and barking, but no boys are selling Roman coins.

To dispel the dream, Travers needs to be above ground and in the open—and he wants to feel the sunrise. The gate is shut, but, remembering the rock, he pushes hard against the door. It scrapes back an inch so he puts his weight into it. When he gets it open a foot, he slides through the opening. He shuts the gate and shoves the rock back in place. As he walks past the ticket booth and up into the ruins, birds sing in the pines. Light tips the marble columns ahead of him, but the partially restored brick walls are dim silhouettes. When he reaches higher ground, he looks over Selçuk's roofs to the eastern hills limned with light.

He sits on a stone bench in the western courtyard so that he can watch first light traverse the fields and orchards out to the Aegean. He presses his palms against the cool stone and rocks slowly, feeling the breeze on his face. Birds begin swooping forays to his left, and up through the pines on his right a light is on in Altay's house. The sun tricks him, flashing first on the distant water and then igniting the hills above Ephesus before touching the back of his neck. Still unable to shake the dream despite the sun's warmth, he stands and climbs onto the top of the curtain wall. He sets his feet apart and stretches his arms as if to bid the dawn some pagan greeting. He raises his eyes to the pale gold sky, and then he glances down.

The body lies crumpled on the rocks at the base of the wall sixty feet below. One black shoe is missing. The legs of the pants are askew, the bulky torso contorted, and the white shirt stained dark at the collar. The head is twisted to the side, the bald skull split as though Sirhan dove to the boulders. Blood discolors his mustache above his frozen grimace. Travers' breath catches. He drops to his knees and teeters forward as though he, too, is going to plummet from the curtain wall.

⚱ 19

Sophia Altay starts when Travers hammers at her window. She whirls from her computer and pulls open a file drawer on her right.

"Sophia!" he shouts through the windowpane. He's sweating hard, and his breathing is ragged.

She hurriedly saves and closes a file and then shuts down her computer. As she steps toward the window, the lamp from her computer table backlights her body in her white nightgown. Her hair flows wildly over her shoulders. Alarm shows in her eyes.

"Sophia!" he shouts again. He can't get out any other words.

Her eyes narrow. And then she seems to know. She turns from him and leaves the room. He stumbles through the rising birdsong toward the patio. The air is cool, but his skin prickles as though he's been in the sun all day. She's already out the door by the time he turns the corner.

Grabbing his shirt with her left hand, she yells, "What, Joe? What is it?"

He chokes down bile and opens his mouth, but words still won't come.

Looking up into his eyes, she wipes sweat from his forehead with her right hand. "What happened?" she asks.

He catches his breath and blurts, "Kenan!"

"What?" She twists the fabric of his shirt. "Where?"

"The curtain wall. The base."

Her hands slip from him. Her eyes brimming, she steps back. Then she leans forward, sagging into him. "No, no, no," she murmurs into his chest.

He swallows bile, but he can't rid himself of the image of Sirhan's crumpled corpse.

She steps back and looks out at the gathering light. "No…no," she says again. "It's already starting."

⚯ 20

Travers needs to walk, but there's no chance of that happening. He stands with a uniformed Selçuk detective in the shade of some pine trees near Saint John's curtain wall. The detective is ruddy and handsome, with thick black hair and a mustache. His English is good, but he's having difficulty understanding why Travers walked into town before dawn, pushed open the gate, and climbed onto the curtain wall directly above a corpse. For his part, Travers is trying not to comprehend why the detective keeps repeating questions about his movements and why, though the answers aren't changing, he keeps writing in his small black notebook.

Another officer is interviewing Sophia Altay separately on her patio. Evidence technicians are milling at the base of the curtain wall, but they seem in no hurry to remove Sirhan's body. In full daylight, the corpse doesn't look any less grisly. The authorities are keeping people out of Saint John's, but a crowd of men and boys has formed in the garden behind Asa Bey Mosque.

Leopold Kirchburg marches through Saint John's nave and atrium toward Travers. His tailored pants and pressed shirt look out of place among the ruins. He frowns, his eyes bright with anger and his face blotched with red spots. He ignores Travers, nods to the detective, goes over to the wall, and looks down at Sirhan's corpse. He then turns back and speaks to the detective in German. Travers gets his name, *direktor,* and *Ephesus* but nothing else.

"Ich spricht Deutsch nicht," the detective says.

Kirchburg switches to English. "Why was I not notified immediately?" His voice is flat, devoid of emotion, but ire burns in his eyes.

The detective stares at Kirchburg for a moment. He is ramrod straight, probably ex-military, and Kirchburg, though imperious, is not his commanding officer. "The investigation follows standard procedures, Herr Kirchburg," he says.

"I must be fully informed about this…," Kirchburg says.

The detective scratches his mustache. "A Turkish citizen has died," he says. "An accident has occurred." He keeps his voice even, but color rises in his cheeks to match Kirchburg's. "Procedures must be followed. The man's relatives must be contacted. In time, information will be available to all interested parties, including any foreigners involved."

Kirchburg pulls himself up to his full height. "I see," he says. A note of condescension creeps into his voice. "I will speak directly to your superiors, the mayor of Selçuk, whom I know well, and to officials at the Ministry of Culture."

The detective jots something in his notebook and then nods. "If you must."

Turning to Travers, Kirchburg says, "Where is Fräulein Altay?"

"An officer is interviewing Director Altay," the detective says.

Kirchburg turns and strides toward the house.

"You must wait until we are finished here," the detective calls, but Kirchburg keeps walking.

⳨ 21

Travers finds Sophia Altay in the office he saw her in at dawn, though that moment seems like a long time ago. As he enters, she slides a black laptop computer case onto the floor next to a bulging backpack. Her desktop computer is off, her file cabinet closed, her chair pushed under her desk. She wears a loose white blouse buttoned to the neck, a long khaki skirt, and brown walking shoes. Her hair is pulled back in a tight braid. Her eyes are bright, but not a tiger's—as much prey at the moment as predator.

It has taken him more than two hours to catch her alone. The police are officially treating Sirhan's death as an accident, but the detective told Travers to remain in Selçuk. Leopold Kirchburg shut down the Saint John's dig until further notice and stationed Teutonic-looking young men at the site's main entrance and along the path leading up from the restoration house. Charles Lee, who arrived half an hour after Kirchburg, quizzed Travers about what he had seen and why he had been, as Lee said, *cat stepping in the ruins at sunup*. Finally, the detectives joined the technicians at the base of the curtain wall, and Altay's elderly foreman drove Kirchburg and Lee in the tractor up Ayasuluk Hill so that they could inspect the excavation site.

Altay is obviously bolting, and so Travers asks only, "How are you?"

"How do you think I am?" she snaps. Then, glancing around the office, she takes a deep breath and says in a softer voice, "Not good, Joe. Not good at all."

He scratches the stubble on his chin. "The police are calling...it... an accident, but..."

Fire lights her eyes. "It was no accident."

He doesn't think so either, and he knows far less than she does. "Why do you say that?" he asks.

She lifts the backpack a couple of inches and then lets it drop. She scans the office again, puts her hands on her hips, inhales, and slowly releases her breath. "He...Kenan...was working for...was going to..."

When she doesn't answer further, he nods at the backpack. "How do you know it wasn't an accident?"

She takes another breath, bites her lip, and looks him in the eye, seeming to gauge him. "Because I'm the target. I'm next."

"What? Why?"

She doesn't answer.

"So you're running?"

"No." She shakes her head. "I'm not *running*. There's something…"

He takes a step toward her and then holds back. She looks both younger and smaller standing next to her backpack. Her gaze is neither hard nor fierce, but her eyes are no longer vulnerable. She didn't tell him what was important the night before, and she isn't going to tell him now.

"It will look like you…" he begins.

"It doesn't matter what it looks like. Not at all." Her voice is low but not soft. "I've got to do this."

"How can you walk away from…?" He waves in the direction of the restoration house and the citadel. "…your job? The Project? You said it was your life."

"It is. That's why… I've got to find… I'm going *to* my work. To what matters most."

"*Where* are you going?"

She shakes her head again.

"Sophia?"

Rolling her shoulders back and tapping her thumbs and middle fingers together, she stares into his eyes. "I need you to do something, Joe."

"What?"

"I need you to…" She stoops, opens her knapsack, reaches in among the neatly folded clothes, and pulls out a computer flash drive one-fifth the size of Monuglu's Zippo. As she stands, she turns the drive over in her hand as though it really were a lighter and she needed a cigarette. Holding it out to him, she says, "Give this to Mr. Glavine."

"Bill?"

"No. Le pére. Personally. Only to him."

He hesitates. A man fell to his death from the wall that runs outside this house. Whatever danger she's in, he'll accept it with the flash drive. But he doesn't even know if he should trust her—or even if he's capable of trusting anybody at this point in his life.

"Promise me," she says, leaning toward him and extending her arm.

He takes the flash drive. The metal feels cool, and the green plastic on its side glimmers.

Her eyes lock on his. "Don't tell anyone else about it. No one."

"Bill's father, yes," he says. The drive feels unbearably light in his hand, as though it might float away.

"Go up the hill," she says, wrapping his fingers around the drive. "Keep Leopold and Charles Lee occupied."

"But Sophia…"

"Check your email. And text messages."

"Kirchburg's men are here. At the gate. In the ruins."

"I know," she says. Hefting her knapsack and computer case, she leads him out to the patio. They stand in the shade, but the morning light floods the orchards and fields all the way to the Aegean. The breeze is scant in the rising heat, and the wind chimes are silent. She takes hold of his forearm, leans up so that her mouth is close to his ear, and whispers, "Le pére, Joseph." Without saying anything more, she walks off into the pine trees toward what he thinks is only a precipitous bluff.

⚰ 22

As Travers climbs Ayasuluk Hill, the tractor and wagon rumble toward him. He is just starting to sweat, and the hike all the way to the citadel would have done him good. His mind won't clear, but at least the image of Altay vanishing into the trees along the bluff is vying with that of Sirhan's corpse. As Travers approaches, the tractor turns onto the narrow, worn path toward the knoll where he noticed Sirhan the previous night. Charles Lee, who wears a dark sportshirt, blue jeans, and lightweight hiking boots, sits on one side of the wagon talking with the young Turkish woman with raven hair. Leopold Kirchburg faces away from them and toward the ruins of the cathedral. His slip-ons are dusty, and his shirt is sweat stained.

Kirchburg shouts, "Dur!" at the old Turk driving the tractor and then, pointing ahead toward the knoll, calls out, "What do you know about this site, Herr Travers?"

Lee and the young woman look over their shoulders at him.

"Nothing," Travers shouts over the noise of the tractor's engine. Both the light and his perspective have changed, but the area beyond the cairn looks to have been tamped down again.

Kirchburg scowls. "The trench digging is obvious," he says.

Travers looks out over Selçuk at the waves of heat drifting from the roofs. The sun washes out the hills to the east. "But without adherence to standard archeological practices," Kirchburg adds. His eyes narrow. "Where is Fräulein Altay?"

"I saw her near the restoration office a few minutes ago," Travers answers.

Kirchburg smiles superciliously, turns, and shouts for the old man to get moving again.

As the driver accelerates, blue-black smoke rises from the exhaust pipe. The woman glances at Travers as the wagon passes, but her dark eyes offer nothing. Diesel fumes hang in the air.

When the tractor stops by the cairn on the knoll, Lee steps down from the wagon. Kirchburg slips off and brushes the back of his pants. The young woman stays on the wagon, and the old Turk turns off the tractor's engine. As Kirchburg and Lee walk about looking down at the chunks of overturned dirt, Travers passes them by, continues to the edge of the bluff, and gazes out at the distant sea. The slope of the orchards and fields down toward the water is particularly beautiful. A figure with a backpack is crossing through an orchard to the right.

When Kirchburg comes over, Travers turns to keep him from looking down the bluff. "Terrible accident," Travers says before the Austrian can ask about Altay again.

"It will have adverse consequences on the work here," Kirchburg answers.

"Did you know him—Kenan?" Travers asks.

"I met him once or twice through Sophia," Kirchburg answers.

"He drove me to Ephesus and the Virgin Mary's House yesterday."

"One of his duties was to transport visitors."

A cloud of gnats swirls in the light.

"I have a couple of questions," Travers says, gesturing back toward the citadel.

Kirchburg glances at his gold Tag Heuer. "This is not a good time for your questions, Herr Travers."

"Another time, then." Travers sticks his hand in his pocket so that his fingertips touch the flash drive. "They're related to my evaluation."

Kirchburg waves the gnats away. "Your report," he says, "has become superfluous."

Travers isn't so sure, but he answers, "Maybe, you're right."

Kicking a clod of dirt, Kirchburg says, "I need to be informed about this site *now.*" He turns and shouts at the young woman, "Asar, kommen sie!"

The woman climbs down from the wagon. Her jeans are dusty, but her red τ-shirt is clean. Lee, too, strides toward the bluff.

"What was going on here?" Kirchburg asks.

The young woman's focus moves from Kirchburg to the ground, then out over the bluff toward the Aegean, and finally back to the dirt by her feet. Her nose is sharp, and her skin dark. Her eyes veil whatever she's thinking. "A dig," she says. "A added…" She looks at Travers as though he can help her find the English words. "A extra…"

"A supplemental site?" Lee asks as he steps into the conversation.

She nods. "That is what Sophia called it. She worked it only after…" She waves back toward the citadel. "…After her other work."

"She herself worked the site?" Lee asks.

Looking Lee in the eye, she nods again. "Yes. In the evening. When her other duties were completed."

"Who else?" Kirchburg asks. "Who else worked it?"

"The diggers sometimes stayed after."

"And Kenan?" Travers asks, trying to deflect Kirchburg's attention. "Did he work up here, too?"

"Yes. At times."

"And what about the missing boy?" Kirchburg asks, his voice more imperative than inquisitive.

What boy? Travers thinks.

"Abrahim?" she asks.

Kirchburg stares at her, his silence ordering her to go on.

"Yes. Abrahim is Sophia's most…" She glances at Travers again.

"Trusted?" Travers asks. "Enthusiastic?"

"Yes, enthusiastic." She nods, a grateful smile briefly crossing her face. "Yes. The hardest worker at Saint John's. Always willing to help. To do extra. To do what was needed."

"And he's missing?" Travers asks.

She looks at him, her eyes again not giving anything away. "He did not come to work yesterday."

"Is that like him?" Travers asks.

"Pardon?"

"Were there other times when he did not show up?" Travers asks.

"Oh, no. He is very…dedicated."

Travers smiles at her use of the last word. "Were you…was Sophia worried?"

She nods. "She was quite concerned at first…when she returned from Istanbul," she says. "But then other matters took her attention."

"And you?" Kirchburg asks. "What about you?"

"Yes, I was worried. Abrahim is my friend."

"Not that," Kirchburg says. "Did you work this site?"

A bead of sweat serpentines down her temple, but she looks straight at Kirchburg. "When I had time. When I was able to finish at the restoration house."

"Where is the most recent trench?" Kirchburg asks.

She hesitates for the first time. "I…I have not been up here for days. Since before Sophia went to Istanbul."

Kirchburg steps closer to her. He is more than a foot taller than she is, and he leans forward so that he blocks Travers from her. "Asar," he says, "which is the newest trench?"

Stepping back, she says, "I am not sure."

"Which one?" he repeats.

"Near the edge," she says to the hummocky earth. "Close to the bluff."

"What did Fräulein Altay find?" Kirchburg asks, his tone now magisterial.

The old Turk fires up the tractor's engine.

Asar swipes sweat from her cheek. "Nothing. She found nothing."

"Why is the site backfilled?" Lee asks.

"You mean, the earth?" she says, wiping her hand on her shirt. She glances from Lee to Kirchburg. "Because the orders were for the work on the citadel *only.*"

"Leopold," Travers asks, "is that what you were confronting Sophia about last night?"

"I…" Kirchburg begins, but then he stops, as though answering Travers is something he need not do. He turns back to the young woman who has already begun to walk to the wagon. "Asar!" Kirchburg shouts, but she climbs onto the wagon's bed without looking up, as though the noise of the tractor's engine is drowning his command.

"What was that about last night?" Travers asks Kirchburg.

Lee stares at Kirchburg as if the answer means more to him than to Travers. His expression is blank, but his eyes shine.

Kirchburg glares at Travers for a moment before saying, "What did you and Sophia discuss last night?"

Travers smiles at him. "We talked about my visit to Ephesus and Saint Mary's house. I learned that her family makes good wine."

Glaring again, Kirchburg says, "We have work to do. Come, Charles."

"I think I'll walk from here, Leopold," Lee says. He shakes his arms like a swimmer trying to get loose before a race.

"Fine," Kirchburg says. He pulls back his shoulders and turns toward the wagon.

Travers looks again toward the west. The color in one of the distant fields has changed, gone to celadon in the few minutes that they were standing there.

⊢⚷⊣ 23

"**N**ice view," Lee says as the tractor pulls out with Kirchburg sitting straight-backed on the wagon and the young woman, shoulders hunched, looking away from the Austrian.

"Yeah," Travers says, "the light's incredible."

Travers and Lee walk back over the hardscrabble to the path and then head down toward the restoration house.

"What *did* you and Ms. Altay chat about last night?" Lee asks, his drawl less pronounced.

"Nothing, really," Travers says as they pass one of the grape arbors. "Mostly I was just trying to get a feel for the place."

Lee nods. "She didn't mention any artifacts?"

"Nothing specific."

"But something?" Lee closes his fists and then splays his fingers. "Anything?"

Shaking his head, Travers smiles. "No. Nothing at all."

Lee rolls his neck. "She certainly left Istanbul in a hurry."

The tractor is parked by the restoration house, and Asar has gone inside—but Kirchburg stands in the shade speaking to the two young men he left guarding the area. Both are fair-skinned and thickly built, and both lean their heads forward while Kirchburg speaks to them.

"If she found something," Travers says as he slows sixty yards from the restoration house, "she certainly didn't tell me what it was. I think she sees me as a hatchet man." Travers has the sense that Lee, like Kirchburg, sees him more as an errand boy.

Kirchburg walks briskly around the side of the restoration house toward Altay's porch.

Lee slaps Travers on the back and steers him off the path. "Leopold is sure that your Ms. Altay is holding something out on him. Something significant."

"He is? Why?"

"The way she's been acting."

"Lately? Or is there more to it?"

"That, Brother Travers, is the question." Lee's voice becomes low, as though he's distancing himself from Kirchburg. "I do believe he kept after her when she interviewed for the job, but then she didn't put out once she was hired. He sees himself as a player, and she wouldn't play."

Travers smiles at the thought that the Cat Woman somehow got to Herr Professor Kirchburg.

"Still makes him mad," Lee adds.

Travers starts to walk again, and Lee falls into step with him.

"Turkey," Travers says, "has been more than I bargained for."

"I guess."

"Have you been here often?"

"Fourth...," Lee shakes his head, "fifth trip. I come in a week every quarter to make sure the locals aren't flushing our money down the can."

"So you've been here to Saint John's before?"

Lee nods. "It's not Texas, but there's worse places. Hard to scare up a good steak, though."

"And the site? It's been running okay?"

Lee's smile is crooked. "If y'all don't mind Ms. Altay digging holes all over God's creation."

"What do you think of Kenan's accident?"

Lee brushes the back of his hand across his chin. "What do you mean?" he asks.

"Well, the timing of it, for one thing. It happening the first night we..."

"Shit happens, Brother," Lee interrupts. "It hits the fan sometimes."

"Did you know Kenan?"

"I'd met him here. But he wasn't too talky. Not like Nihat with his diarrhea of the mouth."

"And Abrahim? What's that about?"

"That little squirrel," Lee says, a hint of disdain in his voice. "Your Ms. Altay doted on that gal boy. She..."

Below them, Kirchburg storms out the door of the restoration house and shouts in German at the two young men.

More shit, Travers thinks, *is hitting the fan.*

⊹ 24

Travers hangs up the telephone in Sophia Altay's office. He called Bill Glavine to let him know about Sirhan's death, but it's still well before dawn in Dayton—and he got only Glavine's voicemail. He opens the file drawer he saw Altay reach into at dawn, but it holds only neatly organized supplies and personal items—everything from a stapler to hand lotion. Wondering if the flash drive was in the drawer earlier, he rotates it in his pocket. Turning on the computer and slipping the drive into the USB port would be easy enough, but it's too risky at this point. He simply has no way of knowing who might come through the door.

Once Leopold Kirchburg realized that Altay's laptop computer was gone with her, he browbeat his minions and then questioned Asar, who seemed genuinely upset that Altay wasn't there. Kirchburg demanded that they get the Selçuk police involved immediately, but Lee pointed out that it was too soon. There was nothing to indicate that Altay had not merely stepped out for an hour.

Travers looks closely at the three photographs on Altay's desk. The first, in an antique silver frame, is black and white. A man and a woman stand on a paved surface with a seawall and water in the background. Both stare somberly at the camera. The man is dark with a full mustache and thick hair. The woman is slender, with sharp features and large eyes. He wears a black suit, she a long white gown. They are holding hands but not otherwise touching. The second photograph shows a young Sophia Altay sitting on a boulder. Behind her is a dark hollow, perhaps the mouth of a cave. With her legs pulled up, she hugs her knees. Her head is tilted, and she is grinning. Even at a distance, her eyes glow. The third photo was taken in the courtyard outside. Altay stands behind the large amphora Travers saw by the cactus. She is smiling, as are the dozen people around her. To her left are four diggers, the old tractor driver, and Sirhan, who stands at attention. To her right are younger people, including Asar who has her arm around a thin young man who's so handsome he's pretty.

When Travers returns to the work area, Charles Lee is just leaving for a meeting at their hotel. As Kirchburg shouts orders into his cell phone, Travers sits in the shade on the section of column he sat on the evening before. The birds are silent in the pines, heat radiates from the nearby piles of stone and timber, and trucks grind through their gears in the distance.

Kirchburg stops pacing, puts the phone in his pocket, stands over Travers, and asks, "What do you know about Sophia's disappearance?"

Travers leans over, scoops a pebble from the ground, and tosses it toward the timbers. Then, squinting up at the Austrian, he says, "Nothing, really."

"You informed me that you spoke to her. You were the last one to see her."

Travers shoos a large black fly. "What about your boys?" he asks, his choice of the last word deliberate. "They must've seen her go."

Kirchburg puts his hands on his hips. "They did not. She must have had assistance."

Travers runs his fingertips over the dirt, finds another pebble, inspects it, and then discards it. "How?" he asks. "From whom? Asar and the old man were with us. You sent everybody else away."

Kirchburg's voice becomes more conciliatory. "Joseph," he says, "the Aegean Association and the Glavine Foundation must work together to discover what has occurred at this site."

"The police are investigating…"

"Not that," Kirchburg interrupts, his tone again sharp. "The work itself. The site must…" His phone rings, and he steps away to answer it without excusing himself. "Ja," he says. "Sehr gut. Jawohl." He flips the phone shut, turns back to Travers, and says, "My diggers have arrived."

Kirchburg leads the six men from another Aegean Association site directly to the knoll. They begin, under his supervision, to uncover the supplementary site. Travers remains seated on the column for awhile, heat rising all around him. A few birds begin to sing again. Asar steps out of the restoration house for a moment, gazes up toward the knoll, glances at Travers, and goes back inside the building without saying anything. Travers would like to ask her what she knows, but he's not sure he can trust *anyone*. When he goes down to the main gate to get a bottle of water, a uniformed policeman stands with Kirchburg's sentries under the Gate of Persecution. Men in baggy pants and loose shirts talk and smoke across the street, but no reporters or TV crews are around.

Travers crosses through the ruins again and sits with his back against the trunk of one of the pines by the restoration house. The water is cool, and the scent of pine reminds him of his childhood. The sounds of picks and shovels as well as Kirchburg's intermittent commands fall from the knoll behind him. With his knees pulled up, Travers can feel the flash drive against his thigh. He wonders what's on the drive—photographic evidence or Altay's notes or both. He has to get to Istanbul fast without drawing attention to himself. He needs to talk as well as walk, and the only person in the country he might speak with about the flash drive has gone to ground.

ⵣ 25

Just before noon, Nihat Monuglu strides through the Saint John's Cathedral ruins, smoking a Yenidje and gazing at the columns and brick walls. His gray pants and white shirt remind Travers of Kenan Sirhan. He's neither ghost nor reincarnation, but even their rolling gaits are similar. Travers meets him near the washtub Asar was using to clean artifacts the previous afternoon.

Monuglu does not shake Travers' hand. "Joseph," he says, "this is a bad thing, a Turk dead at an archeological site run by infidels." His voice is devoid of the glib amiability of their dinner in Istanbul.

Travers agrees with him but not with his choice of words. "Yeah," he says. "It's too bad."

Monuglu dunks the tip of his cigarette in the tub, where it fizzes in the brown water. "What is happening on the hill?" he asks as he places the soggy butt on the tub's rim.

Travers glances up toward the knoll. "Herr Kirchburg," he says, "is uncovering archeological trenches that were filled in."

"And Sophia Altay, where is she?"

"She went out this morning and has not yet returned."

"Really?" Monuglu asks. He scratches his mustache. "Where did she go?"

"No one seems to know."

"And Charles Lee?"

"The hotel, apparently. He had business he needed to take care of."

Nodding, Monuglu takes an old coin from his pocket. "Show me where you found the body."

"I didn't actually find it. I was at the top of the curtain wall and saw it…him at the base."

"Show me," Monuglu repeats. His tone isn't quite antagonistic, but he definitely wants Travers to know that he, Monuglu, has authority—and Travers does not. It was obvious even in Istanbul that Monuglu wasn't merely some glad-handing government greeter, but how much power he really wields isn't yet clear to Travers.

Travers leads Monuglu over to the curtain wall where a ten-foot section has been cordoned. Sixty feet below, a uniformed policeman with an autmatic rifle stands outside a taped-off semicircle, but no detectives or technicians remain in the area. Monuglu climbs on top of the curtain wall, gazes down at the rocks, turns, and looks at the spot from which Sirhan likely tumbled.

"When did you discover the body?" He turns the coin between his middle finger and thumb. The coin's battered face shows the profile of a man wearing a laurel.

"At dawn. I couldn't sleep so I walked over from the hotel."

Monuglu steps down from the ledge and stands silently when the call to prayer begins. Travers looks out over the mosque's dome toward the sea. The sun is close to its zenith; the dome and the water glow, but the fields between waver, more mirage than landscape.

When the call to prayer ends, Monuglu stares at the coin for a moment. "This part of Turkey," he says, "is the cradle of civilization. The Europeans…" He glances at Travers. "…and the Americans who come here agree but do not really understand." He scratches his mustache again. "Look out there." He points beyond the mosque. "You will see all of history. A mosque, Christian ruins, a Roman city, the remains of a Greek temple. But you will not comprehend its meaning. A man is dead…" He looks Travers in the eye. "…because you search for ancient artifacts. You do not understand. You go on digging. For what?" He holds up the coin, which gleams darkly. "We Turks do not even know what we have." He flips and catches the coin. "The boy who sold me this outside the gate had no idea what he possessed."

Travers thinks he understands part of what Monuglu is saying—that life, the life that you are already leading, is more important than any artifact. But he wonders if Altay would agree with Monuglu. "Is it, the coin, real?" he asks.

"Does it matter?" Monuglu closes his fist. When Travers doesn't answer, he adds, "I must see what Herr Kirchburg is doing on the hill."

As they walk up the path, Monuglu puts the coin in his pocket, takes out his gold-plated cigarette case, and lights a Yenidje without altering his pace.

"I have to get back to Istanbul," Travers says, "to make my report."

Monuglu nods. As they turn from the path toward the knoll, they can hear Kirchburg's clipped German over the clang of shovels in dirt. The diggers are already down to shoulder level in the trench that was nearest the edge of the bluff.

"The police told me to stay in Selçuk."

"Yes, I know," Monuglu says. Breathing hard, he stops walking, drags on his cigarette, and exhales. "They are interested in you. And you would make a convenient—what is the word?—*scapegoat*. The desk clerk saw you leaving the hotel only thirty minutes before you reported the body. The time of death has not been established exactly, but it is earlier." He picks a speck of tobacco from the tip of his tongue and flicks it away. "A larger problem is your disappearance for more than three hours last night after your fight with Kenan Sirhan."

"Fight?" Travers looks into Monuglu's eyes.

"You deny that you and Kenan had an argument?" Monuglu's words are more a statement than a question. "That you shouted at each other outside Sophia Altay's house?"

Wondering how Monuglu got that bit of misinformation, Travers shakes his head. "Yes," he says. "No. I mean, yes, I deny it. And no, there was no argument. Kenan yelled at me."

Up ahead, Leopold Kirchburg's voice sounds strident as he stands on a dirt pile. The diggers' heads disappear as they lean into their work, and then their shovel blades flash and dirt flies.

"About what, my friend?" Monuglu's last word isn't particularly amicable.

Travers smiles. "I don't know. It was Turkish. Except for the end."

"The end?"

"He called me *a Son of a Greek.*"

Monuglu drops his cigarette and grounds it with the heel of his polished black shoe. "He *was* angry at you." He claps Travers hard on the shoulder. "But you do not know why?"

"I have no idea. Something about my being American."

Monuglu waves his hand as though he is making a pocket of air vanish. "But at least you can explain your disappearance."

"I took a walk," Travers says, not quite able to keep a defensive note from his voice.

"After your dinner here with Doctor Altay?"

"Yes… No. Kenan and Kirchburg got here before we could eat."

"Ah." Monuglu nods. "That's too bad. You enjoy your dinners with Doctor Altay?"

"I do."

"And then you and Kenan did *not* have the argument."

"I told you, Kenan yelled at me."

"And then you took a walk alone in the Turkish countryside?"

"Yes," Travers says, unwilling to explain what was on his mind. "Under the stars."

"Ah, the night sky," Monuglu says. "It is beautiful in this part of Turkey."

Kirchburg is perspiring even though others are doing all the digging. His gray blond hair is matted, and his neck is red. With his back to Travers and Monuglu, he doesn't see them approach until they've passed the cairn that marks the site. The diggers are thickset men sweating through sleeveless T-shirts. Their labor looks more like ditch digging than archeology.

"Guten Tag, Herr Kirchburg," Monuglu says. "You are back at work quickly after what occurred this morning."

Kirchburg takes a handkerchief from his pocket and wipes his forehead. "It is necessary." He looks at Travers. "Important, to find out what So…Fräulein Altay was doing here."

"Of course," Monuglu says. "But you do not seem to be proceeding with your usual caution."

Kirchburg folds the handkerchief. "I am following the contour of her most recent trench. I will use the most exacting techniques when I discover what she…if she has covered something up."

Facing Monuglu and Travers rather than the trench, Kirchburg doesn't at first notice that four of the men have already stopped digging. The other two, a bald man with thick tufts of graying hair on his shoulders and a heavy man whose arms look stubby compared to his torso, scrape the tips of their shovels in the dirt. Seeing Travers staring, Kirchburg wheels, takes a half step toward the trench, stops himself, and stuffs his handkerchief in his pocket. The outline of a rectangular stone a meter long and three-quarters of a meter wide is visible in the dirt.

"Aus!" Kirchburg yells. "Aus, aus!"

As soon as the men are out of the trench, Kirchburg clambers down with a trowel and whisk broom. He kneels, brushes dirt from the stone, and then digs around its periphery with the trowel, pushing the dirt behind him with the brush. His technique is fast but not fastidious. The diggers wipe their faces and lean on their shovels. Monuglu takes out his cigarette case but doesn't open it. Travers looks west at the light firing the wavering fields.

"Ossuary," Monuglu says, tapping the cigarette case against his palm.

"What?" Travers asks.

"A bone box. Used by Jews in the first century to rebury their dead."

The lid, the color of sand, is decorated with a symmetrical cross surrounded by a circle within a six-pointed star. The smooth stone is barely eroded. As Kirchburg clears a mini-trench like a dry moat around the box, Travers can see that the sides of the box taper inward from the lid. When Kirchburg removes enough dirt to reveal an inscription, he sits back, drops his brush and trowel, and wipes his hands on his pants. He then reaches into his shirt pocket and pulls out a photographer's loupe.

The diggers look at one another but don't say anything. Travers slips his hand into his pocket and touches the flash drive. Monuglu squats and squints at the writing etched into the stone. Kirchburg leans forward, the loupe to his eye, and examines the inscription from right to left. Suddenly, he leaps back as though he has licked an electrical socket.

Monuglu braces his hand on the pile of dirt and then, with startling speed and agility, hefts his bulk into the trench. He hunches over next to Kirchburg, peering at the engraved letters. His head shoots up. His cigarette case falls into the dirt as he, too, steps back against the trench wall.

Kirchburg throws himself forward, clawing at the lid's corners with his long fingers.

"No!" Monuglu shouts. "Nein!"

But Kirchburg is already shifting the lid, getting the tips of his fingers under it, lifting it free. Breathing hard, he holds the lid to his chest. Color flushes his cheeks; sweat rolls down his face and beads in his beard. Even Travers standing above the trench can see that the box is empty, but Kirchburg stares into it, checking every corner. Finally, the lid still clutched in his arms, he straightens and gazes up into the sunsplashed sky. A groan, half sigh and half growl, rises from his throat.

Monuglu turns and looks up at Travers. His thick finger points at the inscription. "Jesus of Nazareth, the Christ," he says.

☦ 26

As Travers looks on, Charles Lee inspects the ossuary standing on Sophia Altay's desk. Lee traces his fingers over the decorated lid—the interconnected cross and circle and star. He then runs his fingers from left to right along the inscription. "Can you read it?" he asks Travers.

"No. It's some form of Aramaic."

"It's also a fake." Lee's tone is even, but his eyes are fixed on the ossuary's symbols.

"What?" Travers asks. Lee's background in archeology isn't any stronger than his own.

Lee reaches out and traces the decorations again. "Discoveries this powerful in archeology are most often frauds. At the end of the day, they don't amount to a bucket of spit." Though his voice remains calm, his index finger trembles as he touches the ossuary. "Even if the box itself is from the right period, the inscription is probably bogus. Establishing authenticity will be hard got. Maybe impossible."

"But..."

Lee looks at Travers, his eyes suggesting that Travers is some kind of rube. "Leopold wants it to be the real deal, but that doesn't make it so."

Travers gazes at the ossuary, at its cross and circle and star. Kirchburg certainly was ecstatic at the discovery, but he was also irate that the ossuary was empty. He did not let Monuglu or Asar or any of the other Turks handle it except to haul it down Ayasuluk Hill. He decided that Altay's desk was the best place for the box, and, after cleaning its exterior himself, is now making self-congratulatory calls on her patio where his cell phone's reception is better.

"And your buddy, Nihat," Lee continues, "whatever he really thinks, he's got to treat the box like it's legit until it's proved otherwise."

Travers nods. On that point at least, Lee's right. Monuglu has gone to the Ephesus Museum in town to speak with the curator before news of the ossuary leaks out. The combination of Sirhan's death and the bone box's discovery will bring media attention to Selçuk in ways the town, Monuglu pointed out, will find difficult to handle.

"But if it's real," Lee asks, "why would your Ms. Altay cover it up and fly the coop?"

That's exactly the question Travers has been thinking about. The ossuary must have contained something that either she is hiding or that she lost. Bones are the obvious possibility, but she definitely wasn't carrying a pile of bones when she left. She was pressed and uneasy, and she didn't have much of anything with her except her computer and some clothes. And what if the ossuary did contain bones? All theological hell would break loose. Christian dogma is going to take a major hit in any case. The Jews used ossuaries, Monuglu informed Travers, to *rebury* the dead. The mere existence of the bone box, if it's genuine, throws Jesus of Nazereth's resurrection and ascension into question. His divinity—the foundation of Christianity—would be undermined, if not destroyed. Finding Christ's remains would be the greatest archeological discovery in history, but a host of powerful people, religious and secular, would have every reason to deny the bones' existence—or, at the very least, question their authenticity. "Why do you think Altay left?" Travers asks.

Lee brushes his hand through his hair. "Because she planted that box," he says, "and somebody found her out. She was going to use the discovery to save her job, at least for a spell, and while she was in Istanbul somebody figured out the hoax."

"Who?"

Lee turns back to the ossuary. He runs both hands along the edge of the lid but doesn't lift it. "You tell me," he says. "According to that Turkish woman, Altay's top employee didn't come to work yesterday. But Altay forgot to mention that fact to anybody. Then her driver has a fatal accident. And now she herself has flown."

Travers admits to himself that Lee's points are true, but he knows a thing or two—the existence of the flash drive and the anxiety in Altay's eyes—that Lee doesn't.

Lee looks again at Travers, his eyes an even darker blue. "Don't be an acorn cracker. Ms. Altay may have done that famous French femme fatale job of hers on you, but something's rotten here at Saint John's. Follow the stench, and you'll find your missing fem."

⚰ 27

As the veiled woman carrying the woven red and gold shoulder bag passes along the path, the young man sitting under the cypress watches her. An aluminum tube is lashed to the backpack lying beside him. This is the first time he has been to Cappadocia, and the tufa fairy chimneys and the web of caves amaze him. Too preoccupied to hike up into the hills, he has spent much of his time at the internet café trying to make contact. But he did visit the open air museum. The churches hollowed out of solid rock chanted hymns to him across more than a millennium. The restored frescoes in the Dark Church whispered prayers. He felt both safe and less alone in the seven-story nunnery with its tunnels and blocking stones for dangerous times.

Now it's finally dusk of the day after he left Saint John's. The sky has begun to darken, and she is keeping her promise. He counts slowly to twenty-five, stands, hefts his backpack, and follows the woman at a safe distance, just as she instructed. She continues along the path as it winds through the brush and rock until, suddenly, she disappears. When he reaches the spot at which she vanished, he sees a cleft to the right. He can just squeeze through it with his backpack. Most of the light has left the small box canyon. Tall sunflowers grow at one end, and water trickles from a crack in the wall. There's a cool breeze, but he can't tell where it's coming from. Standing so that she faces him, Doctor Altay slowly unveils herself. Her expression holds both exasperation and affirmation.

When he comes to her, she gazes into his eyes and says, "Abrahim."

He sloughs his backpack and lets her hug him. He slouches so that she can hold him more tightly, then puts his arms around her shoulders and leans his head against hers. There is nothing sexual in the embrace, but the tenderness almost makes him cry. "I'm sorry," he whispers in Turkish.

She stands back and looks at his fine features, his large brown eyes, high cheekbones, clear olive skin, and full lips. She runs her hand through his thick black hair. Contrition shows in his eyes. Her hands grip his shoulders. "Abrahim," she says, "you should have waited for me."

Staring at the ground, he lets his hands fall to his sides. "I know," he says. "I could not reach you. I heard Kenan talking on the phone. He was going to…"

"He is dead."

He flinches. "Kenan?" He steps back, grimacing. His teeth are bright in the fading light. "Dead?"

She nods.

He makes the sign of the cross. "What…? How?"

"He fell from the curtain wall last…early this morning."

Abrahim is quaking, and only her hands again on his shoulders keep him from taking flight. "You…somebody…?"

She locks her eyes to his. "Who was he talking to on the phone?"

He shakes his head. "German. He was speaking German. And he wanted money. A lot. He kept repeating *euros.*"

Taking a deep breath, she looks around at the light dying on the sheer walls. "Come," she says, leading him to a boulder. He slumps there, starting to sob and to murmur prayers as she returns for his backpack and her bag. Setting the backpack at his feet, she says, "Show me. Now, before it's too dark."

He nods, swipes his cheek with the back of his hand, and unties the aluminum tube. "I got this in a shop that sells posters to tourists," he says. "I thought it would work better."

She takes a clean white cloth from her bag and fastidiously wipes her hands. Noticing the scabs on his knuckles, she asks, "Fight?"

"Kenan…" He drops his eyes. "No… When he…" He fumbles

with the tube's lid, pops it, tilts the tube, and slides out two rolled scrolls. "I have been careful." He looks up at her standing before him. "Kenan is…?"

"Yes." When she takes the scrolls, she feels as if she has been touched for the first time. The scrolls are similar but not identical—the first, the color of Cappadocian sand, slightly darker than the other. The material is brittle but not flaking or worm eaten, the odor at once acrid and sweet. The scrolls feel both light and heavy, fragile and strong. Unable for a moment to believe she's holding them, she is tingling at her core. Her hands quiver as she unrolls one of the scrolls just enough to read the first Aramaic line—*Hear, O Israel. Worship the Lord your God and serve Him only….* By the second scroll, her hands are shaking furiously. *I am John, the one Jesus, the Nazarean, loved….*

The whole day as she was traveling she thought about these scrolls—these testaments. While she was driving to Konya, she went over in her mind the Turkish and French and English translations she was making. After she left her car parked on a side street, she took one bus to Nevşehir and another to Göreme, hoping she was covering her tracks well enough. The Pharisees would discover the car, but they would not find her until she possessed these documents and determined what to do with them. As she rode through Cappadocia, returning to the spires and caves she had loved, the scrolls' deeper implications weighed on her—the words about rebellion and violence… *If you do not have a sword, sell your cloak and buy one…* and *…I have come to bring fire on earth….* And now, her hands will not stop shaking. Before she drops the scrolls, she rolls the second, takes the tube, slips the scrolls in, and presses the lid down tightly.

"Did you translate them?" he asks.

"The first," she says. "The second, not completely yet. The first is a transcription of the words of Jesus of Nazareth. Probably from the time in the Garden of Gethsemane. And it is, I believe, authentic." She doesn't hand back the tube. "The second is written by John the Apostle, in his hand." She does not add, *but later in his life…when he is no longer young like you.*

He looks up at her. "I need to know what they say."

"And I will tell you." She fears the documents' ramifications will be too much for him. "What did you do with the bones?"

He stares at the tube.

"Abrahim?"

He shakes his head.

"Abrahim!"

"The femurs were broken."

She told him in her email what the ossuary's inscription said, and she is sure that he has already made the intuitive leap across two thousand years. "Do not draw conclusions," she says. "The remains must be examined. Where are they?"

"The femurs were broken," he repeats, shaking his head again. He cannot tell her—or anyone else—where he hid the bones. The bones will fracture faith around the world. The gospel truth that not a bone in His body was broken will itself be shattered. He must protect the remains, even from her—though he trusts her more than he trusts anyone else. She understands him better and accepts who he is more than his own family does.

As she slides the tube into her bag, heat runs through her hand. The aluminum isn't hot, but her hand radiates with warmth. She reaches up, brushes her hand through Abrahim's hair, and cups his left ear. The juncture almost sparks, and her fingers pulse for a moment before settling on his neck. She gazes into his eyes.

He cannot look away from her. A shaft of energy passes through her hand and spreads across his skin, along his neck, and down his spine. She could shatter him this second, splinter his soul, send him spilling into a thousand shards. She could compel him to share with her where the bones are, but her eyes are not directing him to. Instead, they offer trust that wings through him like a seraph—faith in him he is certain he is unworthy of.

⌖ 28

Travers stares at the message on the computer screen. It is simple, direct, and cryptic: DELIVERY CRITICAL. He sits back, rolls his neck, clicks on *Reply*, and types OK. Sophia Altay has bolted, he guesses, to those cave churches in Cappadocia she mentioned, and his delivering of the flash drive safely to William Glavine, Sr., is somehow even more important than it was.

Travers sends his reply and then takes a sip of his apple tea. The internet café looks like an outdated parlor replete with overstuffed chairs. It is cramped and crowded, but none of the young people hunched at the other seven computers is American. The two French girls next to him chatter quietly as they take turns keyboarding. Travers logs off the internet and opens the flash drive's single file folder again. The folder contains eleven items, all digital photographs: two of the ossuary, one of bones, and eight of script. Nothing else. No pictures of diamonds spilling from an embroidered sack. No piles of precious stones. No trove of gilded treasure.

He clicks on the first photograph of the ossuary, almost certainly the same box that Leopold Kirchburg uncovered. Both the shape and the markings are the same, and it rests in front of a dirt wall the color of the earth at Saint John's. The second photo, a close-up of the cross within the circle within the star, confirms the similarity. The third shot, taken from a point directly above the ossuary, is more disturbing. The bones are *arranged* in the box, the skull lying on the ribcage, the femurs and humeri forming a cross, and the other bones creating the six points of a star. The femurs, unlike the other bones, are broken. But it's all too neat, as though someone has just finished juxtaposing the bones.

He examines the photographs of the scrolls, but he can't decipher any meaning. He can tell, though, that there are two separate documents. The opening of each is obvious, and four of the images are darker than the others. The language throughout looks like the script on the ossuary, but he can't be sure it's Aramaic. He squints at the incomprehensible second document one last time before closing the files and removing the flash drive from the USB port.

He puts the flash drive in his pocket, leans back, and finishes his tea. He is glad, finally, to have slipped away from the Saint John's site. Nihat Monuglu was right—the combination of the ossuary's discovery and Kenan Sirhan's death knocked Selçuk on its civic ear. The Ephesus Museum's curator and restoration specialists were at Saint John's by early afternoon. Kirchburg is flying in his extended research team from Vienna, and Lee's consultants from the University of Chicago are airborne. BBC and CNN correspondents as well as Turkish and German TV reporters are already encamped—and the American networks' top guns are shooting for Selçuk. The recently leaked news that the Saint John's site director vanished in the few hours between Sirhan's death and the bone box's discovery whetted the international media's appetite for a lurid tale. Even Al Jazeera and Israeli Broadcasting are on the way.

Kirchburg is, at the moment, holding his first full-blown press conference. He and Charles Lee, who's a whole lot less enthused about the ossuary's discovery, were vying for airtime, with the Austrian palpably unable to resist the lights and cameras. The upside for Travers is that neither Kirchburg nor Lee wanted him around to speak to reporters. Travers himself doesn't have anything personal against the press, but in Selçuk this particular evening it does seem to him like a case of flies to shit.

The local police, seemingly more preoccupied with the sudden influx of foreigners than with the investigation of Sirhan's death, have disregarded Travers since the initial interviews. And Monuglu simply told him to check in at the Selçuk Municipal Building in the morning. Travers had a short, pointed, and difficult conversation with Bill Glavine. His old friend's reaction, like Lee's, was that the ossuary must be a fake. Travers' news that one employee had died and that the site director and another employee had disappeared—as had the bone box's contents—disturbed Glavine. And when Travers asked if he could speak privately to Glavine's father, the conversation ended abruptly.

After paying the young man stationed by the door, Travers leaves the internet café. Three guys lean against a white Toyota outside the café. Smoking cigarettes, they laugh and talk and ignore Travers completely. The night is warm but not oppressive. Across the street and half a block back, a swarthy man stands in a doorway smoking.

Travers glances up at the sky, where the quarter moon is just coming up above the rooftops and a few stars glimmer through the haze of ambient light. More edgy than tired, he heads through Selçuk's narrow backstreets. As he walks, he begins again to work through what's happened since he first arrived in Turkey. He should have known—and at some level really did know—that he couldn't escape thoughts about his job, his failed relationships, and, ultimately, Jason's death. Still, he in no way could have expected to find a corpse or lose a site director. He makes a mental note to call his son, Tom, when he gets back to the hotel—he's in New York, working in investment banking, living the life of a single Manhattanite, and they haven't talked often enough in the last year.

Taking a circuitous route back to his hotel, Travers passes through a quiet neighborhood. Turkish music falls from an open window above a closed carpet store. The scent of something like cinnamon is in the air. As he reaches a curve in the road that bends sharply to his right toward the main road, two men round the corner ahead of him. A wiry man with short black hair steps in front of Travers and grins. His small dark eyes shine. "Travers?" he says, pronouncing it *traverse*.

The taller man with the cropped brown hair and thick neck circles behind Travers.

Travers instinctively grabs for the flash drive in his pocket. He looks about wildly, but no one else is in sight. The music seems distant, barely an echo. He suddenly feels as though heat is rising from the pavement. Lights are on in some of the second-story windows, but no one is peering out at the street.

The wiry man flicks a knife open.

As Travers steps back, a fist strikes the left side of his head from behind. He stumbles, his ear ringing and pain flashing across his temple. Turning, he glimpses the bigger man—the nose above the sneer is crooked, the left eyebrow scarred—swinging a second time. Aware that he's moving too slowly to even get his hand up, Travers watches the fist. The uppercut catches his jaw, snapping his head back into darkness.

⚵ 29

Kneeling on the prayer rug, Sophia Altay carefully slips the scrolls back into the aluminum tube and caps it. All around her, the faded red and gold frescoes of the saints shimmer in the dim light away from her headlamp's beam. Before she began her work, she pushed the blocking stone across the cave church's low, narrow entrance. The church is high up a tufa outcropping far from the town, and the only light that can escape rises to the stars through the sheered wall above the stone altar.

Her body still tingles. She has touched the Rosetta Stone and the Elgin Marbles in London, held Phoenician gold and Roman coins, worked with Hittite tools and Greek utensils, and inspected Christian relics and Islamic treasure, but nothing has ever touched her like these scrolls have. She turns off her laptop and places it next to the only two books she brought with her—a paperback Aramaic dictionary and a slim volume of Rumi's poems. She has finished proofreading her Turkish translations. The scrolls were far better for the task than the photos Abrahim took, and she has, she believes, gotten the meaning exactly right.

Just before dawn, she will take the scrolls to the safe place she has chosen. The journey is dangerous in the dark, but she will not risk being seen in daylight. The Pharisees will do anything to destroy these documents—she is more certain of that than ever. They have killed, and they will kill again.

She looks up at the ceiling above her, the light from her headlamp creating a halo. All three symbols are there on the roof—the equal-armed cross, the circle, and the hexagram. All predate Christianity, and each attempts to present meaning—in the cross are the elements of earth, air, fire, and water; in the circle, unity and creation and the cycle of life; and in the six-pointed star, humanity's position between sky and earth, the juxtaposition of women and men, and the reconciliation of opposites.

She brushes her hand along the aluminum tube gleaming in her headlamp's beam. The scrolls possess her. The ossuary's bones would herald and help verify the documents, but she does not possess them. Abrahim, sweet Abrahim, will not give up the bones because he fears their effects and because he suspects she will cast him off once she has all of the ossuary's contents. She will not, of course; she knows a thing or two about not fitting in, having been the French girl in Istanbul and the Turkish girl in Paris and Cambridge.

Abrahim is even more of an outsider, a Christian with Aramaic roots, a homosexual with devout religious beliefs, a brilliant student who could not function in a traditional university, and a beautiful naïve boy who was preyed upon early. He was largely untrained and self-taught when he appeared at Saint John's the previous year asking for work, but he quickly demonstrated a gift, a real genius, for both archeology and restoration, for *discovery*. It doesn't surprise her at all that he was the one to first find the ossuary or that he has taken the discovery so deeply to heart. If only he had been able to wait for her rather than, in his excitement, gone to Kenan. Though Abrahim likes nothing more than to please her, he is also a stubborn child who holds fast to whatever is most important to him. Had he known what these scrolls said, he might never have let go of them.

She stares again at the aluminum tube, her hand reaching for the molten light reflecting from it. She will hold the scrolls one more time, just once more, and then she will conceal them where the Pharisees cannot reach them. As she lifts the tube and starts to open it, her breath catches. She finds herself shaking her head and whispering, "No...no...no." The scrolls must be preserved, protected even from her own touch. Still cradling the tube, she switches off her headlamp, lets her eyes adjust, and gazes out the cut above the altar at the night sky, the brush of stars.

⚷ 30

Abrahim starts. He was fast asleep, dreaming that skeletons were chasing him across a tufa cliff. The specters kept getting closer, their bones chattering, until he could feel their brittle fingers scratching his neck. The cliff steepened, falling away into a void. They raked his back, the blood running hot. He lost his footing and began to slide, their hideous laughter trailing him down the tufa into the abyss.

Sweating under the covers, he grabs himself and curls on his side. He must confess or demons will chase him through all his days and nights. He strokes himself, stops, curls tighter, and begins again. It is not yet dawn. Outside, the birds are singing, but there is no light. The bones were not his to take, and stealing is a sin. Looting that holy box, touching those sacred remains, is sacrilege. But Kenan was going to sell them. To whom? And for what, thirty pieces of silver? Like Judas, Kenan paid with his life. Did he throw himself upon the rocks? Abrahim would have, except that suicide is the one unforgivable sin. He has sinned all too often, and he has sometimes thought that he must take his own life so that he sins no more. But damnation would follow, an eternity of hellfire. Kenan had no such scruples. He was incapable of feeling the unbearable weight of sin, and he did not fear hell. Money bought Kenan base pleasures, and he was going to trade the most venerable of relics for euros without a thought for his immortal soul. Euros! Kenan would never have taken his own life, broken his own bones, when there was money to be made from the ossuary.

Abrahim wills himself to stop stroking again. He forces himself from under the covers to the cool, hard floor. He kneels naked and bends forward, his forehead touching the cold tiles. He must seek forgiveness yet another time. "Confeitior Dei…," he begins, his prayers always in Latin, a sacred language that speaks directly to the Lord. But his Act of Contrition isn't perfect. He still cannot feel truly sorry that he took the bones. He is glad that he stole the documents.

The sweat chills his body, causing him to shiver. He tries to offer praise in place of his failed contrition. "Laudamus te," he chants aloud. "Benedictimus te. Adoramus te. Glorificamus te." He repeats the incantation, but the words do not raise him up or free his mind from what he has done or what he will do. He must find out what the Messiah said. He knows no Aramaic, only Latin and Greek as well as his native Turkish and the English and French he has picked up in the last year. If he had known Aramaic, would he have let Doctor Altay take the scrolls? He trusts her more than he trusts anyone else, but she did not ask him for the scrolls. She simply placed them in her bag. She must already have translated them. She has a gift for languages, moving effortlessly among ancient and modern tongues. But why didn't she tell him what the scrolls say? Just as he is protecting the hidden bones, she is safeguarding the scripture. But is she protecting him—or the words from him?

His shivering deepens, and his knees ache from the cold floor. He looks at the warm bed taking shape as the curtained windows turn from black to gray. He is not supposed to make contact with her today. When at nightfall she pointed him back along the road into Göreme, she told him only that they would meet at the same time and place the next evening. But how is he to make it through an entire day, alone and bereft of her touch or that of any other human?

⛏ 31

At eight in the morning, Joseph Travers limps into the small Selçuk Municipal Building office cluttered with a row of file cabinets, a computer station, a desk, and a conference table with four chairs. Stacks of documents are piled on top of the cabinets as though filing is a century behind.

Nihat Monuglu, seated at the desk smoking and reading a word-processed document, looks up and stubs out his cigarette in the half-filled ashtray. Waving his hand at the mess, he says, "It is the best the mayor could do for me." As he stands, he adds, "How are you, Joseph?"

"I've been better," Travers says. He has shaved and put on clean clothes, but his jaw is swollen, and his left ear won't stop ringing. His head aches, and he's groggy from medication and lack of sleep. Though the meds are doing some good, his right thigh where the fifteen stitches are sewn is tight and burning. The pervasive odor of stale cigarette smoke nauseates him.

"I apologize on behalf of my country," Monuglu says. "What happened to you does not occur to tourists here."

Travers nods but doesn't smile at the irony. Both he and Monuglu know that what happened has nothing to do with tourism. The guys that beat him and then cut the flash drive from his pocket knew who he was and had some idea what he had. Or at least that he had *something.* He was out cold, and the knife wound in his thigh was more message than necessity.

"Please take a seat," Monuglu says, gesturing toward the table and then picking up the ashtray and coming around from behind the desk.

Travers pulls out a chair, sits, and grimaces when the pain snakes along his leg.

Monuglu sets the ashtray on the table, sits down across from him, leans forward, and folds his hands. "Have you spoken with Herr Kirchburg or Mister Lee?" he asks.

Travers can't get comfortable. "No," he says. "Have you?"

"Not since Herr Kirchburg made all of his announcements for

television. Have you heard from Sophia Altay?"

Travers looks around the office. Two laminated posters, one of the facade of the Library of Celsus and the other an aerial view of Saint John's Cathedral, hang on the wall over Monuglu's shoulder. But there's nothing, no personal photographs or talismans or knick-knacks, to let anyone know whose office this really is. "I don't know where she is," he says. "Or even if she's doing all right. You're much more likely to know about that and Kenan's death and anything else that's going on."

Monuglu shrugs. "Perhaps..."

"Damn it, Nihat," Travers says, leaning forward. He's too tired and in too much pain to keep playing this game. "The two guys who jumped me knew my name."

Monuglu sits back, his hands sliding along the tabletop. "What are you implying?"

"You know exactly what I'm saying. Did you send them?"

Monuglu stares at Travers, ferocity flashing in his eyes. He slides the ashtray to the side, presses his hands on the table, and leans forward so that they are almost nose to nose. "You want us to be..." He pauses as though he's not sure of the English word. "...frank..., Joseph? That's good. Then listen to me. A Turk is dead. A young Turkish man, little more than a boy, is missing. So is a woman, a noted Turkish archeologist." A droplet of spit flies from his mouth and hits the table between them. He swipes it with his hand. "So is what was in that bone box, artifacts that belong to the people of Turkey."

"Yes," Travers answers, meeting Monuglu's gaze. "And I was knifed."

"You possessed something related to these events, something you obtained during the investigation. Something you did not tell the Selçuk police or *me* about. Those men who did this did not take your wallet or passport. They only took it, the thing you possessed. You do not even know if they were Turkish, and yet you accuse me."

"I was marked."

"They were not my men."

"You had me followed from the moment I arrived in Turkey." Travers tries to keep his voice even, but anger fires through his words.

Monuglu folds his hands and sits back but does not look away. "You must tell me what you possessed. If you do not, your pain is just beginning."

Travers smiles through the ire. The burning in his leg, the headache, and the ringing stir the sense of loss he holds. "Don't threaten me, Nihat," he says. "It won't work."

Monuglu does not break eye contact. "I did not send those men. I learned about it only after the incident occurred."

Incident? Travers thinks. He doesn't trust Monuglu, but he's starting to believe him, at least on this point.

Monuglu pulls his lighter from his pocket. "I must know what they took."

"Yeah," Travers says. "Okay." He insisted to the medics and police that he had no idea why he had been cut, that there must have been some mistake in identity. But Monuglu knows better. Travers has already broken his promise to Altay. He could out of spite withhold what little he knows, but that won't get him any closer to the truth. Malice never does. He brushes his fingertips across the table's veneer and says, "A computer flash drive."

Monuglu picks up his lighter, flips it opens, and then shuts it. "What was on it?"

"I don't know."

Monuglu stares at Travers again. "You were robbed just after you left an internet café. You sent email messages, but you also *used* the flash drive while you were there."

"It had photos of the bone box, the bones, and documents of some kind. Some ancient writing. I couldn't read it. Not a word."

Monuglu flicks his lighter open, fires it up, and watches the flame. "How did you get the flash drive?" he asks.

"You know."

"Where is she?"

"I don't know." He's got an idea, of course, but, technically, he's telling the truth.

"But you did hear from her?"

"Email—a few words."

"What?"

"Basically, *Deliver the flash drive.*"

"To?"

"The Glavine Foundation. Who else would I deliver it to?"

"An excellent question." Monuglu waves the lighter for a moment before snapping it shut. "I can have the email checked."

"Go ahead. If you haven't already."

"Let us be clear on this. Shortly after Sirhan's death, during the investigation, Doctor Altay asked you to do something...something secretive if not illegal. And you agreed."

"I did."

Monuglu scratches his mustache. "Do you know anything about the discovery of the bone box?"

"Nothing. She told me nothing about it or its contents."

That Travers is telling the truth on this point seems to register with Monuglu. "The photograph of the bones. Where were they?"

"Arranged in the box."

"*Arranged?*"

"Yes. Neatly."

Monuglu stands the lighter on the desk. "Ah, Joseph," he says, "your visit to Turkey has been more eventful than you expected."

"It has."

"Thank you for coming in this morning," Monuglu says, the fierceness momentarily gone from his eyes. "With the night you had, my friend, you must need rest."

"I need to return to Istanbul." The attack, the ambulance, the hospital emergency room, the red tape, the interviews with the cops—all of it was a pain, but none of it was more difficult than losing the flash drive Altay had entrusted to him.

Monuglu nods. "You mentioned that yesterday."

"The police told me to remain here."

"That *is* a problem. You see, the status of Kenan Sirhan's death will, very soon, be officially changed to homicide." He stares into Travers' eyes. "The backs of his legs were scraped, and his wrist was shattered. Not only did he not jump, but he tried to break his fall." Shaking his head, he exhales. "And your possession of the flash drive connects you yet again to the murder." Monuglu tilts his head and raises his eyebrows. "Certain other information received…"

"What information?"

Fixing his eyes on Travers, Monuglu leans sideways and takes a cracked leather billfold from his pants' back pocket.

"I had nothing to do with Kenan's death."

He opens the billfold and glances at a photograph of himself standing with his arms around a dark-haired woman and three round-faced young children, two boys and a girl. "No," he says. "Not directly. But the police here in Selçuk…the incident last night… It doesn't look good."

Travers gazes at the poster of Saint John's ruins. The curtain wall and its sheer drop to the rubble stone are clearly visible in the aerial shot. "Goddamn it, Nihat," he says.

Monuglu slides the family photo back into the billfold and takes out an older picture of himself in a red wrestler's singlet. The photo is faded, the upper right-hand corner veined from wear. He places the picture on the table in front of Travers.

Travers gazes at the photograph and says nothing. In the picture, Monuglu has more hair and less girth, but still a bull neck and thick sloping shoulders. He is not smiling, but his eyes are glinting with pride or, perhaps, fanaticism.

"Greco-Roman," Monuglu says. "I was an Olympic alternate." He leans forward, his bulky forearms pressing on the table. "The honor of wrestling for my country in the Olympics would have been the proudest moment of my life."

Travers glances again at Monuglu's eyes in the photograph.

"Off the mat," Monuglu says, "everyone was my friend. But on the mat, no. Never." He tips the lighter over with his index finger. "I was not the most skilled wrestler, but I always fought hard. Always." His smile curls, and the ferocity returns to his eyes. "If my opponents underestimated my determination, they paid a high price."

"I bet they did," Travers says as he passes back the photograph. "And, I get your point."

Monuglu's eyes soften; he slips the photograph into his billfold and stuffs it into his pocket. "Go to your hotel," he says. "Get some sleep."

"I need to be on the next flight to Istanbul."

"Yes, Istanbul," Monuglu says, slapping the table with his palms. "Call me in an hour." He presses himself up to standing and leans across the table toward Travers. "And let me know when you hear again from a certain noted Turkish archeologist."

"Of course," Travers says, though both he and Monuglu know he won't.

⊹ 32

Sophia Altay can swear in seven languages, ancient and modern. A potpourri of all of them would be appropriate at the moment, but, choosing French, she murmurs *"Merde!"* Dressed as a European tourist, she sits at a computer in one of Göreme's cafés. Her blue jeans are tight, her peasant blouse loose; her hair, parted in the middle, flows down around her face. The sunglasses she wore outside are now propped on her head.

Altay types NO! in caps. The email from Joseph Travers was as disturbing as it was simple: LOST ITEM. COMING TO CHURCH. She needed him to do one simple job, and he botched it. And now he's planning to blunder in here. Having him in the vicinity will draw the Pharisees and their henchmen. An already difficult and dangerous situation will be exacerbated.

Her plan to have the elder Glavine read the documents and then explain to him why he needs to do what must be done is no longer viable. The old man is the only one without an academic, political, or religious agenda. He's dying slowly of heart congestion and colon cancer, and he has outlived whatever megalomaniacal tendencies he may have had while he was accumulating wealth. All he cares about at this point is the archeology—that whatever artifacts are unearthed come to light, that the discoveries are preserved, and that people have the opportunity to learn some truth from those discoveries. She would have valued his aid and advice, but now she alone must be responsible for authenticating and preserving the scrolls. And she has to rethink how to do so without getting herself killed or the originals destroyed.

Before checking her email, she logged onto the BBC and CNN websites. Leopold has been crowing as usual. His photo and his quotes are featured on both sites. Kenan's death was downplayed in relation to the ossuary's discovery, but her disappearance was included on CNN. The head and shoulder shot is of a formal, somber professorial woman who is neither the sashaying European tourist nor the veiled Turkish woman she will now be whenever she is in public.

NO CONTACT! she types. It's probably too late to keep Joe and those who will follow him away, but she needs time to implement a new plan. TAKE A TOUR TOMORROW. She smiles to herself as she sends the message. The tour might do Joe good.

She lowers her sunglasses, gathers up her daypack, and stands. She used Spanish on the boy when she entered the café, and she'll say *adios* on the way out. She takes one step and stops. Abrahim is standing outside the window staring at her like a lost puppy. He really is a beautiful boy, and that stricken look he has melts people. If he stays there any longer, he'll draw a crowd of tourists, both male and female. She'll meet him later, but not here in this public place at this time. She shakes her head once sharply. He steps back from the window as though he has been slapped, but he doesn't immediately turn away. Those large brown eyes cloud and his shoulders slump before he slinks off along the sidewalk.

⚛ 33

As he deplanes in Kayseri, Joseph Travers checks out the other passengers, wondering which was sent to shadow him. He dozed on the flight but didn't sleep. His head throbs, and his swollen, discolored jaw aches. Though he's still woozy, the pain, particularly in his thigh, has helped him stay at least somewhat focused. Without the flash drive, he's insignificant—except that Nihat Monuglu and the others know that he might lead them to Sophia Altay and the ossuary's contents.

Monuglu expedited Travers' exit from Selçuk, reserving a seat for him on the flight to Istanbul and providing a car to the İzmir airport driven by a policeman who spoke no English at all. After arriving in Istanbul just after noon, Travers tried to be covert with each step—checking back into the Blue House Hotel and then stuffing toiletries and a change of clothes into a daybag, taking one cab to the main entrance of the Grand Bazaar and a second from the bazaar's back entrance to the domestic terminal, and purchasing his plane ticket only forty minutes before the flight. But it's all amateur stuff, with a paper trail at the airport if nowhere else, and Monuglu's men will track him soon if they're not already on him.

The Kayseri airport has a single entrance and exit gate. Green and gray benches line the one waiting room, and blue steel grillwork rises along the slanted ceiling. The city is crowded and nondescript, but the early evening sky is luminous. A single cloud shrouds the cap of Erciyes Dagi, one of the extinct volcanoes whose lava originally formed Cappadocia's landscape.

The only other passenger in the Turkish Airlines minibus is a doctor born in Bombay and now practicing in London. Her face is round, and her smile radiant. As they leave the city for the countryside, she tells him that she has traveled the world visiting mountains. She liked the Incan ruins and the mountains surrounding the desert in Chile. "Everest," she says to him, "changed me from the inside out." She laughs often, and she doesn't once ask him about his swollen jaw. The farther they ride, the more the terrain reminds Travers of the American Southwest's high country. It's not a literal likeness, but more a feeling of place. The lone thunderhead in the distance, shaped like a standing bear, gray at the bottom and pink and white at the top, looks somehow like home.

Anger simmers in Travers' belly, but with each passing mile it's becoming less focused. He's no longer sure that it was Monuglu who had him mugged. But if Monuglu didn't send the men, who did? Sophia Altay was, he thinks, the only one who knew he had the flash drive, and she *needed* it delivered to Bill Glavine's father. Leopold Kirchburg certainly would have craved the information on the flash drive. Travers tries to remember if the wiry man who pronounced his name "traverse" had a German accent, but a single word isn't enough. Charles Lee…what would he do with it? Any of the TV networks would want to scoop the world about the ossuary's contents… Governments would…

Travers stops that line of thought. It's unreasonable, and, in any case, his irritation is now directed more inward. The mugging wasn't his fault, but he did, unnecessarily, take the flash drive to the internet café. Whenever anything fell apart in his life, he invariably felt he contributed to it, even when he was not the primary cause. His parents became estranged only after his adoption. Mary's bipolar disorder worsened during their marriage, and Jason's congenital depression deepened after Travers moved out of the house. Christine needed children at a time when he was unwilling to become a father again. Motorola's downsizing necessitated the workforce reduction, and he was adept at doing the job until the moment he fired himself. Rightly or wrongly, he harbors blame, always has since he was a boy.

The doctor's head is cocked as though she has said something he hasn't heard. Her bright, dark eyes are wide, and her smile is forced. "Are you all right?" she asks again.

The van's tires are humming on the pavement. His breathing is shallow, and sweat is breaking on his forehead. His palms are clammy. "What?" he asks. "Yeah. Yes." He takes a breath and exhales as slowly as he can. "Thanks. It'll pass." He leans back in his seat, takes another breath, and focuses on the physical pain in his leg.

The setting sun floods the land. Deeper into Cappadocia, the fairy chimneys appear. The cone-shaped tufa pillars capped with basalt cluster in valleys. Wind and water have eroded them for millennia. People have hollowed the rock and carved out the caves for centuries. This woman sitting next to him in the minibus exudes life, and the world outside becomes more vibrant by the minute. He's heading into territory that is at once unfamiliar and familiar. And there's something important he has to do, though what exactly it is certainly isn't clear to him.

⊹ 34

Charles Lee and Leopold Kirchburg sit across from each other at the table in the corner of the Kalehan Restaurant. Afternoon is falling toward evening, and the smell of roses and lemon trees from the adjoining garden fills the air. Old ceramic plates hang on the walls just below the dark wooden ceiling. The waiter, thin as a blade in black pants and a white shirt, stands a safe distance from the table. No one else is sitting near the two men, but they still speak in low voices.

Both men are neatly dressed, Lee in a yellow sportshirt with a Regent University Law emblem and Kirchburg in a blue shirt with burgundy tie. Kirchburg set up a command center in Sophia Altay's house the night before, but both then and today all of the public information was disseminated from a makeshift podium in the work area outside the restoration house. Media attention on the bone box's discovery has been intensifying, and the citadel standing on the hill in the background and the ancient pillar segments lying nearby have provided the necessary cover shots of an archeological dig.

"We must display a unified front," Kirchburg says as he raises his tea cup. They agreed on this meeting to exchange information about the situation as events unfold. It's a dance they've done before—never much fun for Lee but, given the current circumstances, absolutely necessary. And he got Kirchburg to speak only in English simply by flattering the Kraut's use of the language. Kirchburg sips the steaming tea and returns the cup to the saucer. "I am the one the reporters expect to speak for the Aegean Association." As he smears grape jam across a roll, he continues with his self-aggrandizing bullshit. "Your work is essential, but I am the one they want to see."

"Y'all are," Lee says, drawing out the words with his accent. Though Lee is the money, Kirchburg persists in an Old World condescension toward anyone and anything American. "But," he adds, "as I keep saying, you're barking up the wrong tree. That bone box is not the real deal."

Kirchburg chews his bread and then dabs the corner of his mouth with the cloth napkin. "My evaluation," he says, "*should* be more than enough to persuade you that the ossuary is authentic."

Lee drinks his coffee. Strong and dark, it's one thing the Turks do well. And, because it's percolated, it's safe to drink. "Even if it is, which it isn't, you've got an *empty* box," he says. "And even if it does, by some miracle, turn out to be real, my guys back home are still seriously put out that the bones and anything else that might've been in that box have gone missing." In fact, during his calls in the last thirty hours, a couple of his most eminent clients have gone ballistic—absolutely bat-shit.

Kirchburg glowers, places his elbows on the table, and makes a cone of his fingers. "I have received word," he says, "that the Turk's death has officially been labeled a homicide."

Lee nods. The Kraut always changes the subject when he's about to be beat. "What, exactly, were you told?" he asks, brushing his hand through his hair.

"Physical evidence. Something about a mark on the wall and a scrape on the Turk's leg that make it unlikely that he jumped or fell accidentally."

"Booze?" He's been on the phone most of the day, and fifty laps in the pool would do him good.

"Ja. High alcohol levels." Kirchburg pauses, looking into Lee's eyes. "He had twenty one-hundred euro notes in his pocket."

Immune to the infamous Kirchburg glare, Lee asks, "Two thousand euros?"

"Ja. The reporters know nothing of this yet, but I am told it will be difficult to keep the information from them much longer."

Fully aware that in this particular situation Kirchburg will want him to take the media heat, Lee says, "How are y'all going to tackle it?"

Kirchburg clears his throat. "First, we insist that it is a matter for the local police, not the Association, to discuss."

"Of course. But you still have to throw the media some kind of a bone."

Kirchburg drums his fingertips together. "It is all Sophia's fault," he says.

"Leopold, whatever your feelings about her..." Lee shakes his head, trying not to smile at the Austrian's self-destructiveness. Between his obsession with the Femme Frog and his inbred Teutonic arrogance, he's got himself a pair of Achilles' heels. "...you can't pin this on her. She's about half the size of the Turk, and nobody's going to buy that she lured him out to that wall and pushed him."

"She was the site director. Kenan and Abrahim and the other Turks answered to her."

Yeah, Bubba, Lee thinks, *and you're the executive director.* "So," he asks, "what are you doing about this?"

"I have people working on it."

"And?" Lee watches Kirchburg wipe each of his fingers with the cloth napkin.

Finally, Kirchburg says, "I have nothing to share yet. Have you discovered anything?"

Their *sharing* is always interesting. What they really share is a tacit understanding that each has resources that the other doesn't. But Lee's own connections haven't scared up anything yet. They're supposed to be top shelf, but they're Krauts and Turks. Lee finishes his coffee. "Nothing yet on your Ms. Altay," he says. "But I did find out this afternoon that Joe Travers has also bolted. First to Istanbul and then beyond."

"Really?" Kirchburg drums his fingers on the sides of his tea cup. "Did he contact you before he left?"

"No. Not at all since he was mugged last night."

"He apparently had something from my site with him. Something he stole." When Kirchburg picks up the cup, his baby finger trembles.

"Or something your Ms. Altay gave him."

Kirchburg winces, and then his eyes harden. "Ja," he says, setting the cup hard on its saucer. The waiter looks over at the two men and then steps farther away. "Herr Travers is a…messenger boy."

"Maybe. But he's flown to Kayseri. Wherever that is."

Kirchburg drums his fingers on the table and then glances at his Tag Heuer. "Cappadocia," he says. "Anatolia. Central Turkey. A place of little consequence."

"Why would he head there?"

Kirchburg squeezes his napkin, stands, and tosses the napkin onto the table. "Because Sophia is there."

Lee hides another smile. It's got to gall Kirchburg that Travers is in touch with Altay. "Yeah," he says, "I've got it figured that way, too. And I do believe I recall something about her working in the field in Cappadocia as a graduate student."

"Ja. Two internships."

"She's got to be there, all right," Lee says. "And the bone box's contents…"

"I will handle it." Kirchburg's tone fills with its usual imperiousness.

Lee stands so that the Austrian isn't hovering over him. "Actually, Leopold," he says, "I'm heading there. That's why you've got to handle the situation here alone."

Kirchburg glowers at Lee and then glances over at an elderly couple walking into the restaurant. The waiter goes over to greet them. "You should remain here," he says. "And I will locate Sophia."

"No, Leopold, that's not how it's goin' to play out." The dance is different now. Too much is at stake to keep waltzing, and the Kraut's got to get in step. Lee stuffs his hands into his pockets and looks out the window at the light fading in the garden. "Y'all have to get everything under control here. You've said that yourself. You're the one the reporters want to see. And as CEO of the Aegean Association, you're the one responsible for dealing with everything we've been chatting about." He takes his hands from his pockets and rubs his palms. "Finding Ms. Altay and whatever was in that bone box is real important to the old boys at the Eagle Consortium." Now he does let his smile spread. "And anyway, Leopold, I've already made my reservations."

Color rises in Kirchburg's cheeks. "You have, have you?"

"I leave for Istanbul in an hour. I've got a couple of quick meetings there tonight, and I'll fly to Kayseri first thing in the morning."

Kirchburg's eyes are bright, but he says nothing. He has no formal control over Lee, and they both know it.

Lee gazes out the window again. "What really happened to that Turk?" he asks.

"I don't know," Kirchburg says. "Do you?"

ⵣ 35

At dusk, Abrahim perches on the boulder in the small box canyon, waiting. He arrived when she instructed him to, but she has not yet come. She looked angry with him when he saw her at the internet café. Afraid that they would meet again by chance before the appointed time, he left the town for the rest of the day, walking in the hills and visiting the cave churches. He climbed directly up one ridge to the Church of Saint John. The carved entrance was hollowed out in such a way that no one would notice it before arriving at it. He was transfixed by the images on the interior walls of angels with red wings and saints with golden halos. On one wall,

Saint John sat alone, leaning forward on a rock, lost in thought.

Abrahim thinks about the people who carved the stone by hand and created the frescoes, mixing the whites of pigeon eggs with colored pigments. They lived their faith. Their lives every day centered on their love of God in a way that is not possible in the modern world. God is in this canyon now—in the bowing sunflowers, in the trickling water, and in Abrahim's heart. But he cannot always feel God's presence everywhere in every moment as the Christians who lived in the area must have.

Doctor Altay finally comes to him, veiled, a shadow approaching from the cleft. She is completely covered, so different from the way she looked in the café. There she was a fashionable woman, a woman he would want were he able to want women. As she approaches, he stands. She takes him in her arms immediately, without lowering her veil. Her touch fills him. He smells dust and jasmine in her scarf.

"Abrahim," she whispers, "my beautiful Abrahim."

Her Turkish, which always has a slight French lilt, causes his blood to rush. When she lets go of him, he feels it ebb.

Then, as she sits him back on the rock, she says, "Abrahim, I need your help."

He soars.

She uncovers her head and looks into him with those eyes that enchant men. "An American," she says, "has arrived in Cappadocia."

"Mister Lee?"

"No. The new American whom you have not met."

Abrahim nods. He has liked Americans, though not Lee, who sometimes looked at him as though he were an insect. Some Americans are open and direct without making demands or ordering everyone around.

"I need you to protect me," she says. "To…"

"Will he hurt you?" Abrahim interrupts.

She sits down beside him on the rock so that their forearms are touching. "No," she says. "He is harmless. But others who come after him, who are following him, would hurt both of us."

He nods again, though he is not sure if by *us* she means him and her or the American and her.

"You must meet with him," she says, "but not in town. You must tell him to go away." Her voice becomes vehement. "You must inform him that his help is not needed or wanted."

Her words sting Abrahim even though they are about someone else. He looks up at the evening's first faint stars.

"If you do this for me tomorrow," she says, patting his thigh, "I will let you read the translations when we meet."

He knows that he will do whatever she asks no matter what, but her mentioning the scrolls still causes him to shiver.

⚚ 36

Joseph Travers occupies the back corner seat of the Hiro Cappadocia Tour minibus. He arrived early and took this seat so that he could see the other nine passengers as they entered the minibus. A middle-aged Australian couple is seated next to him, and three French girls in blue jeans and spaghetti-strap tops chat in the row in front of him. In front of them is another couple and the young man from the photograph on Sophia Altay's desk. He made no eye contact when he climbed into the minibus with his daypack and a notebook, but Travers understands that this is no coincidence. Neither is the presence of the tenth passenger, a larger man with brown hair who sits up front in the seat next to the tour guide. Travers thinks he recognizes the guy, even from behind, and his pulse has been racing since the guy arrived.

Although Travers' body is doing its little fight-flight dance in the back of the minibus, his mind is more settled than it was when he arrived in town. After having dinner outdoors at the Sultan, he caught up some on his sleep in his cave room at the Sarihan Hotel on the hill above Göreme. He woke at dawn wondering how he was going to get in touch with Sophia Altay after her email telling him not to make contact, and now he knows. Altay told him to take the tour, and that's what he's doing. He looks out the window at the fields of wheat as the minibus approaches the Caravanserai along the Silk Road. He's still very sore from the beating, and his thigh itches as well as hurts, but he's doing what he needs to do.

He is the last to leave the minibus, and the tour guide, a man with a sharp nose and potbelly who looks to him more like a Navajo than a Turk, is already talking in limited but comprehensible English about how these stone forts were built every hundred kilometers or so along the caravan routes that funneled great wealth into the Ottoman Empire. The walls are not as impressive as those of the citadel on Ayasuluk Hill, but they're substantial—high and thick and at one time impervious to bands of marauders. The ornamentation above the portal is pure stonework, not cement. A mosque dominates the inner courtyard surrounded by the market, the caravan owner's quarters, and the stable. A pigeon with straw in its beak waddles by; the smell of manure is in the air. As the guide leads the group over to the carpet display, Abrahim wanders off by himself toward the owner's quarters. Travers watches the other man furtively watching him. His nose is crooked, and his eyebrow scarred. When the guy checks out the postcards at the stand next to the carpets, Travers looks at his hands. The knuckle of the middle finger on his left hand is scabbed over where it recently split striking something hard. Travers has seen him twice before, in Istanbul and in Selçuk the moment before he blacked out.

The next stop, the Ihlara Gorge, a long narrow canyon with a creek running through it, reminds Travers of the American Southwest, too. The hundreds of steps down to the Church Under the Tree were not put in until 1980. The eleventh century frescoes of the Wise Men are well preserved except that whoever desecrated the church gouged out the eyes. In each corner of the church's ceiling is a blue nazar boncuğu similar to the one painted on the tile in his Istanbul hotel room. As the tour exits the church, Travers makes eye contact with the watcher: he is definitely the guy who lurked at Topkapi's gate and at the steps of the New Mosque—and whose fist snapped Travers into darkness. Abrahim lingers in the church, unable to stop gaping at the blinded Wise Men.

The group hikes along the path that follows the creek, slowly spreading out, the Australians stopping to take pictures and the French girls talking among themselves. Abrahim does not reappear, and the other guy walks far ahead with the guide—a follower, Travers realizes, arrogant enough to lead. Travers and Abrahim and this guy make one strange and inscrutable trinity bound by the contents of the bone box.

Birds swirl through the sky and call from the cliffs. Travers lags behind, gradually losing touch with the group. The creek smells like the Southwest, like home—and suddenly, he *is* finally home, here and now. Completely. Perfectly. He passes under the branches of the poplars and willows and pistachios, listens to the rush of water, and gazes at the light in the riffling creek. The sense he felt coming to Cappadocia deepens. He's somewhere beyond loss but also here in the dappled sunlight and shade. Above him are more churches carved into the cliffs, but he is taken by the flashing water. Light flows down the creek, slowing time. The immense emptiness he brought to Turkey fills, brims, abounds.

He limps, wholly unaware of the pain, through a clearing of wildflowers—white and muted yellow and purple and a splash of orange. There are bits of garbage—the messy hand of the species—along the trail, but the scent of the flowers is strong. He feels at home here, partly because of the redolent odor and partly because of the light. It's almost as though he's flowing with the wind and water. Something akin to the presence he felt at Saint John's Cathedral occurs, but there's more to it now. This ground, at once foreign and familiar, feels hallowed. It would be a good place to pray. He can see praying here five times a day, or five hundred. What he was unable to do in the Blue Mosque, he can do here. Being alive is paradox, an intermingling of pain and pleasure, of the deep anguish of loss and the acute awareness of sweet air coursing through sunshine. And he offers thanks for his life, everything that's happened, all of it, every moment. He sends his thanks along the creek and out among the branches into pure light.

He is completely knocked off his horse here in the Ihlara, the Valley of Beautiful Horses, but he isn't blinded. He would in this moment start his own religion, a faith without rules or rituals. A faith without icons. A faith in which fairy chimneys are steeples and trees minarets. A faith in which birds are the only angels. A faith in which all ground is sacred and all water holy. A faith in which breathing is prayer. But he knows, of course, if Joe's Faith ever caught on, Pharisees would complicate it, devising prohibitions and creating rituals. And he is no preacher, no proselytizer. Still, he is struck by the ground beneath his feet, the air clapping all around, the light burning the branches gold over his head, and the water streaming and purling molten all about him. He becomes the rush of sparkling water across smooth stones. He is an ancient bell ringing. He is a freshening wind.

⚰ 37

Travers doesn't catch up to the group until, almost an hour later, he reaches the outdoor restaurant at the other end of Ihlara Gorge. The guide and the eight others, everyone except Abrahim, are seated at a long picnic table under a wooden lattice frame on a terrace near the creek. The only seat left is directly across from the man who shadowed him in Istanbul and sucker-punched him in Selçuk. The breeze is rustling and the light purling and pooling, but he is already apart, separated from them, again in the company of people. And already in a quandary, the balance between the breathtaking beauty of the day and the sordid affairs of men not at all clear. His years of corporate work taught him that revenge, though sometimes momentarily satisfying, doesn't solve problems, but there isn't any way he can let go of the mugging, drop it as though it didn't happen, as though the pain isn't real.

Travers takes the seat and gazes across the table. The man's small brown eyes are set close together below his scarred eyebrow and above his crooked nose. Covering his left hand with his right, the man glances at Travers' discolored jaw and then looks away at an elderly waiter placing bowls on the next table.

"Hello," Travers says, "I'm Joe." Over the man's shoulder, the gleaming creek cascades down rapids.

The man looks at Travers for a moment before nodding and again glancing at the other table.

"You remember me," Travers says.

The man's smile is wary.

"Of course, you do. Your hand probably still hurts. My jaw certainly does."

The man takes a paper napkin and slips his left hand into his lap with it.

The French girl seated next to Travers eyes his jaw and then quickly looks away again at the tour guide regaling the group at the other end of the table.

Travers leans forward. "What's your name?" he asks the man.

The man studies his soup spoon.

"I'd really like to know."

The man looks up, but then averts his eyes. "Ich bin Günter Schmidt," he says to the red and gold plastic tablecloth.

Travers is surprised for a second that the man speaks German. "Sprechen sie Englisch?" he asks, cocking his head so that the ringing in his ear is less intense and he can also make out the sound of the creek.

Schmidt hesitates before holding up his right hand with his thumb and forefinger half an inch apart. "Small," he says. "Little."

Smiling, Travers nods. "Good," he says. "I'll give you the chance to practice."

A slight old man with a white beard serves bowls of lentil soup from a tray. The tour guide glances at Travers and Schmidt but then goes back to flirting with the French girls.

"It's my first visit to Turkey," Travers says to Schmidt. "How about you?"

Still guarded, Schmidt takes a sip of his soup.

"Is this your first trip here, Günter?"

"I come here before."

"Really? What do you do?"

Schmidt takes a piece of bread from the basket on the table, breaks it in half, stuffs the larger half into his mouth, and chews hard.

Travers tastes the soup, which is very good. "I'd really like to know. What work do you do, Günter?"

Schmidt looks at the bread and soup and plastic bottle of water but not at Travers' swollen jaw. Finally, he says, "I am instructor. Physical education in Vienna. At the gymnasium." He shrugs. "In the summers, I do other works..."

"What work?"

"Last summer I did works at Ephesus."

"I was just there," Travers says. Schmidt has, it seems, already told him what he needs to know. "Tell me about your work," he adds, his tone more amiable.

All through the lunch of chicken and tomatoes and couscous, Travers keeps peppering Schmidt with questions. The man hides his left hand for awhile, but then, as Travers' inquiries gradually disarm him, he talks more freely about the dullness of his life in Vienna and his wanting to visit New York and Las Vegas. Eventually, he raises both hands, gesturing to emphasize points. Travers gazes over his shoulder at the white water, the rhythmic rush and tumble. Schmidt may be a boxer and probably Kirchburg's boy, but he's no killer. He's not the one who shoved Kenan over the curtain wall.

When the sliced watermelon is brought to the table, Travers stands abruptly. The French girl looks up at him. Her shoulder-length hair is brown, her face round, and her expression quizzical. He places his palms on the table and leans toward Schmidt. "It's good to meet you, Günter," he says. "I don't think you know what you're involved in."

He brushes his fingers across his swollen jaw. "Hell, I don't, and I'm the one that got knifed."

Schmidt wipes his hands with his napkin and, his eyes becoming dull, looks at Travers.

Travers gazes out for a moment at the light flashing along the rippling creek. "I forgive you, Günter," he says, "but I won't forget. There was no reason to knife me."

The conversation around the table dies.

Travers extends his right hand. "Whatever the intended message was, I didn't get it."

Schmidt looks at Travers' extended hand but doesn't shake it.

"I'm staying here until all this is finished."

Schmidt doesn't move; the French girls and the others stare up at Travers.

"Ihlara Gorge is gorgeous today, Günter. I hope you noticed it."

Schmidt looks down at the napkin he is squeezing in his left hand.

Travers steps back from the table and takes a breath. "Tell your boss to stop," he says, his tone not threatening but forceful. "Tell him that the bones and the documents don't belong to him."

⚔ 38

When Travers boards the minibus, Schmidt, up front with the driver, stares silently through the windshield smattered with dead bugs. Abrahim hunches over in his seat writing furiously in his notebook. The others on the tour are subdued, as though they've just witnessed an accident; nobody addresses either Travers or Schmidt. As the bus travels, Travers looks out at the rolling hills, some green and some brown—and all suffused with light. Gradually, the French girls begin to chat among themselves, and the Australians open their guidebook and read to each other about Cappadocia's underground cities. At one point, Travers sees in a distant field an old man leading a donkey with an old woman sitting on it.

When the bus reaches the underground city of Derinkuyu, Abrahim doesn't go with the others to the entrance of the subterranean site. Travers follows along for the first three levels through tunnels, storerooms, kitchens, dining rooms, chapels, and even a school. It's all a hollowed-out warren replete with stables and a winery. Electric bulbs illuminate the stone passageways, but the walls are still close and the ceilings low. Each time the group descends to another level, another tour group is squeezing up the narrow steps. The first levels were likely carved out by Hittites as storage spaces, but the subterranean city reached its heyday in the seventh century when tens of thousands of Christians lived on fifteen levels at depths of more than three hundred feet. The city provided a safe haven against the Arabs that intermittently pillaged Anatolia. An immense stone blocking wheel allowed the residents to seal off the entrance from attack, and secret portals enabled them to sneak out and hack apart their enemies from behind.

Schmidt stays close to the guide, seeming to listen attentively to the guide's tales of mayhem. Travers slips back to the entrance and fresh air and natural light. The town above-ground is pretty desolate. Three-dozen small houses spread in no discernible pattern from the central square with its souvenir stands and open-air carpet shops. The carpet peddlers beckon to Travers, but he buys only a couple of bottles of water from a veiled woman waiting for Derinkuyu to disgorge its next group of tourists.

Travers finds Abrahim sitting on a wooden bench in the shade of a tree behind one of the carpet displays. His notebook is open to a pen and ink drawing of the Wise Men from the Church Under the Tree. With liquid streaming from each man's gouged eyes, the rendering is both amazingly artistic and deeply disturbing. Because of the monochromatic drawing, Travers can't be sure if the flowing imagery represents blood or tears. Without saying anything, he holds out a bottle of water.

When Abrahim looks up at Travers, his eyes, a beautiful brown almost the color of bronze, shine. "Deo gratias," he says, accepting the bottle. "Pax vobiscum."

Abrahim's speaking Latin throws Travers even more than Schmidt's German. "Et cum spiritu tuo," he says before realizing what he's doing.

Abrahim smiles. His olive skin is so smooth and clear that he seems more a girl or young boy than a man.

"Do you speak English?" Travers asks.

"I am learning," Abrahim answers, closing his notebook.

"May I sit down?"

"Please," Abrahim says. He shifts so that there's more room on the bench for Travers.

Travers takes a seat, twists the cap off his bottle, and drinks deeply. The sky is clear, and a single bird sings in the tree that shades them. "The tour doesn't interest you?" he asks.

"I am interested only in the churches," Abrahim says without any irony in his voice. "In the saints."

And their relics, Travers thinks. "Is this your first time in Cappadocia?" he asks.

"Yes." Abrahim sets his notebook on the daypack next to him, stows the pen in his jeans pocket, and tilts the bottle so that the water swirls. "The cave churches give me joy."

"But not the Church Under the Trees."

"No." Abrahim squeezes the bottle. "It was sinful for the Islamists to defile the icons. Very evil."

Travers nods. Abrahim's knuckles are cut, too, but there's nothing else about him that looks like a fighter. "And Saint John's Cathedral," he asks, "did working there make you happy?"

"Yes," Abrahim answers. He glances at Travers, unscrews the bottle's cap, and takes a quick sip of water. His lips glisten as he says, "My life was good there. It was… I was good…for a time."

"Did you like working with Doctor Altay?"

"Yes, very much, very much," Abrahim says, but then he suddenly looks away. When he turns back, he looks like he's going to cry. "She told me to tell you to go away," he blurts.

Travers sits back, listens to the townspeople hawking their souvenirs in broken English and German, and takes another drink of water. "I am not going to go away, Abrahim," he says.

"She says that she does not need your help." The skin below Abrahim's right eye twitches. "She does not want your help."

Travers takes a deep breath. "Look at me, Abrahim," he says, his voice low. He turns so that his swollen jaw is more prominent. "I have fifteen stitches in my leg." He points to his thigh. "And my ear won't stop ringing. Leopold Kirchburg had me beaten. Tell her that. And tell her that Herr Kirchburg took the computer files."

Abrahim flinches. "The Christ's letter?"

Travers' pulse races. *Jesus Christ's letter!*

"And Saint John's letter?" Abrahim says. "Herr Doktor Kirchburg has them?"

Letters! Blood rises in Travers' face; his ears buzz as well as ring. *Christ! John the Apostle?* When he tries to take another breath, he coughs. He wipes the back of his hand across his mouth and then, trying to keep his tone even, repeats, "Tell her all that, Abrahim."

Abrahim fidgets with the bottle cap for a moment. "Who is that man?" he asks. "The other one?"

It takes Travers a second to focus on the question. Though he himself suddenly has many questions, he understands that Abrahim won't have the answers. "You mean, the man on the tour?"

"The one you ate with." Abrahim's right eye twitches so much that it must be difficult to see clearly.

"He works for Herr Kirchburg, I think." *Letters from Jesus Christ and John the Apostle!* "He was sent to watch me, just as you were."

"She sent me to give you the message." Abrahim reaches up, not quite touching Travers' jaw. "Is that man the one which hurt you?"

Travers hesitates. "Yes, but..."

Clenching his fist, Abrahim lowers his hand. His voice becomes suddenly strident. "He will hurt Doctor Altay!"

"I don't think so."

"He will!" Abrahim says. Then, he opens his hand and lets his shoulders drop. His voice softens. "I saw you praying."

"What?" Travers is surprised by Abrahim's abrupt shift in tone.

Abrahim looks directly at Travers. "By the river," he says. "When the others were gone. You were praying."

"Yes, Abrahim. I guess I was."

"Pray for Doctor Altay."

"I'm not going away."

"Pray for me," Abrahim says, his voice sad.

⌖ 39

From his corner table at the Sarihan Cave Hotel's rooftop terrace, Travers gazes out across Göreme at the fairy chimneys in the valley. Nearby, doors and windows are carved into many of the conical spires. Farther away, some of the tufa and volcanic ash formations are cylindrical and capped with darker basalt. Beyond them, mountains range to the horizon. The air is still, but hosts of small birds dart for insects in the fading light. As Charles Lee strides toward him, Travers drinks his apple tea.

Lee says, "Hey, Joe. Good to…" When Travers turns, Lee stops and stares at his swollen jaw. "Y'all sure got your clock cleaned."

"Yeah," Travers says, waving toward the white metal chair across the table. "Have a seat." When Travers returned to the hotel after the tour, there was a note from Lee saying that he had arrived in town and that they needed to meet ASAP. Travers left a return message, showered, and redressed his leg wound before coming out to the patio. He is wearing walking shoes and light nylon pants so that once this meeting is finished he can head out of town. He's not feeling jangled like he did the morning he hiked to Saint John's curtain wall at dawn, but he still needs to walk. He wants to roam for awhile to make sense of what he learned on the tour. And, he wants to regain, if only for a moment, that singular feeling of oneness—if he can.

The waiter that followed Lee over to the table takes his order for a can of Coca-Cola and a glass but no ice. Lee then leans forward, resting his forearms on the edge of the table. His carefully pressed blue sportshirt, the color of his eyes, has a golden eagle monogrammed on the pocket. He looks even more tan and fit than he did when he arrived in Istanbul. "I'd ask," he says, "how you've been, but..." He smiles.

"I'm all right," Travers says, returning Lee's smile. "In fact, I'm pretty good."

"Even if you don't look so good." Lee's drawl is diminishing again. "How was that tour today?"

Travers looks down from the rooftop at the rosebushes and at the amphoras set at angles in the hotel's courtyard. "Charles," he says, "the Eagle Consortium has no vested interests in any sites in Cappadocia. None at all in the region. Why are you here?"

Lee's smile broadens as he leans farther forward. "Why are you here?"

"My stay in Selçuk didn't go well."

Lee sits back. "No, I believe it didn't. And that's something we have to talk about." He looks down over the roofs of the town. "But that's not why you came to a place halfway between East Gibbip and Bumblefuck."

Travers smiles again. Lee is apparently immune to the landscape. "I came to see the cave churches and the underground cities." There is, he suspects, more truth to that than Lee will believe.

The waiter brings the can of Coke and a tall glass. Lee takes a paper napkin, folds it, and wipes the top of the can before opening it. He lifts the glass, inspects it, puts it down, and drinks straight from the can. "Cut the crap, Joe," he says.

Travers shrugs.

Stifling a burp, Lee leans forward again. "You may not have figured it out yet, but we're on the same side in all this."

"Really?"

"Yeah. And, things'll go better if you work *with* me."

Travers smiles, shakes his head, and looks at the sky. Sparse clouds line the horizon, and overhead the first stars are appearing. "And what does that involve?" he asks.

Lee drinks from the can. "We both know that Sophia Altay took off with whatever was in that bone box, and she's here with it, or you wouldn't be here."

"But why do you care? You've already told me the ossuary's a fake."

Lee slams the can onto the table. Half an ounce of Coke arcs from the can and splashes onto the table. "Because she's dragging the Eagle Consortium, all of us, through the mud."

Travers glances at the spilled Coke and then looks into Lee's eyes. "The Eagle Consortium—*you're* not at risk."

Lee grabs the folded napkin and wipes the Coke from the table. "Don't be an acorn cracker," he says. "That Turk back in Selçuk, his death is now officially a murder investigation." He tosses the napkin to the center of the table. "If you're not the suspect, she is—and you're abetting her, sure as shit."

Travers looks again at the deepening night sky. Even with the hotel's ambient light, stars are spreading above him. He uses the Big Dipper to locate the North Star. "It *is* good," he says, "that we can talk frankly." He spreads his hands. "I don't know where Sophia Altay is or exactly what she has. But I do know that she's afraid of whoever murdered Kenan. And I know that she doesn't want my help. And she sure as hell isn't going to want yours."

"What was stolen from you?" Lee's voice rises.

"Ask your friend Leopold."

"What?"

"It looks like he has it."

"What did you have?"

Travers finishes his apple tea. "Sophia Altay entrusted me with a computer flash drive which I lost. A couple of guys mugged me for it. One of them was Austrian, Viennese, a P.E. teacher who was in Turkey before. He'd worked around Ephesus."

Lee's eyes darken, and his hands grip the edge of the table. "How do you know that?"

"He's here. I talked with the guy this afternoon."

Lee grabs his can of Coke and takes a long gulp. "And he told you he works for Leopold?"

"Not in so many words."

Lee sets the can next to the empty glass and wipes his mouth. "What was on the flash drive?" he asks.

"Photos of the ossuary and bones and a couple of scrolls. But they were in some ancient script." Travers watches Lee's right fist clench. "I have no way of knowing what they said."

"What were you supposed to do with the flash drive?"

Travers notices a black Mercedes pull up the hill to the hotel's front entrance. "Deliver it directly to the Glavine Foundation."

"Why?"

As Nihat Monuglu steps out of the car's passenger door, stretches, and glances around, the driver opens the trunk and takes out a blue garment bag.

"Why the Glavines?" Travers asks. "Or why me?" Before Lee can answer, he adds, "In the first case, I'm the Foundation's rep here. That's something you get." He doesn't mention that he was supposed to deliver it only to William Glavine, Sr., not Bill. "In the second, she probably thought it was a good way to get rid of me." He pushes back his chair, stands, and looks down at Lee. "I have to go," he says.

"Sit down. We're not finished."

"There's stuff I need to do," Travers says. "But it's been nice talking with you."

"I said, *sit down.*" Lee's eyes are ablaze.

Travers drops an American twenty dollar bill on the table to cover both of their tabs and then limps toward the exterior stairwell which will take him to the street without passing through the lobby.

⚛ 40

Abrahim clears his throat and spits again. He scrubs his hands with the cool water trickling from the crack in the rock, and then he lowers his head so that he can splash water onto his swollen right eye. Fire erupts, and he jerks his head back. With his left eye, he stares at his trembling hands, but a passing cloud shrouds the moon and stars so that in the darkness he cannot see if he has completely cleaned them. He rubs his hands together hard and then dries them on his jeans. Unable to control his breathing, he goes over to the boulder on which she has twice before seated him. He shakes his hands, hoping the shuddering will stop, and when it doesn't he clasps them tightly. Flames burn behind his right eye, the blaze spreading to his scalp and ear. "Confiteor Dei omnipotenti," he begins aloud, and he lets the Latin pour out of him into the darkness. He missed their meeting, and it is now past their fallback time. She should have been here by now. Fear wells, and his breath catches despite his ongoing prayer. *Dearest God, was he too late to save her?* He will go on praying until she appears or his flesh falls from his bones.

When she finally arrives, the veiled woman passing through the narrow cut in the rock, he is tremendously relieved, but the roiling inside him still will not stop. She sets down her bag, gazes at him in the dark, and gasps. When she holds him in her arms, he can feel his distress pour into her. She will never, though, be able to take on his burden. And he would not wish it on her.

She steps back, holding his right shoulder and lifting his chin so that she can see his tumid eye. "Oh, Abrahim!" she exclaims. "What happened, my Abrahim?"

"I gave the American your message," he says because that is the least of it.

She raises her hand from his chin but doesn't touch his eye. "Oh, Abrahim…" she repeats. "Did he do this to you?"

"No," he says. "He would not. He would never hurt…"

She sits him back down on the boulder. Her hand strokes his hair, but even her touch cannot pacify him.

He shakes his head, the pain firing from temple to temple and un-furling down his neck into his chest. "He said he will not go away, and he is telling the truth. He prayed by the river. I liked him."

"I understand," she says. "I'm beginning to like him, too." Waiting for him to go on, she pats his shoulder.

"Herr Doktor Kirchburg had his hellhounds beat him and cut him. That is how he lost the files. He wanted me to tell you that Herr Kirch-burg stole the files."

When she grips his shoulder hard, he feels her fury. She and Herr Kirchburg despise each other. Something occurred between them before Abrahim came to Saint John's, and since then the problems have all been personal masked in archeological disputes. Herr Kirch-burg wanted everything done exactly to his specifications, but he nev-er did any work himself. Doctor Altay had a better sense of where to unearth artifacts. After all, she grew up on archeological sites. She also treated her workers better. She was highly educated and very intelligent, but she never disdained the diggers as Herr Kirchburg did. Abrahim would do anything for her—and nothing for him.

"Did Joe, the American, explain *how* Leopold knew about the flash drive?" she asks.

"No," Abrahim says, beginning to shake again. "He asked about me. If I liked working for you at Saint John's."

"He knew you?"

"Yes." Abrahim's hands burn, the heat searing from the inside. "He approached me at Derinkuyu while the others were underground." He clutches Altay's wrist. "The hellhound," he blurts, "followed him, Sophia."

It is the only time he has ever called her by her first name, and, startled, she pulls her arm from his grip. When he gasps, she lays her hand on his head. "Who, Abrahim?" she asks, her voice tight.

"The one that beat him." He leans forward so that the left side of his head rests against her hip. The tremors will not abate. "The one that came here to harm you," he whispers.

She strokes his hair again. "The one that hurt you?"

The conflagration in his temples raging, he nods once. She says nothing for what seems to him an eternity, but her touch gradually banks the fire. He smells the soap in her long skirt, feels the heat of her through the cloth, tastes metal in his mouth, and hears their breathing—hers even and his own erratic. Crickets chitter, and farther away tires roll across pavement. The cloud slips from the moon, and pale silver light falls onto the dirt he stares at through his tears.

"My Abrahim," she says finally, "I brought the documents for you to read."

He sits up, the flames bursting again behind his eye.

"But you must try to get hold of yourself."

He nods, but he knows, as she does, that he has never been able to control himself fully—and never will. His desire, though, to know what the scrolls say is so strong that he wipes the left side of his face and takes a series of slow, deep breaths.

She pulls her computer from her bag, sits down next to him, opens it, and turns it on.

The screen's glow halos her face. Her eyes, staring intently, are emeralds. After she selects a file, she slides the computer to him.

His vision is blurred, and he can barely make out the typescript. The letter begins, *Hear, O Israel! Worship the Lord your God and serve Him only.* The Turkish translation is clearly worded, the document a call to faith, a summons to serve God in every circumstance. But it is also a diatribe against hypocrites, the high priests and those who wield power. Rebellious and messianic and frightening, it does nothing to settle him. His sobbing beclouds his vision even more than his tumescent eye does. This voice is *revolutionary,* he thinks, but he does not say the word aloud. The Christ he worships, the Christ to whom he prays, is kind. He heals the sick and feeds the hungry. The voice in this letter is not evil, but neither is he gentle or compassionate.

She leans across him to open another file. The second document declares, *I am John, the one Jesus, the Nazarean, loved. He called my brother, James, and me the Sons of Thunder, but now I am old.* As he reads on, his hands quiver and his throat constricts. He begins to shake again, his breath coming in those fitful gasps of his childhood. Although she is showing him the letter to help him, it only hurts him more. When she rests her hand on his shoulder, he cringes. The letter strikes him— but not as she expected.

This second letter lays upon him the unbearable weight of disgrace, of shame and sinfulness. He lies mired far too deeply in the vile valley of his deeds to hear Saint John's final call. And though he could repent, his act of contrition would be imperfect. Because he is not absolutely remorseful, he is beyond redemption. As he tries— and fails—to read the letter a second time, he becomes inconsolable. The words *despair* and *malice* and *loathing* and *hollowness* burn deeply. He cannot, through his tears, even make out the words in the last two paragraphs. Had he seen the letter just one day earlier, even a few hours earlier... But he did not.

"Abrahim?" Sophia's voice, that beautiful lilting voice, cannot reach him. "Abrahim!"

Saint John's letter is all the proof he needs that he does not deserve to live.

ⵣ 41

The hammering on the door jars Joseph Travers from a dreamless sleep. The Sarihan's cave room is cool and pitch black except for the glow of the travel alarm. It is 4:13 A.M., and the knocking doesn't stop. When he sits up too quickly, the room spins before settling.

"What?" he shouts. "What is it?"

"Open the door, Joseph!" he hears. He would not recognize the voice as Nihat Monuglu's except for the use of his name. As he stands, pain snakes down his right thigh. Wearing only blue boxers and a white T-shirt, he limps to the door, unlocks it, and starts to open it.

The door swings by him, scraping across his left toes as he tries to step away. A flashlight's beam blinds him. Two people larger than he is push past him, almost knocking him over. A hand grabs his T-shirt and twists it tight around his neck. He's shoved back onto the bed.

"Stop, goddamn it!" he shouts.

The ceiling light flicks on, but the flashlight remains aimed at his face. He squeezes his eyes shut and turns his head. "Hayır!" someone yells from the bathroom. Drawers scrape open, slam shut. "Hayır," he hears again. And then it's suddenly quiet. The flashlight turns off. His breathing is shallow; others are breathing above him. Outside along the walkway, a door opens and quickly shuts.

He sits up and blinks at the three figures, Monuglu flanked by two large, dark men in brown uniforms.

"What the hell, Nihat!" he says. He avoided Monuglu earlier in the night by walking far into the heart of Cappadocia. He got fresh ekmek and water at a café on the outskirts of town and then trekked into the night for hours. Skirting the clusters of partying young people coming and going, he climbed hills and rounded bends as the night sky spilled moonglow and starshine all about him. He didn't think consciously about Altay and the bone box or anything else but rather let his thoughts shuffle and turn until he was certain that he would stay in Cappadocia through to the end, whatever happened. He returned to his room after midnight wholly unaware that whatever would occur was already happening.

"The Austrian is dead," Monuglu says, his voice edgy.

Travers plants his feet and sits up straight. As his vision clears, he can see Monuglu's unshaven frown and the somber faces of the uniformed hulks behind him. "Kirchburg?" he asks.

"You are not funny."

"Who?" Travers rolls his neck. His clothes are strewn around the room. The toes on his left foot sting. The nail of his big toe is ripped, and his blood marks the rug.

"Günter Schmidt," Monuglu says as slaps the flashlight against the palm of his hand.

"The guy from the tour?"

"The man you ate lunch with yesterday. The man who followed you out of town last night."

"Followed me? But..." Travers pauses as the implications become clear. "Where? How?"

Monuglu takes a step closer so that he is almost straddling Travers. "Two backpackers...wanting to be alone for a little extra fun...found him in a cave. Half-naked. His cock almost severed." He scratches at his mustache. "His neck broken."

Travers flinches for the first time. "His dick cut?"

"Bitten. Flies swarmed the bloody pulp. It reportedly upset the young woman a great deal."

Travers lowers his head and shakes it.

"You must come with me," Monuglu says, his voice fatigued as well as caustic. "The police will question you."

"Yeah, okay," Travers says. He's not afraid for himself, but Schmidt's death is bad on a lot of levels. He scans the mess they made of his room, looking for his pants.

"I came to get you as a courtesy," Monuglu says.

Travers squints at Monuglu. "A courtesy?"

"The police are not so kind." Monuglu points the flashlight at Travers with one hand while he wipes his head with the other. "You should not have come to Cappadocia without informing me, Joseph. I am the best friend you have in Turkey. The sooner you understand this, the better off you will be."

ⵜ 42

Abrahim climbs barefoot through the darkness. His right eye has swollen completely shut, and his depth perception is curtailed so much that he has already slipped three times. He has on only black cotton pants and a gray T-shirt. Carrying a two-liter bottle of water, he chants in Latin, a soft whisper that does not carry into the night much less rise to heaven. He is long past weeping, alone in this vast valley of darkness. After he left Doctor Altay, he returned to his hostel and threw away the shirt specked with blood—the spots on his chest she hadn't noticed in the dark. He brushed his teeth repeatedly and then showered for a long time but could not cleanse himself. The lukewarm water stung his eye all the more, and the welt on his back burned as though he had been branded.

He treks through the valley beyond the valley. No light reaches him from the town. Although the moonshine is strong enough to lead him through this darkness, he wants no guidance. He is lost. And that is as it should be. His feet are already bleeding, but he must suffer more severe mortification of the flesh before his eternal damnation. He brought the water so that he can prolong the awareness of his suffering. Saint John was right: out of hopelessness comes malice. Others may be forced to pay for your vengeance, but you will always be caught in your own heart. And your baleful acts are, ultimately, hollow. Although people may be made whole again by love, he will not. He has always been evil, and now he is irredeemable.

He rejects the first six caves he finds. They are neither deep enough nor damp enough. In the seventh, the dank stench of decay is strong. He bumps his head on a ledge in the darkness, but pain cannot be added to infinite pain. The right side of his face twitches below his eye. When he sits against the rough cold wall, he can feel the tufa rub the welt where the man gouged his back a moment before he took vengeance.

Before long, he is shivering. He drinks a small portion of the water, then hugs his knees to his chest. He cannot stop the shaking. Even if he could, he would not. The mouth of the cave offers no way out, no escape—and that also is how it should be. He lifts his head, leans hard against the wall, and begins again to pray. His words bounce about the walls, trapped in the cave every bit as much as he is.

☥ 43

When the two techno-boys start talking, Sophia Altay stops keyboarding. In her Spanish tourist guise, she is the first customer in the internet café. She had a difficult night followed by a disquieting morning. Abrahim's injury and his reaction to Saint John's letter perturbed her. She knew that Saint John's words would speak to him, but she expected the antithesis of his devastation. He became upset, then incoherent, and then stubbornly unwilling to talk. A document which should have given him hope made him so disconsolate that she finally had to shut off the computer and guide him most of the way back into Göreme. When she left him by the road, he acted as though he were leaving on a long journey—or forever. He clung to her, muttering good-byes. This morning, she woke in the darkness before dawn with a premonition of disaster. Her chest was tight, her breathing short. Though she tried a series of yogic exercises, none worked. When she reached town, military police and television camera crews were in the streets.

Now, a boy she has not seen before has brought tea and news to his friend who opens the café each day. She wipes her sweating hands on the gold silk scarf tied around her waist, a scarf that accentuates her hips but could also be used to cover her head should she need to change her appearance quickly. The boys are talking freely because they think she does not understand Turkish. Every word they are saying makes her heart pound. If they have *any* of their facts right, something has gone terribly wrong.

She leans forward, feigning deep concentration, sets her fingers on the keyboard, types utter gibberish, and listens: *Two backpackers fucking their brains out in a cave found a corpse. The dead man was a German who worked for that archeologist who discovered the Christian tomb in Ephesus. The poor bastard was castrated and mutilated. His nose was sliced off and his eyes gouged out. His cock was in his mouth. An American also connected to that German archeologist was arrested in the middle of the night. He fought the cops. A fucking stupid thing to do. He had to be beaten into submission. The American was unconscious when they carted him off to the hospital. Or the police station. Nobody's sure where they took him.*

Altay's chest feels like it's caving in on itself. She straightens her back and lifts her head, but it does little good. Her mind races even faster than her fingers. *The murderer had an accomplice, a woman. A fucking French woman who somebody said just turned herself in. She's the one that castrated the bastard. Bit his cock off while he was still alive.* The techno-boys laugh nervously at that detail, then take quick sips of their tea. The visitor, who keeps shifting his weight from foot to foot, continues. *A military convoy came to keep order. Those MPs are tough sons of bitches. Tv crews are arriving from all over the world. Especially the States. The whole world's watching. Göreme is going to be famous.*

Altay stops keyboarding and logs onto the CNN site. There's still stuff about Leopold and the ossuary, but nothing yet on a murder in Cappadocia. Nothing on the BBC site either. Göreme's not yet on the media map much less the center of anything, and she needs information fast. Who was killed? Where and when? Why? Was Joe Travers arrested? Would Joe fight with the police? What would he tell them? If it wasn't Joe, then who was it? She logs out, gathers her bag, and freezes. *Abrahim,* she thinks. *Oh, merde! Abrahim!*

ⵣ 44

Sunlight blinds Joseph Travers for a moment when he steps out the police station's side door into the parking lot. A crowd of reporters and onlookers has gathered beyond the military police cordon. Travers walks gingerly, the swollen toes of his left foot pressing against his walking shoe. The sun feels hotter than it did the day before, and the crowd's murmuring rings in his bad ear. The uniformed men who trashed his hotel room march on either side of him.

As Nihat Monuglu leads him to an old black Mercedes 280, reporters shout questions at him in English, German, and Turkish. He keeps his head raised, scanning the crowd, but he doesn't say anything.

He is not handcuffed. In fact, he's not sure whether he's still officially a prisoner. During the six hours of questioning, the lead interrogator, a thin man with a pockmarked face and garlic breath, threatened Travers repeatedly but never hit him. Travers did not ask for or receive any help or counsel from anyone. Early on, the interrogator got in Travers' face and shouted in bad English a lot about Travers rotting in a Turkish prison and wishing he were dead. His rapid-fire questions all led to a single point: a quick confession would make the whole ordeal far easier for him. The interrogator had no good-cop counterpart, but Monuglu periodically appeared in the bare, dank room, arms folded across his chest, saying nothing. Neither the interrogator nor Monuglu paid any attention when Travers repeatedly insisted that there would never be a confession because there was nothing to confess.

At one point after the interrogator took a short break—Travers wasn't sure exactly when because time was playing tricks on him— the questioning abruptly refocused on what had happened to Travers on the street in Selçuk. Travers admitted that he figured out during the bus tour that Günter Schmidt was one of the men who attacked him. When asked if he was aware that Schmidt had worked for Leopold Kirchburg, Travers responded that he had no way of knowing that. The interrogator pounded the gray metal table and screamed that Travers was a liar—that every word he'd said was a damned lie.

Half an hour before it ended, the interrogation suddenly stopped being adversarial. It became, bizarrely, a reasonably friendly interview about why Travers came to Cappadocia, what made him take the tour, and what he still planned to do in the area. Finally, the interrogator picked at a sore at the corner of his mouth and told Travers that a car was waiting for him outside.

Monuglu opens the Mercedes' door for Travers and slides into the backseat after him. The uniforms get in front. The lot has been cleared of other vehicles, but a wooden cart holding clay pots stands under the overhanging branches of a tree. An MP waves the Mercedes through the cordon. When the crowd shuffles to let the car out, Travers notices a woman in traditional Turkish dress who briefly lowers her gold silk veil just enough so that he glimpses those stunning feline eyes.

As the camera crews scramble to their vans, the Mercedes turns a corner and heads out of town. A military transport truck pulls in behind the Mercedes but slows so that no other vehicles can follow. The Mercedes speeds up the hill past the open-air museum, the tourists along the road gaping angrily. Travers gazes out the tinted window at the dark entrances to the cave churches dotting the tufa spires. Monuglu takes a Yenidje from his cigarette case and lights it without opening a window. He drags silently on the cigarette, the car's air conditioner blowing the smoke back into the space between Travers and him. Travers sits back and turns from the smoke.

"I cannot determine," Monuglu says, "if you are a lucky man or an unlucky man."

Travers turns toward him but says nothing. Monuglu's shirt is rumpled, and he needs a shower.

"Certainly a man who talks with you is unlucky." Monuglu picks a piece of tobacco from his lips and flicks it on the floor. "At least that was true of Kenan Sirhan and the Austrian."

Travers looks out at an orchard sloping down into a narrow valley.

Monuglu takes a deep drag on the Yenidje. "It seems," he says, exhaling through his nose, "that you are once again my problem."

The Mercedes climbs a steep hill and makes a sharp turn at speed. Travers glances over his shoulder, but there's no one coming after them.

"It would have been more convenient for my friends in Göreme if you had confessed." Monuglu shrugs. "Or if more of the evidence had pointed to you. Once the Austrian was connected to your mishap in Selçuk, everything fit, motive and opportunity…" He shakes his head. "…except for certain details. God is in the details—who was it who said that?"

"Gustave Flaubert," Travers answers, though he knows the question was rhetorical.

Monuglu glowers at him for a moment. "Yes, the Frenchman," he says. "The Austrian's cock was half bitten off. Have I mentioned that?" He pulls on the Yenidje and exhales a billowing cloud in front of Travers. "But you returned to your hotel from your nocturnal walk in the same clothes you left in. They had no trace of blood." He stubs out the cigarette in the ashtray. "A dark blue T-shirt with blood stains was found this morning in a garbage can outside a hostel. The examiners also found tissue and blood under the Austrian's fingernails. But the blood type is not the same as yours, and the DNA testing will, I am sure, exonerate you completely. Which is too bad for the Göreme police. You were so very convenient." He finally cracks his window. "And then there is the matter of the French woman."

Travers flinches.

"It seems that during lunch, she eavesdropped—is that the word?—on your conversation with the Austrian. She was, I do not know why, more interested in you than in the tour guide who was entertaining her friends."

Thinking, *Oh, the French girl,* Travers sinks back in his seat.

"This morning, as news of the murder and your arrest spread through the town, she came forward to tell the authorities that your lunch conversation with the Austrian had been almost friendly."

His name was Günter Schmidt, Travers thinks.

Monuglu takes another Yenidje from the case and tamps it against the back of his wrist. "Indeed, she mentioned that at the end of your lunch you forgave the Austrian for something and gave him a message for someone." He brandishes the Yenidje in Travers' face. "Failing to admit that you knew that the Austrian worked for Leopold Kirchburg was your only error the entire time you were questioned." He slips the cigarette into his mouth but doesn't light it. "In any case, the young woman's testimony destroyed the convenient revenge motive." He smiles. "You seem to have a way with French women." His smile falls into a frown. "Which brings us back to our earlier...conversation. How is Doctor Altay?"

"I wouldn't know." Travers is tired of questions—Monuglu's, the interrogator's, and anyone else's. His toe burns where the nail ripped, his stitches still throb, and his head feels like he's been kicked in the temple.

"But your walk last night. It was to see her. To speak with her in private."

Travers exhales slowly, blowing a pocket of clear breath into the smoke. "No," he says. "It wasn't. I haven't had any contact with Altay since I arrived here. None at all."

Monuglu rolls the Yenidje between his thumb and first two fingers. "Really?" he asks, and it seems to be a genuine question. "A reasonable man would conclude that when you slipped out of town you were on your way to see her." He snaps the cigarette in two and then mashes the pieces in his palm. "Certainly the Austrian and at least one other person made that assumption."

"I went for a walk."

"Ah, another of your strolls to look at Turkish stars." Monuglu gazes at the crushed cigarette as though he's not sure how it got into his hand. "You like the night sky here in Cappadocia as much as you did in Selçuk, do you?"

"Maybe even more. I'll let you know."

"But you admit," Monuglu says, "that the Austrian must have followed you into the countryside, thinking that you would lead him to Doctor Altay."

When Travers doesn't respond, Monuglu throws the crumpled Yenidje out the window he cracked. "So, as I have stated, you are once again my problem. People around you die, but you are not, it seems, the cause. When you are near, people disappear. Or reappear." He smiles morosely. "That sounds like a bad American song. Mister Lee, who, I trust, you had a productive meeting with, is already here, and Leopold Kirchburg will arrive soon. And that young Turk, the one who also vanished from the Saint John's site, I wonder if he is enjoying his tour of Cappadocia as well. The police visited his room this morning, but he was not there."

The Mercedes winds down a hill into a town far less touristy than Göreme. A bent old man leads a donkey up the hill. Two old women draw water from a roadside faucet into large metal containers.

Beyond an open gate, another old woman sits on a wooden stool in the shade of a tree and shakes a large bowl filled with grain. The car turns into the driveway in front of the red-brown Alfina Cave Hotel built into a rock massif. After pulling behind a cluster of trees in the courtyard, it stops near the office entrance.

Travers hears the call to prayer, waits for it to end, and then asks, "Why the hell did you do that...stuff...at the hotel last night?"

"It was a bad night." Monuglu scrapes his fingers through his mustache. "And I needed to be certain that, if you were in trouble with the police, you did not have in your possession any antiquities that belonged to the Turkish Ministry of Culture and the Turkish peoples." He lays his hand heavily on Travers' shoulder. "And what I told you is true. I am your friend." He lifts his hand and waves at the Alfina's entrance. "Look, I have arranged new accommodations for you. A place away from all those reporters. My men...," he gestures toward the front seat, "...have gathered your belongings, even your suitcase from Istanbul, and brought them here for you. And, Joseph, they will be staying here at the hotel in case you need anything."

⚵ 45

"He was your boy, Leopold," Charles Lee says. He has his right hand on the silver Mercedes L360's steering wheel. He's tapping the top of the window well with the fingers of his left hand. He's got his Ray-Bans on to reflect the glare, both the sun's and Kirchburg's. He picked up Kirchburg at the airport in Kayseri so that they could have this little chat before they got to Göreme. The Mercedes rides well even on this two-lane road that's supposed to be a major highway. Some lone mountain juts off to the left, but it's all wasteland to the right.

"Nein," Kirchburg says, "Herr Schmidt was not my employee." His long legs are bent in front of him, but his hair still almost grazes the car's roof. He turns and stares hard at the side of Lee's face. "He was my…our staffer last year. Not *this* year."

Lee glances at Kirchburg whose pinched face is flushed, his finically trimmed beard almost aglow. "Then what in God's name was *your* ex-employee doing *out here?*" he asks.

"Perhaps *you* can tell me." Kirchburg keeps staring. "After all, we are on the same team."

Lee passes some rattletrap flatbed truck that looks about forty years old. Neither of them has ever believed that *same-team* shit, but their interests have coincided—at least until Sophia Altay's gal-boy dug up that bone box. "Yes," he says, his tone not at all conciliatory. "I do believe we are. And, no, I don't know why Schmidt was here." He waves his hand at the vast barrenness.

"What *do* you know?" Kirchburg asks.

Lee guns the Mercedes. The car flat out flies through the Turkish countryside. Kirchburg is an effete intellectual snob who tries to get the upper hand in any argument, but that's not happening this time around. "I *know* y'all look pretty bad, leaving Selçuk and shucking your Aegean Association duties."

Kirchburg puffs out his narrow chest, and his hair brushes the Mercedes' roof. "The ossuary's contents—the bones—are here!"

"Sophia Altay is here, and it looks like you're too busy sniffing after *her* bones to take care of Association business."

"I…"

Lee slices the air with his hand, cutting Kirchburg off. "Y'all don't get what you're stepping into. Schmidt's murder was brutal. And the media's on it like bottle flies on dung. They're swarming Göreme." He pauses, looking directly at Kirchburg. "The local police have already connected Schmidt to you and to the theft of the files from Joe Travers in Selçuk."

"I had nothing to do with any of that."

Lee sniggers. "That ossuary you left at Saint John's—and those bones that've gone missing—they're all snowballing into one helluva story. Nihat Monuglu is in town with a couple of his gorillas. And the Turkish military. And Arabs. And Israelis—the Mossad, Leopold. And it looks to every mother's son like y'all created this whole shit storm." He takes the wheel with both hands, closing his fingers tightly around the leather guard. "Do you have *anything* more on that bone box?"

Kirchburg does not answer at first. He looks out at the rolling countryside. "Sophia..." he murmurs.

"Jesus, shit!" Lee says. The Kraut may be brilliant, but his narcissism makes him thick as a brick. The issue here is the bone box's contents, not Altay's sweet ass. "A man, one of your gofers, was murdered at Saint John's on your archeological site. Since then, it looks like you had two goons mug the Glavine Foundation rep for some damned computer file. Then one of the goons, who just happens to be your countryman and employee, gets himself killed in a particularly gruesome way. When this gets out, Leopold, all of your funders, but especially my Eagles, are going to have your butt in a sling." He drums his palms on the steering wheel. "The Aegean Association will collapse, and you'll be the king of squat."

"You know that is not what happened. And not what will happen." Kirchburg's tone is disdainful. "I would never be involved in something that sordid." His face is so flushed now that red blotches are appearing above his beard. "Herr Travers stole an artifact from m... from an Aegean Association site. Schmidt apparently stole it from him. I told you, I had nothing to do with any of it."

In a way, Lee marvels at the Kraut's belief that his word is, ipso facto, all that matters. But if he sticks to that particular story, the American and European media will fry him. "It wasn't an artifact, and Altay *gave* it to him," he says. "And, it doesn't change the fact that it looks to everybody like y'all had your funder's rep knifed."

"Sophia Altay...," Kirchburg mutters.

Lee comes up behind a minibus like the ones hippies used to drive, lays on the horn, and blows by the beater. "What have you dug up on the ossuary?" he shouts.

Kirchburg shakes his head. "I have nothing..."

Lee hammers the steering wheel. "Damn it…" He pauses, regaining control. "If you want me to save your…if I'm going to provide you support here…" It galls him to use that phrase, but often the only way to get through to the Kraut is sycophantic bullshit. "…y'all have got to level with me."

Kirchburg rubs his knees with his bony fingers. His gold university ring with the red stone glints in the sunlight. "Killing Günter Schmidt was a direct attack on me."

The fingers of Lee's left hand tattoo the window well. The Herr Professor's faith that the universe revolves around him and his highfalutin academic horseshit just keeps getting more amazing. "I thought he wasn't your *ass*et," he says, emphasizing the last word's first syllable.

"He is not. But he was. I've made a monumental discovery. The greatest find in the history of archeology. I am about to obtain the Christ's relics. Murdering Schmidt, my countryman, is an obvious attempt to discredit my work here. To assault me."

Lee lifts his sunglasses and rubs his left eye. "Who's doing this, Leopold? Who the hell is attacking you?"

"Ich… Sophia stole the relics from me." Saying the name aloud causes a brief tic in Kirchburg's left temple. "She knows I will get them back."

ⵟ 46

Abrahim has not gone to hell. His face burns but not from an infernal, unquenchable fire. The taste of his swollen tongue is metallic but not sulfuric. Darkness did not swallow him whole. He lies in the mouth of the cave, his head and shoulders in the sun. He could not will himself into eternal damnation. He sat shivering against the cave's wall until the deeper, slower tremors of hypothermia set in. All he had to do was drift into sleep, and he would have awakened in the sea of fire. But he could not. He wanted to suffer for his sin, but something more profound occurred, a paradox he did not understand then and doesn't quite fathom now: the more he wished for death, the more he clung to life. The more his remorse weighed on him, the lighter he felt. The desire to live, even as an unspeakably sinful sodomite, surmounted his need to die.

He dug himself into the cave's sandy floor, curled tight like a cur, and lay there until the shuddering ceased. And then a cycle began. Each time the shaking stopped, his shame and depravity beat him against the wall. And each time he gave up on himself, life itself pulled him from the dark wall and held him close. His physical appetites, his weakness always, became the strength that kept him alive.

And, now, exhausted, he feels the sun blister his skin. When he thinks about his actions, he loses hope—but remains alive. Guilt wracks him, but he listens to each breath as though it is his first not his last. He can taste the tufa, gritty against his cracked lips. He can see the light, strobing red and gold, through his closed left eyelid; the swelling over his right eye has gone down enough that light shimmers through the slit. He can hear the wind murmuring in the cave mouth... Feel the prickle... Smell the dust.

When he squints up at the sky with his good eye, the sun is well past its zenith. The sun has cauterized him as he lay here unaware of time's passing. Now, the air around him shimmers in the heat. It wraps and holds him, stroking him with each breath he takes. He presses up on his palms and snakes back into the cave. He must forsake the world. The beauty out there would break his heart again. Inside, there are no paintings, no blind saints to sing of his sins. There is nothing but tufa and sand and shadowy darkness. He cannot go back, not after what he has done. But he cannot die either. He must not walk among people, and yet he craves human touch, Sophia's or anyone else's.

He takes the bottle and drinks. The last of his water, still cool, slides down his throat and ripples through him. It, like air and light and the ground beneath him, is life—and he begins to weep again. If only

Saint John spoke to him a day earlier, he might be saved. *Over the years, I came to see the hollowness of my acts…. I have seen light as well as darkness…. Only love has made me whole again…* The words burn into his mind now, all others before them, even the gospels, pallid in the light of their flame.

⊹ 47

Returning to the Alfina from his walk, Joseph Travers stops at the Local, the restaurant next door to the hotel. It is just after ten, and the townspeople have gathered there for a dance under the stars. The music is Turkish, but with an amplified big band sound. The young women dance together in their long skirts and loose blouses. The older women, heads covered with scarves, sit at tables around the patio's periphery, talking and gesturing. The older boys and men stand in clusters smoking. The younger children dart about among the groups. It is, Travers thinks, like a square dance but with more arcane rituals and taboos. He leans on the low wall along the street and watches the girls in colorful swirling skirts sway with the music. The rhythm is slow and the movement beautiful. Monuglu's two men, whom Travers has come to think of as Hulk Major and Hulk Minor, give him twenty yards leeway. They have changed out of their brown uniforms into dark pants and light shirts, and now they stand together smoking and watching the young women with an intensity far greater than Travers'.

Travers lets the music fill him and waits for whatever's going to happen. He got the message, handwritten in English and unsigned, when he went by the hotel's office before dinner—

Take your walk at dusk, but remain local after ten.

How Sophia Altay found out where he was staying wasn't clear, and he didn't understand the second part of the message as he reread it over his lamb stew served in a clay pot at dinner—but he assumed the message had been analyzed by any number of interested Turks. After dinner, he cut the toe out of his left shoe to get it on over the swelling. He then hobbled into Ürgüp, which, with its few souvenir shops and clubs around the main square, hadn't seemed to have decided yet whether it was going the way of Göreme into the modern world. As he climbed back up the hill toward the hotel, Monuglu's hulks followed at less than a discrete distance. The evening call to prayer followed the trio, and it was only when Travers slowed by the Local that the message made sense.

As he headed farther out into the hills above Ürgüp, the darkening sky lifted him. Physically, he was a mess, a general achiness from having been rousted and interrogated permeating every part of him that didn't feature a specific pain. But he was outside, trekking under a rising moon and spreading stars in a light breeze—and Altay was going to contact him upon his return.

Slowed by his injuries, Travers didn't try to lose Monuglu's hulks. Their dark heavy shoes were made for standing around looking menacing not for hiking. Neither man was built for clambering over boulders, and so Travers took it easy, wanting to lull them into complacency, which, from the look of them slouching along the wall outside the Local, has worked. Hulk Major lights one cigarette from another and nods toward two young women gliding arm in arm across the patio.

Travers scans the Local, wondering if Altay is one of the veiled women. The knots of older women are so tight, though, that it seems unlikely. An empty flatbed truck flying a Turkish flag from its cab rumbles by. A song ends, and static scratches through the Local's sound system before the next tune begins. The crescent moon and its trailing star hang above the massif into which both the Alfina and Local are built.

A motor scooter whines by heading down into Ürgüp. Travers shifts his weight so that there is less pressure on his left foot. The skirts and blouses wave with the music. One of the young boys tackles another on the lawn, and both roll around laughing. The scooter's whine Dopplers back through the music. He turns to look just as it fishtails to a stop near him.

"Joe!" a voice shouts from beneath the full visor of the rider's blue helmet.

The scooter is already moving again by the time he has his leg over the back. He throws his arms around her waist, almost swinging off the other side of the scooter. They are already up the hill and leaning into the turn before he even thinks of looking back at Monuglu's hulks. Sitting up higher than Altay, close in against her, he tucks his head behind her helmet and feels the new pain where he just singed his calf on the scooter's tailpipe. The bike is a Peugeot, sleek, metallic blue and silver—and she winds it fast over the road. The sky wheels, and the scooter bumps onto a dirt track. Altay's stomach is firm against his palms, her breath even. They rise gradually, the headlight's beam jiggling past low shrubs and rocks. Another sharp turn, a grove, and she cuts the lights and motor into dark silence even before the scooter stops.

Travers, having traveled from a festive dance to an isolated valley in ten minutes, doesn't let go immediately. She takes his right hand, peels herself free, and slips off the scooter. He slides off, too, but onto his left foot, causing a quick jig. The burn hole in his hiking pants is only the size of a cigarette, but the material is stuck to his leg. She removes her helmet and shakes out her hair. Even in the pale moonlight, her eyes shine. She pushes the scooter behind a thick stand of bushes, lays the helmet on the seat, and pulls out a broom of brambles lashed to a stick.

"Wait here," she says as she disappears into the night.

He locates the North Star, but, in truth, he's all turned around. He couldn't find his way back here to save his life.

When she returns, whisking the broom over the ground behind her, she says, "Follow me."

He does, but not over any trail he can make out. Tufa spires rise around them, and, as they climb, the valley falls to darkness below. The pain in his leg intensifies, but he doesn't lose sight of her back.

Her hair, bouncing in the moonlight, gleams darkly. They crab across a boulder and then squeeze between two massive rocks before heading upward again. When they can go no farther, she doubles back across the face of an outcropping—and vanishes.

Vertigo isn't exactly the problem, but even as a boy in Prescott he never much liked precipitous heights. He's glad it's dark. Seeing the situation more clearly might freeze him. They are high up an escarpment away from any trails, and he has no idea how long or rough the slide is down into the darkness of the valley. Taking a series of deep breaths, he pauses before stepping out above the abyss. He might as well be blind. Raising his arms to horizontal, he turns toward the rock and slides along it face to face. His hands provide balance but little purchase. The grainy tufa feels as though it might disintegrate under his sweating palms.

ⵂ 48

Altay pushes the blocking stone across the low, narrow entrance as Travers stands, panting, in the center of the cave. A section of the roof has sheered away, and the moon provides just enough light for him to see her movements. The cave, about thirty feet long and twenty feet wide, is, even in the dimness, obviously a church. The stone altar stands below the oval of sky. Faint images of saints adorn the walls above the low ledge running along the sides. Indentations, perhaps stands for icons, are cut into the walls at intervals. Altay's computer lies on her backpack, a dark lump among other lumps in the corner farthest from the sky hole.

"It's good to see you, Sophia," he says once he has caught his breath.

Combing her fingers through her hair, she nods. Her khaki pants are tight, and her blue T-shirt is loose. With her helmet on, she might have been mistaken for a boy as she flew by on her scooter. She shakes her head so that her hair falls loosely on her shoulders. "You lost the files I gave you," she says, her tone like it was that first evening in Istanbul.

"They were stolen."

"You were carrying the flash drive with you on the street?"

"Yes. I'm pretty sure the guys who mugged me, Günter Schmidt and another man, worked for Leopold Kirchburg." He sits down on the ledge. "Did you know Schmidt?"

"Not really. I knew who he was. He worked security for Leopold last year. But not at Saint John's. At another site." As she steps over closer to the altar, light catches her eyes. "How did he know you had the flash drive?"

"I was being watched, I think. Since Istanbul." He rolls up the leg of his hiking pants. The burn, the size and shape of one of Monuglu's Yenidjas, feels much larger.

"*Since Istanbul?*"

"Yes. Probably even before our dinner. But I recognized Schmidt from the next day. He followed me. And somebody, I think, followed him."

She chews on her lower lip. "But how did they know you had the flash drive?"

"I used it at the internet café—when I emailed you."

She rubs her palms on her hips. "You read the files?"

"I looked at them. I couldn't read anything."

Exhaling, she shakes her head.

"How did you find me?"

"There's not much between Göreme and Ürgüp." She shrugs. "I had a boy from town deliver the note."

He scratches the side of his nose. "I have another question."

She folds her arms in front of her chest.

"What was Kenan yelling at me about that night when he brought Leopold to your house?"

She sits on the ledge next to him. Closer to him, she is more of a shadow. She smells like the desert he knew as a child. "About your firing me," she says. "About how you Americans are such arrogant pigs. Always stomping in and acting like you own everything." Her smile is sad. "About closing down the Saint John's site…firing him."

"And Kenan's death?" he asks. "What made you so sure right away that it was murder?"

She looks at him for a moment. "He was trying to sell the bones and the documents."

"To whom?"

"Abrahim didn't know. But he overheard Kenan speaking German on the phone."

"And so Abrahim took the bones and letters?"

"Yes. To save them. At least in his mind, he was…" She touches Travers' calf below the burn. Her voice becomes softer. "I'm worried about him."

Travers is, too, but maybe not in the same way. "He was all right when I saw him…" Taken by how recent it was, he stops for a moment. "…yesterday afternoon."

She goes over to her backpack, unzips a pocket, and takes out a small, white plastic box. "He didn't meet me this evening. He was hysterical last night when I… Someone had hit him hard, injured his eye." She returns with the box and opens it in her lap. "Muffler?" she asks.

He nods as he asks, "Which eye?"

"It was swollen shut."

"Which eye, Sophia?"

She pauses, turning her shoulders. "His right."

"What have you heard about Schmidt's murder?"

"That it was macabre." She takes a tube from the box, opens it, and squeezes ointment onto the tip of her index finger.

"What, specifically?"

"Hold still," she says. "There are a lot of rumors. Some involving you and me. But all of them suggest that Schmidt was mutilated. His genitals…"

He flinches when she dabs the burn. A sharp inhalation cuts his words. When he can speak again, he says, "The gouged eyes of the saints at the Church Under the Trees in Ihlara Gorge upset Abrahim during the tour."

"He is a complex boy." She takes out a sterile pack of gauze and tears it open without using the finger with the ointment.

"Sophia, I saw a drawing in his notebook…"

"He would go to extremes to protect me…" Her voice sounds as though she is crying.

"If he thought I was coming to see you last night and that Schmidt was following me, would he…?"

She carefully unfolds the gauze and places it lightly over the burn. "He would not mur… I don't believe that he would ever kill someone. Not in any circumstances."

"Not even to protect you?"

She looks away, and they sit in silence for awhile. As his eyes adjust more, the saints' halos appear in the faint light. She wipes her finger on the gauze's packaging, closes the box, and stows it again in her backpack. She rummages in a bag against the wall and comes back with a liter bottle of water.

When she sits, she says, "He's always hard on himself." She twists off the cap and hands him the bottle.

"And?"

She leans back against the wall, a shadow shifting. "I don't know where he is or what he's doing, but I know him well. If he hurt Schmidt, he will only hurt himself more."

He killed Schmidt, Travers thinks.

They are quiet again, this time for longer. He drinks from the bottle and hands it back to her. She takes a sip and caps the bottle, then stands and crosses to the oval of sky. She raises her head and gazes upward.

Turning back toward him, she says, "So you're sure Leopold has the flash drive?"

"Am I sure? No. But it looks that way."

"And Schmidt followed you here to Göreme?"

"And Lee. And Monuglu. And Kirchburg." Shaking his head, he clears his throat. "And half the reporters in Europe and the Middle

East. Both the police and the military seem interested in my movements, too."

"Mon Dieu, Joseph!" she says before they lapse into silence a third time.

He pats down the edge of the gauze so that it sticks to the ointment better. Then he stands and comes up next to her. As he looks up into the night sky, he is close enough to smell her and to hear her breathing, but he doesn't touch her. A cool breeze wafting through the skylight brushes them. "I need," he says, "to read the letters."

ⵚ 49

When Altay turns on the computer, light splashes up the cave's walls to the roof. Travers looks around rather than at the screen. The two saints on the arched ceiling hold each other. Their inner robes are white, their outer robes red. Their hands, still clear after all of these centuries, clasp one another. Each saint's eyes gaze into the other's. They share one overlapping halo. Another figure, a smaller angel-saint all in white robes, hovers to their right.

Altay slides the computer onto Travers' lap, but she remains close to him on the ledge. The screen is bright, and he glances at the sheered oval.

"We're near the top of the cliff," she says. "Light only escapes *up* from here. No one can see anything."

This manuscript, he thinks, *is illuminated in a way that would shock medieval monks.*

"There are two documents," she says. "This one was written before Jesus of Nazareth died. I don't know if he dictated it to a scribe or if someone there in the Garden recorded the words."

Feeling her breathing next to him, he begins to read.

Hear, O Israel! Worship the Lord your God and serve Him only. Love the Lord your God with all of your heart and all of your strength. Hear me, all of you, and understand. Fear the Lord. The Kingdom of God is at Hand. The Day of God's vengeance is upon us.

I have come to deliver you, O Israel. I am the Son of Man. I am God's hand. I have rebuked the wind and stilled the seas. I have made the blind see and the deaf hear and the lame walk. I have forgiven sins. I have cleansed lepers and cast out demons. I have raised the dead.

Serve no Lord but God. Do not think I have come to abolish the law or the prophets. I have not come to abolish them but to fulfill them. Beware of the teachers of the law. The deceitfulness of riches and the desires for other things choke the words of the Scribes and the Pharisees. This is a wicked generation. Caiaphas and the high priests are a brood of vipers. The men of Ninaveh will stand up at the Judgment with this generation and condemn it. The Pharisees who nullify the word of God for the sake of tradition will be punished most severely. The Temple is called a house of prayer, but they make it a den of robbery. Woe to you, teachers of the law and Pharisees, you snakes!

When you pray, do not be like the hypocrites who love to pray standing in synagogues and on street corners. Be careful not to practice righteousness in front of others. When you give to the needy, do not announce it with trumpets, as do the hypocrites in the synogogues.

Serve no earthly master. Do you think I have come to bring peace on earth? No, I tell you, but division. Do not suppose I have come to bring peace, but a sword. I have come to bring fire on earth.

A prophet is not without honor except in his own town. Whoever is not with me is against me. They have hated me without reason. Woe to the man by whom the Son of Man is betrayed. Whoever disowns me before others will be disowned before the angels of God.

You will be betrayed even by parents, brothers and sisters, relatives and friends. Brother will betray brother to death, and a father his child. Children will rebel against their parents and have them put to death.

They will seize you and persecute you. Be dressed ready for service and keep your lamps burning. If you do not have a sword, sell your cloak and buy one. You will be hated by everyone because of me, but the one who stands firm to the end will be saved. The Son of Man is coming on the clouds of heaven, with power and great glory.

When Travers finishes reading, his eyes burn. He takes a breath that hitches twice, and then he exhales through his nose, a sound to him like steam escaping. Altay's eyes are on him, gauging his response. He meets her gaze but doesn't immediately say anything. These words, revolutionary two millennia ago, are probably even more inflammatory now. Their release will cause controversy, maybe even chaos. "And you're sure it's authentic?" he asks, nodding to the screen.

"Absolutely!" Her eyes narrow. *"You* know it is."

He feels the tight, stitched burning in his thigh and the scorched spot on his calf, whose pain he didn't notice while he was reading. His mind flashes to his dealings with Monuglu and Kirchburg and Lee and Schmidt and the smaller man who cut him. "Where's the original?"

"Safe." Her lips purse. "I have it in a safe place." The finality in her voice, like that when they first spoke on the Blue Hotel's rooftop and when she was about to flee from her house's veranda, shuts him out once more.

He skims the print on the screen, stopping at, *I have come to bring fire on earth.* "Who else has read this?" he asks.

"Abrahim." She takes a breath. "Leopold, if you're right about him having the files. He reads some Aramaic."

He bites his lower lip. "And you're going to release it when it's authenticated?"

"It's authentic," she snaps. "I will disseminate it as soon as I safely can." She shifts her weight away from him.

He stares at the final sentence. *The Son of Man is coming on the clouds of heaven, with power and great glory.* "Sophia...," he starts but then stops himself. He runs his tongue over his front teeth. "Won't it stir up a firestorm of would-be prophets and self-styled saviors?"

She turns from him and says to the cave's darkness, "It is the truth." In the computer's light, the muscles around her jaw look like they are knotting. "I have discovered it. It must come out."

His mind races through a tumult of images—Israeli hardliners on the attack, Palestinian rockets and suicide bombers, Middle Eastern messiahs and caliphs rising in the desert, inciting tens of thousands, and jihadists rallying to destroy the enemy of Allah. Anyone who feels directly ordained by God—or pretends to—will use these words as a righteous call for insurgency. The Talaban and other tyrants will justify the oppressive terrors of their theocracies. Demagogues will rain death on infidels, and, in fact, anyone who disagrees with them. Christian fundamentalists everywhere, but especially in America, will declare the End Times at hand and call for the creation of the New Jerusalem. And those already paranoid political, religious, and economic power-brokers will suppress dissent—everywhere. His voice low, he asks, "Have you thought through the possible consequences?"

As she turns, her eyes lock on him. "I have." Her voice is sharp. "And I've thought of the consequences of *not* releasing the truth." Her eyes narrow. "Rumors about the ossuary's contents are already flooding the internet."

"Impia fama," he says.

She cocks her head.

"Evil rumors spread fast."

"They will be much worse than the truth."

He's not sure. He doesn't necessarily disagree with her—he just doesn't know. He needs to walk, to think. Turning the computer screen, he asks, "When did Abrahim read this?"

"Last night when he came to see me." She clasps her hands. "He was distraught. I thought it—or at least John the Apostle's letter—would settle him down. They only made it worse. I did not know what he...what had happened."

"Does he know where the original is?"

She shakes her head. "I am the only one."

Her face is olive in the light from the screen, and her eyes are the green of sea glass. People will kill—have killed—to possess this document. And people will kill—have killed?—to suppress it. Kill her, and the voice is silenced. He gazes up through the slashed rock at the night sky, the scimitar of stars. "What are you going to do?"

She takes the computer from his lap. "I was going to talk that over with Monsieur Glavine."

"But you don't want to email the translation?"

"I do not trust the internet."

He looks into her eyes, now otherworldly in the computer's light.

"I trust neither those eavesdropping on the web," she adds, "nor those in the Glavine Foundation offices."

"But you've already made English and Turkish translatations?"

"And French and Spanish."

He takes a long, slow breath. "Whom do you trust?"

Her eyes glint, as if to say, *I trusted you.*

"Sophia?"

"I don't know. Certainly no one from the Aegean Association or the Eagle Consortium. I *mistrust* government officials. And all reporters." Her smile is fleeting. "I would trust a few of my mother's colleagues and friends, but they're all gone. Two of my retired dons at Cambridge, whom I've been unable to reach."

"And what about the bone box's other contents?"

"Abrahim hid the bones, even from me. He believes they are the Christ's. But the femurs are broken."

"Are they Christ's?"

"The ossuary is authentic, but I have not seen the bones. Even if I had, I lack the expertise…"

Travers looks into her eyes again. "And the other document, John the Apostle's letter. Have you translated it?"

"It is of less import."

"Still, I need to read it, too."

☦ 50

As Altay closes the file and opens another, he watches the light play across the saints on the walls and ceiling. When she slides the computer back onto his lap, she says, "This, Joseph, was written later. The papyrus is different. The hand is less hurried, but more uncertain. Each word is carefully wrought, as though writing were learned only late in life."

He rubs his eyes, takes a breath, and begins to read once more.

I am John, the one Jesus, the Nazarean, loved. He called my brother, James, and me the Sons of Thunder, but now I am old. I have lived almost three times again as long as I did before I stood on Golgotha. All of the disciples with whom I broke bread are gone, betrayed and persecuted and martyred in the name of the Nazarean. Saul of Tarsis and Timothy and so many others are gone, too. But I am still here in this world. Jesus said of me, "If I want him to live until I come, what is it to you?" So reports spread among his followers, Hebrews and gentiles, that I would not die. But I have come to understand that he will not return. He will not rescue me. His time is not our time.

When he hung on the cross, he said to his mother as I stood there, "He is your son." He said to me, "She is your mother." While his brother, James the Just, was alive, I took vengeance upon those who crucified him. To watch him suffer and die on that tree was the most painful moment of my life. I was never again with man or woman. We are meant to lie with others, but I lay alone for the rest of my days. I despaired, and out of despair came malice.

I took vengeance on the Pharisees, one by one. Cloaked, I went about like the Sicarii taking revenge. I was truly, as he said, the Son of Thunder. I was the terrific silence between lightning and thunder. I did not cease until Jonathan lay in his own blood on the Temple floor.

"The Sicarii?" he asks.

"Religious fanatics. Assassins."

"Jonathan?"

"The Jerusalem Temple's High Priest, killed in 55 CE." She taps his arm with her index and middle fingers. "Keep reading."

Others, the Sicarii and disciples and strangers, paid for my acts. I suffered for what I did, but only at my own hand. Neither his mother nor mine nor my brother James nor James the Just nor any of the others ever knew what was in my heart.

I was never caught, except in my own heart. Jesus came to accept men and women like me. He believed in those who believed in him. I strayed from that path into despair and loathing. With time comes understanding. Over the years I came to understand the hollowness of my acts.

I have seen years of persecution, years of hatred. I have seen women stoned and boys thrown from the Temple roof for what they believed. I have seen crowds, at the bidding of the Sanhedrin, tear people apart. I have seen Roman burnings and beheadings and crucifictions. I have hid from the Pharisees and fled from the Roman wrath. I will never honor Caesar. I will never offer sacrifices to Roman gods or to any emperor. I worship the Lord my God and serve Him only.

My brother James was beheaded. When Ananus and the Sanhedrin had James the Just stoned to death for blasphemy, I finally took their mother away from Jerusalem. We came to Ephesus, far from the revolt and the coming slaughter and destruction and annihilation. I cared for her all these years as a son will. We lived among the gentiles near this city but apart from it. She died slowly, her breath becoming more shallow over many days until she no longer breathed. After I buried her under the trees near the spring she loved so much, I moved from that hill to this that I love. I can look down across the city and harbor at the shining sea. I can watch the fishing boats come and go. Each morning is my prayer. Every day is a blessing. The light among these trees bathes me in God's love every moment.

I have seen light as well as darkness. I have seen years of charity, years of love. I have seen men share their last loaves of bread. I have seen women suckle the newborn and bathe the dying. I have been broken not by the cruelty of the Pharisees or the brutality of the Romans but by my own acts. Only love has made me whole again. This I have, over time, learned, and this I have taught. It is difficult, as my brothers and sisters have learned. In the end, there is no other way. I have come to love my neighbor and my enemy. I have come to understand the truth of this and many other things since Golgotha.

I, like Jesus the Nazarean, have been betrayed. The fierce storms, the lightning and thunder of my youth, are gone from me. I will neither denounce the gentiles to the Hebrews nor the Hebrews to the gentiles. I will denounce no one to the Romans. Because I will not take sides in the discord here, my time has come. I will not live to see the Temple rebuilt in Jerusalem. I will never see the one who loved me come upon the clouds of heaven.

Travers stops biting his lip when he tastes blood. Jesus of Nazareth was messianic, and he died brutally for his zealotry. John, his disciple, was more complicated, a vengeful murderer who survived the calamitous machinations of his generation—the Jewish revolt, internecine fighting among the Jewish sects, the Romans' obliteration of Judaea, the sack of Jerusalem, the destruction of the Temple, the extermination or enslavement of the Jews, the diaspora of the survivors. He eventually found some balance, even meaning, in the world. But he was apparently betrayed and murdered, too. The statements *I have seen light as well as darkness* and *Each morning is my prayer* and *Only love has made me whole again*—all echo. Altay is right that Saint John's is the less important historical document, but it speaks more deeply to him, providing something of a counterbalance to the revolutionary zeal of Jesus. He feels for just a moment as though he's on a hill among the ruins of a cathedral as well as in a cave church carved high in an escarpment. On a path along a creek in sunlight and wind and birdsong as well as in quiet darkness lit by a computer screen.

He rereads the final two paragraphs. *It is difficult as my brothers and sisters have learned. In the end there is no other way....* Finally, he clears his throat and asks, "Where's the original?"

"I told you, *safe.*"

"And you're going to release it? Go public with *both* of them? Both letters *together?*"

"I intend to." She moves her hand close to his leg so that they are almost touching. As she gazes across the cave rather than at him, she adds, "But I have to get them verified without getting myself killed."

"And you're not worried that their release will cause havoc?"

"Yes, Joseph, I am." She turns so that their knees touch and their eyes meet. "Of course, it worries me."

"But you'll release them no matter what?"

She turns off and shuts the computer, causing the cave around them to vanish. "The ossuary and its contents belong to the world." She lifts her hand, barely visible, and waves it between them.

"Yes, but…"

"No!" she interrupts him. "No *buts*…" Her eyes are firing in the scant, shadowy light of the cave. "These documents are real. I discovered them. The world must know the truth."

His palms itch; his mouth tastes like copper. "But people will distort…"

"People," she interrupts him again, "have always distorted truth." Her tone is caustic. "Religious…political fanatics." As she shakes her head vigorously, her energy ripples around him in waves. "But that never means that truth should be withheld or suppressed. Or annihilated."

Her hair is darkness flowing through deeper darkness. When she stops moving, he can see almost nothing. The burn's pain pulses up his leg and mixes with other aching and fatigue, but he's lightheaded. Monuglu and Kirchburg and Lee and the media and the military are marshalling. She neither needed nor wanted his help, but with Abrahim out of touch and her lifelines to William Glavine, Sr., and her archeological mentors cut, she can't go it alone. "Okay," he says. "Okay."

"I have no one else, Joseph," she says, her voice less harsh.

"I guess not," he answers, aware that her last statement may be disingenuous. It's possible that she choreographed the whole meeting so that he would volunteer to do something, but he doesn't care. It no longer matters whether he can trust her. He has a sense—an irrational notion—that he is doing it more for himself and for John the Apostle than for Sophia.

"The reporters," she says, "want a story." She places her hand on his forearm. "You'll deliver one. The more the media gathers, the less likely...." Her voice, softer still, trails off.

"They won't believe me."

Brushing her fingers along his wrist and down the back of his hand, she says, "They want to believe."

He knows, historically, what has happened to messengers, but he stepped into harm's way when he accepted the flash drive, or earlier when he looked down at Kenan's corpse, or much earlier than that—even as the 737 tore down through the clouds toward Atatürk International Airport. Though a deep sense of loss and of isolation persists, his penchant for life has never been stronger. This is it, his necessity here and now.

⚴ 51

As Travers climbs the Alfina Cave Hotel's steps, he can smell the smoke of Nihat Monuglu's Yenidje. All of the cave rooms are accessed only by exterior stairwells connecting concrete terraces, and his room is on the highest terrace. Monuglu sits on an old metal patio chair in the shadows in front of Travers' door.

The terrace lights are off, and the glow of Monuglu's cigarette jiggles as he says, "Sit down, Joseph. We don't want to disturb the other guests."

Travers takes the chair to the left of the door, settling into the darkness. He is sweating from his walk. Altay dropped him along the road a mile outside of Ürgüp. At the outskirts of town, he hid the new flash drives in plastic bags in separate spots under the rubble of a derelict wall. It's late now, everyone gone from the Local and the street outside the Alfina deserted.

"You are taxing my patience," Monuglu says. As he inhales, the Yenidje burns brighter. "You have embarrassed my men and abused my hospitality."

At the very least, Travers thinks. "I apologize, Nihat," he says—and he means it.

Smoke curls into Travers' face as Monuglu turns his head toward him. "It was necessary," Travers says, blowing the smoke away.

"How is Doctor Altay?" Monuglu asks.

"Good, all things considered."

"Yes. All things considered." Monuglu drags on his cigarette again. "I would like to speak with her myself."

"I don't think that will happen, at least not in the short run."

Monuglu drops the butt onto the concrete and grinds it out with the sole of his shoe. "She would be better off speaking with me."

"Just the same," Travers says, "she isn't exactly sure whom to trust right now."

"Did she give you any Turkish artifacts…anything at all?" Monuglu is not even a shadow with the Yenidje extinguished.

"She has, I think, learned her lesson."

"Just the same," Monuglu says, "we will check before you enter your room."

"Of course," Travers says.

As Monuglu reaches over and taps the burn hole, he asks, "From a blue and silver Peugeot motorbike?"

Travers winces. "Yes."

As Monuglu takes a cell phone from his pocket, he mutters, "At least they got that right. My men knew she would contact you. But they were expecting someone with less—what is the French word?— *élan.*" He punches one number, barks "Evet," and places the phone face up on his thigh. "I don't think you will be taking any more walks," he says.

"They do me good. In the last few years, they've kept me sane."

"Sanity," Monuglu scoffs. "You Americans are obsessed with it. But you still do crazy things."

Travers hears shoes scuffing up the steps.

"The Göreme police wanted to ask you more questions about the Austrian's murder," Monuglu says. "But unfortunately I could not produce you."

The scuffing stops at the top of the stairs. A light flashes on and finds Travers' face just as he turns away. He's pulled from his chair, pinned against the wall, and frisked. A sharp stench like onions gone bad clogs his nostrils.

"Hayır," he hears, and, as the hands let go, he leans back against the wall. He can see only weaving red and yellow spots. The smell of onions recedes as that of smoke intrudes.

"Do not take any more of your walks without my knowing," Monuglu says.

"I..."

"Is that clear?" The voice, close to his left ear, is suddenly irate.

"I can't promise..."

A heel stomps Travers' left foot. Biting his lip to stifle the scream, he crumples to the concrete.

⌖ 52

Travers descends the Alfina Cave Hotel's steps like a child—right foot first, then left to the same step, and right to the next. There's no other way to do it. He can barely walk. Any pressure on his left foot slings pain from his toes to his hip. He slept fitfully for a few hours, washed his hair in the sink, shaved, and dressed in his last clean shirt.

Hulk Minor trails him as he hobbles toward the hotel's office. It's early, and there's not much traffic out on the street. Two veiled old women are straightening chairs on the Local's patio. A hot breeze ruffles his hair. Before he opens the office door, he turns to Hulk Minor, extends his hand, and says, "I'm Joe. What's your name?"

The man stares at him with bleary brown eyes. He's unshaven and disheveled, his white shirt yellow under his arms. He shakes Travers' hand but remains silent.

The desk clerk, a thin young man with a crisp shirt and a gap between his front teeth, is more jovial. When Travers asks him for a taxi, he glances at Hulk Minor in the doorway before saying, "Of course, sir. Where are you going?"

"The Göreme police station," Travers says.

"Göreme polis," the clerk repeats, his smile beginning to look forced.

Hulk Minor pulls a cell phone from his pocket.

"I'm guessing my friend will be going with me," Travers says. "Two of us."

His smile crashing to a grimace, the clerk says, "Yes, sir. Of course." As he picks up the desk phone's receiver, Hulk Minor is already speaking fast Turkish into his cell. By the time Travers reaches the door, the two Turks are speaking tersely to each other.

Outside, Hulk Minor brushes by Travers and lumbers over to the Mercedes. In half a minute, he has it turned around and idling next to Travers.

"Thank you," Travers says as he gets into the front seat.

The air-conditioning blows the smell of stale cigarettes into the backseat. Travers doesn't even glance at the derelict wall when they pass it, and neither man says a word as they wind along the road toward Göreme.

Travers gazes at the infrared transmitters jutting from the television vans lined across the street from the police station. As soon as the Mercedes stops in the lot next to the side entrance, Travers swings the door open. He pulls himself out and, leaving the door ajar, limps toward the vans.

"Dur!" Hulk Minor shouts, but there's no way to stop Travers without tackling him in the parking lot, and the men talking across the street by the vans have already noticed him.

When Travers slaps the BBC van's windshield, the man sleeping in the driver's seat jerks forward and grabs the steering wheel. He has black hair and dark brown eyes that bug as he turns toward Travers.

"Sorry," Travers says through the half-open window. "Are you the reporter?"

"Who the hell are you?" The man looks Pakistani, but his accent is British.

"Joe. Joseph Travers. I need to talk to a reporter."

The man leans back to get a better look at Travers.

"I need to speak to a reporter," Travers repeats. He looks around. The technicians from the other vans are sauntering toward him as a group. Over in the parking lot, Hulk Minor is standing by the open passenger door of the Mercedes talking on his cell phone. "Tell him I have information about the murders here and in Selçuk. That I want to talk about the ossuary, the bone box."

"Her," the guy says as he reaches for his cell phone.

"What?"

The guy taps the number 1 on his phone. "She's a woman. Allison Wade, mate. You must have seen her on the telly."

Travers watches Hulk Minor enter the police station's side entrance.

"Al," the guy says into the phone. "Sorry to wake you." He smiles. "I've got a bloke here. Joseph Travers, he says his name is. Wants to talk to a BBC reporter." He laughs. "Truly. I shit you not." He laughs again. "Will do." He hands the phone out the window to Travers.

"Hello," he says.

"Joseph Travers?" He hears rustling as though she is getting out of bed or already dressing.

"Yes." The other men from the vans are gathering around Travers in a loose circle.

"From the States?" Her voice is husky, perhaps from sleep. "From the Glavine Foundation?"

"Yes," he says. "I need to talk with someone on air about what's happening, the ossuary and the killings."

"Good, yes. I'm Allison. Al, to friends." There's more rustling. "Wait right there, Joe. May I call you *Joe?*"

The man in the van's cab is smiling at him, his eyes flashing and his teeth bright white.

"Sure," Travers says. "But I'm about to be dragged into the Göreme police station again. As soon as I come out, though."

"You're not turning yourself in?" She sounds genuinely aghast.

"No." He wonders for a moment who's playing whom here. "More questions, that's all."

"You'll do an interview immediately upon your release?"

"Yes. Right here in front of the police station."

"An exclusive?" She sounds breathless.

"What?" He sees Hulk Minor exiting the police station's front entrance with two uniformed officers. "No," he says. "A statement, answer questions." He smiles at the grinning man in the van's seat. "But, yes, an exclusive interview later. Definitely. I promise. They're coming for me now, Al."

"Put Ravi back on!" she shouts. "He's got to shoot them taking you."

☥ 53

His hands folded on the table, Travers sits alone in the stark interrogation room. The hour or so he has been left alone in the room has given him time to think through what he will and will not say to the media. The walls, cream fading to gray, are bare. The dark steel table and chairs gleam harshly in the overhead light. Scuff marks mar the wall, but the room is clean, kept that way, perhaps, to isolate a person totally from other people and from the world out there. The wiry interrogator with the pockmarked face, the same guy who had questioned him in this room the day before, seemed haggard this morning, more exhausted than Travers. His questions covered no new ground except for intermittent inquiries about a young man who was on the Cappadocia tour bus but made no contact with the other tourists. Travers provided the interrogator with no information he didn't already have.

Travers' thoughts turn now to what he wants to tell his son, Tom, about what's happening to him here in Cappadocia and what he's about to do. The mugging in Selçuk prevented his calling the other night, and he doesn't want Tom to get the only news of his father from CNN. Travers hasn't been back in touch with Bill Glavine, either, since their call in which Travers asked to talk directly with Bill's father.

Travers wonders, too, what Jason would be doing were he still alive. What music would he be into? What gadgets would he be tinkering with? What large ideas would be sweeping him away? What grand but implausible schemes would be taking him? These are thoughts that Travers has had before, ones that inevitably usher in sadness.

And, Christine, Travers thinks, what is she doing at this very moment? Sleeping? Or waking to the darkness before dawn? And even Mary—has her pain made immeasurable by her son's suicide in her car abated any? And vanished Abrahim, out there somewhere, according to Sophia, torturing himself? And Kenan Sirhan and Günter Schmidt, both lost to some deadly game Travers is part of but still doesn't fully understand? And so many others. *Only love has made me whole again,* John the Apostle said. *I have come to love my neighbor and my enemy.* In this stark room, as much a cell as any cell, there is no sign of neighbor or enemy whom he should love. Or of the world outside.

Finally, the door behind him opens, and he turns to see Nihat Monuglu step into the room. His white shirt and brown pants are clean. He has shaved, but his expression is dour.

Travers stands, bracing his hand on the tabletop to keep weight off his left foot. The pain is constant, but putting pressure on the toes spikes it.

"You arranged a press conference?" Monuglu asks.

"No. Not exactly."

"Yes," Monuglu says. "Exactly. The reporters are waiting outside." He pats his pocket but doesn't take out his cigarette case.

Travers doesn't smile, aware that he has put Monuglu in an untenable position. The Turk can keep him, uncharged with any crime, locked in the station while the reporters become increasingly impatient; he can escort him forcibly away, hobbling like some wounded prisoner of war through a picket line of video cameras; or he can let him speak to the world. None of the options will enhance tourism or foreign relations or Turkey's standing with the European Union, but letting him talk is the least damaging.

"I will say nothing negative about Turkey, the government, or you personally," Travers says. "After all, you are my best friend here in Göreme."

Monuglu glares, seemingly wary, but unable to find any irony in Travers' voice. "Do not…" he begins, but then stops. "I will be at your side at all times. Remember that."

⳨ 54

Travers squints in the sunlight. It's even more of an event than he imagined. A dozen reporters and their camera crews stand before him in the parking lot. Behind them, a crowd stretches across the lot in a semicircle. There are old men with white beards and children with bright clothing, veiled women and sunburnt backpackers. Leopold Kirchburg is easy to pick out because he's taller than most of the others. His head is tilted to the right, his face pale above his beard. To his left in the same patch of shade under a tree, Charles Lee stands, hands clasped behind his back, slowly rolling his neck. Both men are frowning.

Travers scans the reporters, finds the woman with the BBC microphone, and nods. Her blonde hair falls to her square shoulders. Her face is round and pink; her wide blue eyes are focused on him and Nihat Monuglu, who stands so close to him that his right elbow touches Travers' left arm.

"First let me say…" Travers begins, speaking loudly so that his voice will carry to the crowd as well as the reporters, "that I will provide you with information about the contents of the ossuary discovered recently at the site of Saint John's Cathedral in Selçuk, Turkey." He looks directly at Kirchburg and Lee. "But let me point out at the start that I am speaking to you as a private citizen, not as a representative of the Glavine Foundation, which funds the Saint John's site."

Travers shifts his weight so that the electric eel slithering up his left leg won't seize his breath. "The ossuary," he says, "contained human remains and two documents. All were taken from the archeological site, but Doctor Sophia Altay, the director of the Saint John's site, has recovered the documents. As you know…" he glances again at Kirchburg, "…Kenan Sirhan, an Aegean Association employee, was killed at Saint John's, and Günter Schmidt, also employed a year earlier by Doktor Leopold Kirchburg, was murdered outside of Göreme the night before last. Because of these two deaths, Doctor Altay does not feel it is safe at this point to come forward with the documents. I was beaten and knifed in Selçuk when I was serving as a representative of the Glavine Foundation, so I believe her fears are justified."

Monuglu's elbow presses into his arm. Sweat serpentines down to the small of his back.

"I have, therefore," Travers continues, "agreed to serve as her intermediary in this matter. I have read the English translations of the documents. The first was apparently dictated by Jesus of Nazareth shortly before he died."

Murmuring flows through the crowd, and three of the reporters are already waving their hands.

"The second document, a letter written by Saint John the Apostle in Ephesus, dates from decades later. I believe that people…" he pauses, gazing over the reporters at the crowd, "…around the world and of all faiths will find the documents meaningful."

He wipes the sweat beading along his hairline. "Doctor Altay will release the documents online at three o'clock—I'm sorry—at fifteen-hundred. I will provide printed copies in Turkish, English, French, and Spanish at the Sarihan Hotel at four…sixteen-hundred. I will at that time discuss the contents of the documents, but only after you have had a chance to read them. I will try to answer any other questions you have now."

The CNN correspondent, a tan, square-jawed man wearing a floppy military hat, shouts, "What proof do you have that these letters are authentic, that this is not some hoax?"

Travers repeats the question in case someone didn't hear it. Then, smiling at the man, he says, "None."

"The bones?" a black-haired woman in a white blouse asks. "Are you telling us they're Christ's?"

Travers wipes his mouth. "I'm not suggesting anything about the remains," he says. "I have not seen them, and neither has Doctor Altay."

"Where are they?" the woman asks. "Who has them?"

"I don't know." Travers looks over at Kirchburg and Lee. The American has his arms folded across his chest, and the Austrian is leaning toward him lecturing heatedly. "If I find out anything more about the remains, I'll tell you this afternoon."

There's silence for only a moment before another reporter asks, "Have you personally seen the documents?"

"No," he answers, "I've only seen the transcripts, the English translations. But given what has happened since the ossuary's discovery, I don't doubt their authenticity. And, I trust that Doctor Altay has them in a safe place."

"Who stole the artifacts from the site?" a reporter with a salt-and-pepper beard asks.

"I did not say that the artifacts were stolen," Travers answers. "I said that they were *taken.*" He scratches his nose. "I honestly don't know exactly what happened. But Kenan Sirhan and another man found the ossuary while Doctor Altay was in Istanbul. It's likely that one or both of the men took the artifacts in an attempt to protect them."

"Who is the other man?"

The question comes at Travers so quickly that he's not sure who asked it. He doesn't want to lie or to reveal the truth. "He's called Abrahim," he says, "but I don't know if that's his legal name. I didn't meet him at the site, and I don't know where he is currently." He notices a green and gold hot air balloon rising in the distance. Though he's physically a wreck, he still suddenly needs to walk, to get out into the hills and canyons.

The reporters begin to fire questions.

"Where are the bones from the box?"

"I think I've already answered that. I don't know."

"Where is Doctor Altay?"

"I don't know."

"But you met with her?" This is from the CNN correspondent who has turned up the front of his floppy hat.

Travers feels the reporters and crowd closing in. "Yes."

"When?"

"Last night."

"Where?"

Monuglu's elbow digs into Travers' arm. "She came to my hotel."

"So she's in the area?"

"She was yesterday. But I don't know where she is now." Glancing over, he sees that though Kirchburg is still under the tree, Lee has gone.

"You mentioned that you were beaten and knifed." Allison Wade is giving him the opening he needs. Though her expression is serious, her eyes are twinkling as if she wants him to withhold any additional information about Altay until her exclusive interview. "Is it true that Günter Schmidt was involved in that incident?"

"Schmidt was not the man who cut me, but, yes, he was one of the men who attacked me." As other reporters shout follow-up questions, Travers nods to her and clears his throat. "I look forward to discussing the translations of the letters. Remember, four this afternoon—sixteen-hundred —at the Sarihan Hotel." He takes a quick awkward step to his right. "Any further questions about Kenan Sirhan or Günter Schmidt and the ongoing investigation would best be answered by Turkish officials." He turns, gesturing to his left. "This is Mister Nihat Monuglu, who, I am sure, can answer your questions far better than I can."

Monuglu's scowl suggests that he's really going to hurt Travers the next time they're alone.

⟊ 55

While Nihat Monuglu is fielding questions, Travers meets Allison Wade in the shade of a tree near the police station's side entrance. Ravi is still shooting Monuglu so they have a moment alone. Almost as tall as Travers is, she carries herself erect, with her shoulders held back. She is in her late thirties, but her unblemished skin makes her look younger. Her smile is skewed to the left.

"It's good to meet you, Ms. Wade," Travers says, shaking her hand.

"Call me *Al,*" she answers. Her tone is amicable, but there's fire in her eyes.

"Sure, Al," he says, balancing on his right foot. "I take it you want an interview?"

"Righto, Joe. Absolutely."

Leopold Kirchburg strides around the corner of the building but stops when he sees the reporter with Travers. He jams his right hand into the pocket of his light linen pants and glares in their direction.

"I'd like you to cover me retrieving computer flash drives along the road into Ürgüp," Travers says. "In half an hour. I'll also provide you…the BBC…with one of the drives." He pauses. "I can give you exclusive access to other stuff, too."

"Sophia Altay?"

"That, I can't promise." He smiles. "At least, not yet."

"Well…" She cocks her head, looking askance at him for a moment. Then she nods. "Righto. Yes. I'll get my crew on it." Glancing at Kirchburg, who's stalking in tight circles shouting curt German into his cell phone, she adds, "What about him?"

"You should definitely interview him, too."

Her laugh is clipped. "You know I didn't mean that. You're the one he wants to…"

"Rip a new orifice for?" he says. "Yeah. And I do need to talk with him for a few minutes."

As Wade pulls a small digital recorder from her black leather shoulder bag, she says, "It's a long way from Chicago to Cappadocia."

"Yes and no." He nods. "It must look like a winding trail."

"Why are you doing this?" she asks as she turns on the recorder.

"People need to know what the letters say. I've come to understand that." He takes a quick step and rebalances on his right foot. "Both of them. John the Apostle's as well as Jesus Christ's."

"Of course," she says. "But, given the risks—two men already dead—you must have other motives, other reasons."

He shakes his head. "The letters really are that important." He sounds to himself like Altay.

"And?" The intensity in Wade's eyes deepens, and lines form at the corners of her mouth as she tightens her lips.

"And…" He takes a breath. "And, we can't change what's already occurred, but maybe we can have some effect on what will happen."

"Do you mean, *politically?*"

"Yeah, I guess." He shakes his head slowly. "No. There's more to it than that."

She looks into his eyes as she asks, "Are you referring to Sophia Altay?"

He smiles again. "Not really," he repeats. "She may be part of it, but there's a lot more."

"But I didn't get any sense back there that you're looking for that infamous American fifteen minutes of fame."

"No, that's not it at all." He watches Kirchburg stuff his phone back into his pocket and strut toward them. "I'll explain…" But he knows he's not going to at this point. He's not even sure he could, and so he adds, "Here's your shot at Herr Doktor Kirchburg."

"Herr Travers," Kirchburg says as he approaches them, "I need to speak to you…" He glances at Wade. "…privately."

Travers gestures toward the reporter. "This is Allison Wade, from the BBC."

"Guten Tag." Kirchburg nods to her and turns on Travers. "*Now,* Herr Travers."

"Yeah, okay," Travers says. "I need to talk to you, too. But somewhere outside."

"Nein, we will speak…"

"Allison," Travers interrupts, "wants to interview you."

"Nicht jetzt," Kirchburg says. Red marks rise on his cheeks.

When Wade shuts off her recorder, Travers turns to her. "Give me half an hour," he says. "We'll continue our business. On the road."

"What business?" Kirchburg asks.

"Yes, Joe," Wade says. "Righto." She then turns to Kirchburg and holds out her hand. "We should set a time to talk, Herr Doktor."

"Ja," Kirchburg says. He seems to really notice her for the first time—the blonde hair and blue eyes and clear skin. He takes her hand but doesn't shake it. "Fräulein…"

"Ms. Wade," she says, her smile fixed. "This evening. Somewhere mutually convenient." She lets go of his hand. "I'll have my producer arrange it with you." She turns quickly from the two men. Her gait as she walks away is strong and purposeful, with no hint she's aware that Kirchburg is watching her.

⚷ 56

Travers begins to limp across the police station's parking lot in the direction of the Sarihan Hotel. The morning is clear and bright with little wind. Heat is starting to rise from the pavement. Travers' mouth is dry, and each step sends currents of pain across his left foot and up his calf.

"Herr Travers," Kirchburg calls after him.

Travers can't outpace Kirchburg so he stops. When Kirchburg reaches him, he hobbles ahead without saying anything. John the Apostle's words run through his head. *I have come to love my neighbor and my enemy,* he said, but he also admitted that it was diffficult.

"Your comments," Kirchburg shouts after him, "were ill-advised, inappropriate, and counterproductive."

Travers turns the corner, and, in order to avoid the town center and bus terminal, heads along a side street on which there are fewer people. Jesus of Nazareth's words vie with those of John the Apostle: *If you do not have a sword, sell your cloak and buy one.*

Kirchburg catches up with him again, grabbing his elbow. "Herr Travers!" he says sternly.

Christ's words still echoing in his mind, Travers says, "Get your hand off me."

Kirchburg loosens his grip.

Travers stares into Kirchburg's eyes and pulls himself free. "Inappropriate? Counterproductive? You had me beaten and stabbed."

"I did nothing of the kind." Kirchburg's tone is spiteful. "You took from an archeological site something belonging to the Aegean Association. When... I would *never* order that."

Travers shakes his head. He hasn't eaten anything so he steps over and buys a loaf of flatbread and a half-liter bottle of water from a street vendor. Staring again into Kirchburg's eyes, he asks, "Where's Charles Lee?"

Kirchburg's eyes shine with anger. "Your comments were not appreciated."

"Not appreciated?" Travers opens the bottle, takes a long pull, and feels the water cool in his throat. Inhaling the bread's aroma, he tucks the bottle of water under his arm, breaks off a piece of bread, and offers it to Kirchburg. "Where's Charles?"

Glaring at the bread, Kirchburg says, "Herr Lee needed to contact his superiors in the States. Despite your performance, he still does not believe that the documents are authentic."

Travers starts walking again, and Kirchburg follows. They pass an open two-story carpet store. The largest rug hanging on display would cover the floor of Altay's cave church. "But you've read the letters, and you know they're real," Travers says. He takes a bite of the bread, which is still warm.

"I have not. I have never seen the documents." Kirchburg rubs the tips of his fingers against the palms of his hands as he walks. Clearing his throat, he says, "I...The Aegean Association has made an invaluable discovery. The contents, the documents and the remains, must be returned to me. Those bones may be the Christ's. Do you have any idea what that means for the field of archeology?"

Or the world! Travers thinks as he chews the flatbread.

"All of the relics must be turned over to me." A thin sheen of sweat lines his mustache just below his nostrils. "Immediately!"

"That's not going to happen." As the two men turn onto the narrow cobblestone lane that leads up to the Sarihan Hotel, Travers takes another deep drink of water, finishing the bottle. The incline causes pain to fire in his leg.

"What is your business with the Englishwoman?" Kirchburg asks.

"Allison Wade is going to tape me."

"You are taking the Englishwoman to Sophia?"

"No," Travers says, though it's not a bad idea. Cameras running when Altay comes out of seclusion would enhance, if not ensure, her safety.

"You know where Sophia is. Take me to her. I must…"

Travers shakes his head. "I'm not going to do that."

They climb past a rough stone building with a thatched bramble roof. Telephone wires pass above it, and twenty yards beyond it solar panels line the roof of another building. Kirchburg's leather slip-ons slide with each step on the cobblestones.

"Where is she?" Kirchburg demands. "I must speak to her about her responsibilities to…the Aegean Association."

His tone is disdainful, but Travers thinks he hears another note as well. The ground beneath the Austrian is apparently shifting; tremors are rippling around him.

Breaking off another piece of bread, Travers says, "I really don't know where she is. That's the truth."

Ahead of them, red roses bloom in the Sarihan's courtyard. Light shimmers on the rock formation above the hotel.

⚑ 57

Abrahim crouches next to one of the rough wooden stakes driven into the ground. His water long gone, he has crept down from the cave and skirted the valley until he found this grape arbor. His lips are cracked, and his tongue is bloated. The welt on his back stings like a cut from a lash. Grit covers his pants and shirt. The scabious cuts on his bare feet have torn open, but he bleeds little. He's too dry, too parched, to bleed out.

The beauty of the day stuns him but does not, as he feared, break his heart. The sky is clear, the breeze soft, the tangled vines a sea of light and color—green here, russet there, rose, silver, even gold flowing like fire on water.

Although he is incorrigibly evil, he is somehow not damned. He remains very much alive in this world that is for him, as for everyone, not hell but purgatory. Though he has not yet punished himself enough, he can not resist life. He scuttles sideways, tears off a bunch of grapes, and huddles in the dappled shade of the vines. Each grape blushes, a delicate glistening beyond beauty. He pulls a single grape free, holds it up before him, and prays. His prayer is, as always, one of remorse and sorrow, but also, for once, thanksgiving as well. Gratitude for all he has been through. Everything.

When he bites the grape, the juice bursts in his mouth. It is both sweet and tart, cool and warm, a taste that's life itself. Light shimmers in the sweet air. The juice of the second grape pricks his lips, but that of the third washes his tongue. And then he is stuffing the grapes into his mouth, juice drizzling down his chin and smearing his hands. He swallows seeds and skin, chokes, and goes on gulping, sinking his face deep into the bunch.

Suddenly, he jerks his head back, his mouth full, swallowing and gagging at the same time. It is all too much like his sin. The depth, the enormity, of his evil strikes him. He flings away the remnants of the bunch, spits gelatinous grapes into the dirt, and stares at his stained, shaking hands. He crawls away, climbs to his knees, and mutters,

"Mea culpa, mea culpa, mea maxima culpa…" His hands, red from the dirt, continue to tremble.

The air goes rank. The tufa spires jutting above him become phallic monstrosities. The fairy chimneys are priapisms! He must suffer more for his sins. Far more. But, unable to stop himself, he rips off his shirt. Hyperventilating, he grabs three more bunches and rolls the grapes into his shirt. He looks up into the wide, blank sky and begs forgiveness.

⚜ 58

As soon as the black Mercedes stops on the side of the road thirty yards from the crumbling stone wall, Joseph Travers pushes open the door to escape the cigarette smoke. When he steps out of the car, the air is still, the sky clear, the sun at its apex. The dirt and stubble and stone look bleached, the day itself high noon in the Arizona desert. He and Nihat Monuglu did not speak on the way out of Göreme. When Travers circled back to the police station parking lot to tell Monuglu that because he could not walk, they needed to go for a ride, the TV crews had already packed up.

As Travers limps around the front of the Mercedes, he can see Hulk Major and Hulk Minor staring fixedly through the windshield, but a blue fog of smoke obscures Monuglu. Travers is supposed to be providing theater, a sideshow for everyone, those in Göreme and those around the world, but the fierce tension in the Mercedes on the way here was all too real. Sweat is already rolling down his back again. He drank another half-liter bottle of water at the Sarihan Hotel, but it wasn't really enough. He taps on the tinted backseat window. As the window lowers, cigarette smoke curls out. Monuglu scowls through the smoke.

"Nihat," Travers says, "we need to talk."

Monuglu flicks the Yenidje's lit butt past Travers. "Making me speak to those foreign reporters," he says, "was not a good idea."

"You handled it well."

"What," Monuglu asks, "are we doing on this trip into the Cappadocian countryside?"

Travers touches the window's well but then jerks his hand from the hot metal. "Retrieving the flash drives that I received from Doctor Altay."

"A better idea," Monuglu says. His smile is yellow with nicotine.

"She made a copy for the Turkish government," Travers says. "She wanted to ensure that it got into the right hands." This part is his idea, of course. Altay cares only about the preservation of the original letters. But he's certain that Monuglu will seize all three flash drives if he doesn't offer him one. He glances up the road to make sure his timing is right.

"I see," Monuglu says, taking a Yenidje from his case. "And you will retain a flash drive for yourself?" Hulks Major and Minor continue to stare straight ahead.

Travers nods. "There are three, one for you, one for me, and one to share with the BBC and other interested media. You could take that copy, too, but…" Stirring dust, the BBC van pulls off the road in front of the Mercedes. "…In a minute, the uplink will be hot, and Ms. Wade will be broadcasting everything live."

Monuglu taps the cigarette fast and hard against the case. "These games you…," he says, glaring past Travers at Allison Wade stepping out of the van holding her phone to her ear.

"This is no game," Travers says. "Not at all. I'm trying to…"

Monuglu shoves the door open. As Travers stumbles back, Monuglu leaps from the Mercedes. Cat quick, he's on Travers, yanking his collar tight around his neck, before Travers can get his balance.

"You son of a Greek," Monuglu shouts in Travers' face. Spit hits Travers' nose and cheeks. "That ossuary… Those documents…" He twists the collar, cutting Travers' breath. "Those bones… Everything belongs to the Turkish peoples." He clamps Travers' neck more tightly, an electric charge seeming to flow through his fingers.

"Hey!" Travers hears Wade's voice. "What the hell...?"

As Travers turns his head away, his vision blurs at the edges.

"Look at me!" Monuglu growls.

His legs wobbling, Travers turns.

Monuglu's glare is maniacal as he tightens his grip. "This is no game either. No threat. Your life is..." He presses his thumb against Travers' carotid artery. "Understand me..."

Color drains from the world around Travers. His footing is unsure, his breath choked. He has no idea whether Monuglu's last statement is a question or a command—and he couldn't speak even if he had an answer.

⚵ 59

"**M**erde...merde," Sophia Altay murmurs. "Merde!" She is seated at the computer farthest from the door in this narrow, dimly lit internet café on a side street in Ürgüp. She wears a long beige skirt and a bulky white blouse. Her scarf, a muted yellow and brown, covers her head. Though she remains still, her skin prickles as though she has been stung a thousand times. Her breath is stuck in her throat. All hell is breaking loose *before* she has had a chance to release her translations of Jesus of Nazareth's testament and John the Apostle's letter.

Despite her meticulous planning, the internet chaos she feared is already thundering about her at 14:46. She made the list of thirty-five global media outlets yesterday—everyone from Al Jazeera to Fox News. Her cover note is clear and concise, her translations from the original Aramaic exact. She scouted this café where she could—or should have been able to—blast the net and vanish into Ürgüp in less than five minutes. She has devised alternative escape routes. The man sitting by the door—dour, aging, paunchy, asthmatic—is far more interested in the football game on his monitor than in her. The only other customers, two German girls with flaxen hair and tight black T-shirts, provide a perfect diversion.

Altay assumed that turmoil would ensue *after* her release of the documents. But not now. Not this heinous attempt to poison the well. Not eight or more ersatz transcriptions flooding the web in the last few minutes. Two versions using her address! And six others differing from hers in a single character: sophia.altay@sfj.org or sophea.altay@stj.org, or sophia-altay@stj.org, and so on. Each with variant translations of the documents. Each version proclaiming that any other version is a fabrication. Each asserting that all others are anathema. Each diverging from the truth. Each fomenting and escalating the confusion online. Each already causing controversy. Consternation. Division. Derision.

A couple of the fraudulent versions are subtle, making only minor alterations like changing each use of the word *Man* to *God* in the phrase *Son of Man*. But others are heavy-handed and overtly apocryphal. One turns Jesus into a megalomaniac: *Worship the Lord your God and serve me only* and *Serve no earthly master but me*. Another calls for the equivalent of jihad—*The one who kills in my name will be saved* and *The Son of God is coming on the clouds of heaven, with power and great glory, to cast my enemies into a lake of eternal fire*. The versions of Saint John's letters are, in some ways, even worse. One gloats about the murder of the High Priest, Jonathan, and another completely replaces the text with rantings from *The Book of the Apocalypse*. Yet another denounces both Hebrews and gentiles. And still another states, *Jesus came to love me and lie with me*. It's absurd, but people are all too willing to believe what they want to believe—and whatever serves their purposes.

Altay's eyes fill with frustration and anger. The German girls are giggling and jiggling. Lighting one cigarette from another, the callous man is glancing salaciously at them. She cannot stand and scream; she cannot shake her hair and snarl. She rips off the tip of her left forefinger's nail, slips it into her mouth, and bites down hard. She slows and deepens her breath, pulling her belly in with each exhale. Slowly, slowly she lengthens each breath.

Joseph Travers' news conference will be a disaster; the media hyenas will tear him apart. He had a sound idea but no specific plan—and certainly no sense that his diversion would become catastrophic. They agreed that neither would attempt to contact the other until 19:00. Her phone, one of three inexpensive burners she purchased with cash on the street in İzmir as she was fleeing to Cappadocia, is stowed, and she has no way to warn him except through email, which he won't check in the next hour. He has, she believes, the wherewithal to survive, but not unscathed.

And Abrahim? Poor, sweet Abrahim. She has lost contact completely. She cannot believe that he killed Leopold's henchman, but he was perturbed beyond anything she had seen in him before. And whatever happened, he is certainly castigating himself, if not actually self-flagellating or indulging in some other form of Christian self-mortification. She has learned that his belongings, including his shoes, remain at the hostel, but he has not, apparently, been seen since she left him disconsolate along the road three kilometers outside of Göreme.

She must finish here in the café and get out fast. Anyone able to wreak this internet havoc will also be able to track her through the web. She taps *Send,* and, watching the *Outgoing Mail* icon turn blue, adds her translations, the only authentic documents, to the swell of misinformation stirring controversy on the internet. She hears the computer's swish of finality as her message takes flight. She grinds her fingernail with her molars. Leopold, that egomaniacal, confrontational Pharisee, has mounted this massive attack on her.... He is so pompous and so obsessed with her that...

Her fingers freezing above the keyboard, she flinches as though she has been slapped. Leopold's need for self-aggrandizement is total, but if he desires credit for the discovery of the ossuary, why discredit the letters? Unless his need to destroy her overleaps his ambition. No, he is far too egotistical to have undermined his own reputation and that of his precious Aegean Association. He has too little technological savvy and too few human resources. He is too aristocratic and autocratic to have sullied himself with this sort of... Joseph Travers and, admittedly, she herself, have drawn erroneous conclusions. "Merde!" she mutters aloud. "Merde!"

⌖ 60

At five minutes to four, Charles Lee accosts Joseph Travers in the Sarihan Hotel's pale stone and wood-paneled lobby. Lee wears a blue tie and a starched button-down white shirt with a gold Jerusalem cross monogrammed on the pocket. His face is red, as though he has just been working out, and his jaw is set. He clasps Travers' arm and says, "Hey, Joe, we need to have a chat."

Yanking himself free, Travers says, "I tried to find you this morning, Charlie. Missed you entirely."

Producers bustle by each other as they cross the lobby between the cave rooms where they're encamped and the garden patio where they expect the action to be.

"We need a Come-to-Jesus meeting," Lee snarls. "Now!"

Travers wishes for a moment that he had a cloak to sell. The internet is, by all accounts, abuzz with controversy over contradictory versions of Jesus of Nazareth's testament and John the Apostle's letter. "I really don't have time right now," he says. A dozen people have asked him for interviews or for more information about the letters, but he has been too busy getting press packets made from the flash drive he now carries in his pants pocket.

Allison Wade and Ravi shot footage of him removing one of the flash drives from the chink in the stone wall and presenting it to Nihat Monuglu, who, though he had almost strangled Travers minutes before, accepted it with stiff formality. *Perhaps,* Travers thought, *like a wrestler receiving a medal after a championship match.* Everything since then has been a blur of activity.

A muscle twitches in Lee's jaw. "Goddamn it, you acorn-cracking dipshit." Lee's voice is vicious. "You're dead on your feet. And y'all already look like the fuckin' village eegit in the media!"

Shaking his head, Travers exhales slowly. "I wonder *who* caused that."

"You've got no evidence that those letters are real," Lee whispers, seemingly aware for the first time that what he's saying isn't stuff for a hotel lobby three minutes before a news conference. "None." His deep blue eyes darken. "They're a fuckin' fraud. Any moron can see that."

Travers takes a press packet from the pile on the table to his right and waves it once in front of Lee. "Oh, the documents are real, Charlie," he says. "If they weren't, we wouldn't be having this conversation."

"You're goin' to get yourself fuckin' pan fried."

Spittle smacks Travers' eyebrow. He wipes it off with his sleeve. "Probably."

"Act like y'all are somebody."

That, Travers thinks, is what he's doing. He told Sophia Altay he would hold the news conference, and he announced it to the world. He's going to carry it through.

His shoulders tensing, Lee glares at him. The muscles in his jaw dance. "If you go out there, you'll betray your country."

"My country?" Travers smiles. "Our country has nothing to do with the documents, and you know it." He's happy to be an American. Proud, even. At least, much of the time. Always has been. But what the documents say goes beyond the borders of any particular nation, especially the United States where freedom of religious belief has historically been protected, even championed.

Lee sets his feet and balls his fists.

Or, Travers thinks, *the letters have everything to do with our country.*

"For God's sake, you fuckin' cracker...," Lee begins.

"God isn't on our side," Travers says. "Or any other side." He taps the packet against Lee's chest.

Lee pushes the packet away.

"Charlie, your *superiors…*" Travers lets the word hang between them for a moment, "…won't like it if you attack me here in front of all these reporters."

Lee's voice becomes a low savage drawl. "When I'm done, y'all are going to wish you were dead."

Travers smiles. "You've got that wrong," he says. "I'd never wish for death."

⚷ 61

The afternoon replicates Prescott, Arizona—clear and bright and hot enough to fry an egg on the pavement. The first question, hurled at Travers by a dark-haired, round-faced reporter with a Texas accent, is an unadulterated accusation. The guy uses the word *fraud* three times before actually asking anything. Travers, who faces the crowd and the hotel and the mini-forest of infrared broadcasting towers, feels lightheaded. He's already sweating, and his balance is off. He figures he should recognize the guy, but he gave up watching network news after the orchestrated recitals of the second Iraq war—*Operation Iraqi Freedom,* the spin doctors dubbed it, and the networks lapped it up. Smiling at the reporter, he holds up the printed packet he picked up in the lobby. "As I mentioned this morning," he says, "I have not seen the original documents. But I have stood on Ayasulak Hill where the letters were discovered and walked in the ruins there. And, I'm telling you that these letters are real. I can't at this point prove to you that they're authentic, but that doesn't make them any less real."

"Mr. Travers," a reporter in the middle of the scrum yells, "visiting an archeological site doesn't make you an expert." His English is perfect, but there's a hint of an accent Travers thinks is Middle Eastern.

Travers expected skepticism from the press, and this hostility likely comes from the spread of the spurious documents on the internet. "I'm not an authority," he says, thinking he has already been clear on that point. The reporters want the story, but it's open season on him. He's fair game. And once he gives them Altay, he'll be roadkill. He's not stuttering, but words aren't forming very well. "I'm only the...messenger."

"Mister Travers..." The CNN guy with the floppy military hat is waving a fax. "...how are we supposed to believe anything you say when you've already been fired by the Glavine Foundation?"

Sweat breaks on Travers' forehead, and his stomach drops. If it's true, he had no idea. He doesn't think Bill Glavine would turn on him so quickly, but he doesn't know what pressures—political, social, or even personal—have come to bear. And, he hasn't spoken to Bill since...he can't remember. He inhales, shakes his head slowly, and says, "I'm trying to speak with you about these documents, not about me..." He looks around but doesn't see Allison Wade anywhere among the reporters. "I'm talking to you as a private citizen on behalf of Doctor Altay, not as the representative of any organization."

"Then when will you provide hard evidence?" a reporter shouts.

"Where is Doctor Altay?"

"Where are the letters?"

"When will we see the originals?"

Travers holds up his hand to stem the flow. "You'll see the letters when it's safe," he says. "As early as tomorrow morning." He surprises even himself with that answer. Nihat Monuglu might or might not be willing to provide security. He might or might not be trusted. But he hasn't reappeared since he got his hands on the flash drive. In any case, Travers doesn't know if he can ever ensure Altay's safety.

"Doctor Altay will come forward then?" a reporter with a thick black mustache asks.

Trying to settle his stomach, Travers takes a deep breath. The heat rolling over him in waves buffets him but also takes him home. His head throbs, and he's tottering behind the microphones, but his mind is starting to clear. "I think so," he says. "I hope so. But that's her decision. I'm only acting as her intermediary." He notices Leopold Kirchburg standing on the hotel's terrace roof near where they ended their meeting in the morning. The small man next to him looks like the cutter from Selçuk's street. Maybe not the same guy, but similar—wiry and sharp-featured.

Travers grabs one of the microphone stands to steady himself. He looks out over the crowd. There are a lot of people—and well more than the hundred press packets he had printed. Perhaps twice that number.

"What about the radical Zionism?" a female reporter shouts. She is dark with bright flashing eyes that show both fervor and scorn.

Travers doesn't answer immediately. As he scrolls mentally through Jesus of Nazareth's testament, murmuring emerges from the crowd packed around the reporters. "I'm not a scholar," he says, "but the intent seems pretty clear. Jesus is speaking out against the hypocrisy of the Pharisees and other authorities." *Jesus was a Jew who adhered to scripture,* he thinks. "And it seems to me that John remembers Jesus as a teacher, a rabbi, not a rabble-rouser."

"If the intent of these unauthenticated documents is so clear to you, Mr. Travers…" It's the Texan again. "…do you admit they're advocating homosexuality?"

The crowd is muttering. The waves of heat are strobing in the light.

"Advocating?" Travers wipes his forehead. He clutches the microphone stand and gulps air.

The Texan is sneering as he raises his press packet. "It says right here, *Jesus came to love me and lie with me.*"

Travers squints hard at the Texan, trying to stop the world's wheeling. He glances down at his packet, turns the page, and finds the line. The sentence reads, *Jesus came to accept and love men and women like me.* It's not just the internet that's been compromised. Even some of the press packets, it seems, have been adulterated. He has been set up perfectly. He's not sure how deeply he's been undercut, but this might be the last moment anybody's ever going to listen to him. "The only thing John the Apostle's letter advocates is love," he says as the

Sarihan's cave entrances unhinge. "Compassion. Caring for others."
He brushes sweat from his face. "Sophia Altay's documents, the real
letters, will speak to you. Some of you must have the authentic copies. You'll recognize them. You'll know them when you read them."

Reporters are shouting at him, a babel of accusations and recrimi-
nations. They're becoming a mob; an incensed multilingual din surg-
es around him. The crowd, the broadcasting equipment, the hotel's
white facade, the tufa spires beyond, the vast sky above—everything
is skewed, the world listing as though it might capsize at any moment.
He takes a breath. His whole body is sweating now, a chilling damp-
ness despite the heat. But he's *not* going to take the fall here in front
of an international television audience. Bile is sour in his throat. He
bites his lower lip. He's not going to sink into darkness.

⚳ 62

 S ophia Altay, standing in the crowd on the cobblestones, takes a single step forward, then stops herself. Joe is clutching a microphone stand, swaying as though he will topple into the
crowd at any moment. Reporters and cameramen are jostling each
other. The crowd is swelling—not stampeding but pressing in on him.
She can't see if the newsmen are still questioning him or trying to
tear pieces out of him, but, stifling her own urge to help, she pulls
her veil more tightly across her nose.

Coming here was rash, wrongheaded, even stupid, but she could
not stay away. She is completely covered except for her eyes, but she is
still concerned that she will be recognized. Her eyes have always been
her best asset, and now they are her greatest liability. She can blend
in a little—a veiled woman is not meant to be noticed—but the other women are young and European, Westernized right down to their

hiking boots, or Turkish and older, squat and gathered in gaggles. Even nondescript, she may well be conspicuous.

The afternoon is hot and still, more torrid than any she remembers from her student days exploring the cave churches. The crowd is close, and among the Turks and Europeans are Americans with crew cuts and Arabs with straggly beards. A couple of dark well-built men may be Israeli. Many of the people hold printed copies of the Turkish, English, French, and Spanish translations of the documents. Joe said he was going to get one hundred copies made, but there are far more than that number circulating among the crowd.

The BBC van and seven others including Al Jazeera have their infrared towers raised like royal palms, their dark cables winding down their trunks like snakes. More than a score of media reps encircle the patio where Joe totters, and people press around the reporters. A squad of machine-gun toting Turkish military police rings the throng, eyeing those still coming up the narrow lane. Travers' ploy has worked—too well. Conversations, discussions, even arguments are already occurring. Her epochal discovery is *already* being misused to further rend a world torn by animosity. She would like to weep, to melt into the stone—but she will not let herself.

In the glimpse she caught of Joe when she first arrived, he looked beleaguered—haggard and beat-up. He suffers from that American tendency to wing it rather than consider secondary or tertiary causes and consequences, and he really seems to have no clear concept of what he's going to do next. She also saw Leopold on the Sarihan's terrace, a story above the crowd but not quite at the height of the infrared dishes. He was with a short, pale, ferret-faced man she didn't recognize. Leopold wiped his forehead with a handkerchief, which he then folded fastidiously.

The little man pulled out a pack of cigarettes and offered one to Leopold, who nodded and took it in his spindly fingers. If she hadn't known Leopold better, she would have thought the pair comic. As Leopold waited for the man to light the cigarette, he snapped the head off one of the gardenias in the flower box next to him and began to scan the crowd below him. Her heart raced for a moment even though she knew that Leopold couldn't see her, much less identify her. Angry with herself for still reacting to the arrogant Pharisee that way, she counted to ten before again looking up. The little man was lowering his lighter from Leopold's cigarette to his own. Leopold took a deep first drag and tilted back his head. As he exhaled, Leopold said something, dropped the gardenia's crushed petals into the box, and smiled dourly.

Now, a swarthy man brushes against her shoulder, trying to get a better look at the chaos around the podium. Jostled by the crowd, she needs to get away from the Sarihan immediately. She glances up at the rooftop terrace, but there's no tall Austrian there. Leopold is coming down from the roof, will be somewhere about, probably heading her way. Joe, the poor bastard, continues to run amuck. Though she has not seen either Charles Lee or Nihat Monuglu since she arrived, they must be around. Any number of reporters might recognize her.

She tightens her veil, turns, and, pushes against the flow of the crowd. By the time she reaches the periphery, she has regained some control. Fifteen meters from the military police cordon, she notices Leopold's little ferret-faced friend working this side of the crowd. He slouches along, hands in pants pockets, glancing at each individual. He's sauntering, a gait too nonchalant for the circumstances, his gaze covertly scrutinizing each person.

When the ferret's focus falls on her, she veers toward an MP with his gun at cross-arms. He is young and broad-shouldered, with a stoic visage and pockmarks on his cheeks. He was supposed to staunch the overflow coming up the lane, but the real action is the people mulling and muttering within the cordon. He, like the other MPs, faces the lane but repeatedly glances over his shoulder toward the Sarihan Hotel.

The ferret follows her. She glances back only once, but it is enough to see that his narrow eyes have locked on her. He can't know who she is, but he has apparently caught her scent—a woman alone who must be his prey. She quickens her pace, the MP now turning to look toward her hurrying in his direction. She keeps her eyes lowered but steps directly up to him. "The infidel following me," she says, "attempted to molest me in the crowd." She gazes up, seeing the MP's face darken, the pockmarks turning scarlet. She lets him look into her eyes, bows her head, and bustles by him down the narrow, crowded lane.

"Dur!" she hears, but she doesn't look back. Over the rustle of the crowd, there's a thud—a rifle's stock striking someone hard.

⯰ 63

Glinting polyglot babble showers Joseph Travers. The air is stifling as the crowd goads him. One swarthy guy is waving a white flag...no, sheets of paper, the press packet. A fat man grabs at him with fingers that look like sausages. Travers has to get away from the crowd, needs to find out how much damage has been done. And he's got to get in touch with Sophia Altay—though if she knows what happened here, she may not contact him at all. Fending off people with both arms, he quickens his pace up toward the Sarihan Hotel's main entrance.

Her shoulders thrown back, Allison Wade steps in front of him. Though her wide blue eyes are fervid, he doesn't look away. Ravi stands behind her with his camera on his shoulder, but its lens is pointed down toward her heels. "You bloody bastard!" she snaps.

Travers doesn't say hello, but he doesn't push past her either.

"That flash drive...," she says. "Eight different versions of the documents were emailed to the BBC."

"The one I gave you is real," he answers. The throng stops pressing, apparently waiting for the next skirmish involving this American idiot. Three cameras are trained on Wade and him, but none of them is Ravi's. She is now *in* it with him.

"You conned me!" Wade is standing straighter so that they are eye to eye.

He looks into her eyes. Her gaze is strong, but without, he thinks, a lot of depth.

"No!" he says. "It's real." He reaches into his pocket and pulls out the flash drive. *"This…"* He shakes his head. "The others are fake!"

"You've already been completely discredited in the American media," she snarls.

They're shooting the messenger! he thinks.

"An out-of-work technocrat!" She's breathing hard, and her pink skin is going red. "Exploiting the situation!"

Still holding up the flash drive, he shakes his head again. Her eyes may be pretty, the blue specked with green, but he sees ambition with only a modicum of concern. John the Apostle's letter doesn't speak to her as it does to him. The documents are newsworthy. They'll alter careers, influence governments, and affect the geopolitical landscape—but they will not touch her to her core. The fact of the letters' existence and the news they stir are more important than what they actually say.

"This circus," she sneers, "you set everybody…"

"No!" he interrupts her, waving the flash drive. He's angry, but as much at himself as at whoever doctored the documents. "Sophia Altay was set up. I was set up! There are multiple versions of the *printed* copies, too." He turns the flash drive over and stuffs it back in his pocket. The air is suffocating; his whole body is sweating. The crowd around him is oscillating, the light at the edge of his vision strobing. "You yourself said there were *eight* electronic versions!" All of his remaining energy is in his voice. "That news conference wasn't *news!*" He pauses, trying to catch his breath. People around him are talking, but he barely hears them. "We were all duped. Everybody. Everything's tainted!"

Ravi raises his camera so that he can shoot over her shoulder.

Wade pulls her phone from her pocket. "Righto, Joe," she says, her voice irate. She raises the phone. "But if you're going to stop the proliferation of the *tainted*"—she spits the word—"versions, contact Altay! Right now!"

"No," he says, "it doesn't work that way."

"Here's my mobile." She hands it to him.

He takes the phone, glances at its screen, and looks again into Wade's eyes. There's no way he's going to contact Altay with Wade and this crowd hovering around him—even if he could.

Wade curls her upper lip. "If you want her version to have any bloody credibility, you've got to provide the originals. You've got to get Altay to come forward with them."

Still gazing into her eyes, he hands back the phone. "You'll get your story, Al. An exclusive. And it'll be real news. I promise. But Sophia isn't going to answer her phone now."

"Then voice mail her," she says. "Or text her. Or email her. But do something." She shakes the phone in front of his face. "Every second you waste makes her original letters look more bloody dubious."

⚰ 64

The moment Travers hobbles away from Wade, the crowd descends on him again. He's only forty feet from the Sarihan Cave Hotel's main entrance when he trips over one of the black television cables and goes down hard, scraping his elbow and forehead. People press in on him, blocking light. There's no air at all. A dead grasshopper lies in the tangle of cables. Everything hurts, the headache and queasiness joining with the older injuries in an excruciating whirl. He places the palm of his right hand on the flagstone, rises to one knee, and looks up. Video cameras aim at him from among the clamoring mob. One man has glistening folds of fat rolling down from his chin. Another has forests in his nostrils.

When Travers stands, he reels with nausea, doubles over, and pukes. As the vomit splatters on the flagstones, the circling crowd shuffles back. He coughs, clears his throat, and coughs again. He drank a lot of water, but he hasn't eaten anything all day except for the flatbread as Leopold Kirchburg badgered him on the way to the Sarihan in the morning.

He spits onto the flagstone and takes two swaying sidesteps. His torn toe throbs, and blood trickles from his elbow. Emphatic Turkish volleys around him, but no one grabs at him. The puke, it seems, has made him untouchable. The flagstones shift and bob when he again staggers toward the Sarihan. The ring of people swirls as he wends through the crowd.

Nihat Monuglu stands by the rosebushes to the right of the hotel's arched stone entrance. "Joseph," he says, "I will help you." His face is flushed, and sweat is beading on his forehead and neck.

Travers takes a stutter step and stops. His saliva is gummy, the taste sour.

"Hayır!" Monuglu shouts at the people following Travers. "Dur!"

Those closest to Travers stop jabbering.

Travers finds his balance, plants his feet, and beats back the pounding in his head. "I've had enough of your help," he says. Blood trickles from his elbow.

Monuglu takes a long drag from his Yenidje. As he and Travers stare at each other, he exhales smoke through his nose. "You must come with me," he says, his voice low.

The video cameras form a semicircle around the two men.

"Arrest me, if you want," Travers says.

"We..." Monuglu glowers at Travers and reaches for his arm but stops before he touches him. "I will take you to your hotel. You need to..."

Travers swallows bile. "If you're going to arrest me, do it."

Monuglu's scowl erodes. "Come with me," he says.

Travers wipes his mouth with his sleeve. His chest is tight, and his stomach churns. His sweat goes cold again. "It was you," he says to Monuglu, loud enough for the reporters to hear. He pulls the flash drive from his pocket and holds it up to the light. "You had the documents. You tampered with those translations."

"No. You are wrong." Monuglu's face is impassive, but his eyes burn. "You do not know what you are saying."

Travers raises the shining flash drive. "You…," he says. "You…."

Monuglu clenches his fist. "You are making a mistake," he says. His voice, though firm, sounds sad.

The world goes on wavering as Travers slowly turns. The pink and red roses ripple. Above the crowd, the trees' white blossoms bow. The dwellings carved into the tufa spires shift and surge. Half a dozen polychromatic hot air balloons drift across the sky. It's all very bright, very colorful, but it's not making any sense at all.

⊬⚲⊦ 65

Abrahim slips through the cleft into the box canyon, but his passage, he is sure, has not gone unnoticed. The sun is still strong, and the tourists along the road he crossed pointed at him. One old crone ululated. And he must have presented a savage, even diabolic, sight. The scabs on his bare feet have cracked open, his black pants are filthy with grit, and his shirt is sullied with sand and stained with grape juice. His sunburnt and grimy face must look feral; his hair is matted and caked with red dirt. He can see with his swollen eye, but it still feels the size of a pomegranate.

Panting, he looks toward the boulder, but she is not there. She is not foolish enough to venture here in daylight as he did. It is not merely that he is stupid, though trekking from the cave and threading his way through the tourists was idiocy. No, it goes deeper. He *needed* to move among people. His depravity drives him from humans, but his humanity inevitably pulls him back. And, he could no longer stand the isolation of the cave. He could not remain apart, much less go on seeking death. He needs her touch, or any touch, even a brutal one.

And so he has returned here, where she has been, where they last met. He crosses to the boulder and brushes his trembling fingers along its surface. His hands are sticky with grape juice, and the black flies are already sizzling around his hair and shirt. They haven't yet swarmed as they did in the mouth of the cave, but they will soon. He turns, leans against the boulder, and buries his face in his hands. He is beyond despair in some dark terrain so arid that each breath he takes cuts his throat.

The flies whir about his head and hands and shoulders, scribing arcs in the air. The cacophony rises as he falls into the depth of his seclusion. The flies sing a nefarious song, their chorus a litany of his iniquities. And above them, a deeper voice chants, *Kill yourself. Do it. Do it. Do it!* But a faint voice beneath the chorus and soloist whispers Saint John's words: *Love has made me whole again.* The buzzing, though, becomes remorseless, and he claps his hands over his ears. *Do it!* the voice hisses. And the faint murmuring continues, too: *In the end, there is no other way. I have come to love....*

Unable to stop the polemic, he stands, yanks his bespattered shirt over his head, and tosses it across the boulder. The flies follow it but return to him a moment later. His back bubbles with pain. His wrists that he scraped with sharp stones sting, as does the side of his chest. The light smearing the walls doesn't fall on him, but the heat distends heavily from the rock wall, pressing him to his knees. His bones feel as though they are ossifying. Millennia crumble into seconds. His bones become those desiccated bones he has hidden. He can't live with the knowledge that he alone is responsible for those fractured femurs, that ancient sternum and clavicle and skull. He must stay alive until he understands—or she tells him—what to do with those holy and unnerving relics. The baked air burns his lungs. When he closes his eyes, the flies' black voices take up the soloist's chant—*Do it! Do it! Do it!* The flies do not bite but their dirge chafes him until he swats at his ears and eyes and temples.

Water. If he cleanses himself, the refrain may cease and his bones regenerate. The diatribe may drown. He careens to the rivulet trickling from the crack in the rock. Like that small voice repeating Saint John's words, the water merely whispers. But it is cool as it runs over his palms. He cups his hands, hurls water at his face. The sharp wet slap stops the dark canticle for a second. Then he is scooping and splashing, scraping wetness across his cheeks, wringing it through his hair, flinging it against his bare chest. He pants, his nipples hard. Blood courses. Breath catches, then deepens.

The voices still themselves for a moment. But then they return. No, these are different voices. External. Exterior voices. Someone is coming. The hellhounds are coming for him. He rises from his knees and turns, his hands at his sides. Water pulses from his fingertips. He could fight, but it would be futile. He could hide, but there are only boulders and sunflowers. He could be lifted aloft by a host, but miracles are for saints not sinners. The flies swarm him, their drone deafening. And the soloist wails: *You are worthless. Give up. Give up!* Saint John's entreaty fades beneath the cacophony.

⳨ 66

As Charles Lee and Leopold Kirchburg sit at the white corner table on the Sarihan Hotel's rooftop terrace, Lee scrubs his Coca-Cola can's lid. Minute black particles he can't rub off stick to the aluminum. Kirchburg scowls across the table at him, his trademark glare not worth a bucket of spit now. Kirchburg is staying at the more upscale Ottoman House, but Lee, who remembered his chat with Joe Travers at this table, wanted the meeting here so that it's outside and away from the Kraut's turf. This meeting has also gotten the bad taste of that earlier talk with Travers out of Lee's mouth.

The media vermin have slithered away from the Sarihan's grounds, and the acorn cracker's credibility is in the crapper, flushed down and leading the parasites through the Turkish sewers to Altay. The sun has fallen behind the rock the hotel's cut into, and the air has cooled. The patio has, all in all, proved a fine spot in which to hang Herr Kirchburg.

"They wouldn't dare do that!" Kirchburg proclaims. The blotches on his cheeks look like reddish puddles.

Lee wipes the lid once more, drops the napkin on the table, and, remembering that a dollop spilled the last time, carefully opens the Coke. "I think they can and will," he says flatly. "I tried, but it looks like a done deal." It was, in fact, his idea to cut the Kraut's funding, but Kirchburg doesn't need to know that. He's bound to do something rash, and Lee is not about to become his target. "Your second *asset* got his ass arrested," Lee says. "And my superiors don't like it a lick. Y'all are smearing shit on *our* boots."

"Nein. Herr Lang was detained, not arrested. And he was not my *second* anything. I met him *today*…here at this hotel just before Herr Travers… *He* approached *me* with information… His accuser disappeared without filing charges… He… This…"

Kirchburg stops himself, apparently because even he can figure out that nitpicking over these issues now—as though this is some asinine academic debate—is pointless. The little rodent was taken into custody minutes after he was seen with Kirchburg at the Sarihan. In fact, CNN got a shot of the two of them smoking together on this rooftop. The Kraut is up to his withers in dung, and Lee can't help smearing him even more. "I'd wager," he says, "that his accuser was Sophia Altay."

"She… I will have *you* removed from *your* position," Kirchburg sputters.

Lee expected the Kraut to piss his pants like this. "Leopold," he says, "act like y'all are somebody." He picks up the Coke can, inspects it one last time, and takes a sip without quite touching the lid to his lips. "*My* board made the decision to withdraw funding. *Your* board will sure as shit hang you out rather than lose the dollars." Although funding of archeological sites is the Eagle Consortium stated goal, he has to be done away with so that the Consortium's unstated and categorically more urgent goal can be met. It's that simple. In fact, Lee's got to finish off the Kraut and the Coke and get back to his fundamental task.

Twisting his gold university ring, Kirchburg mutters, "Amerikan-isch Arschloch!"

Lee gulps most of the Coke, sits back, and crosses his legs. There it is again—that inbred Teutonic arrogance. Their scorn for Turks is perfectly understandable. And the French. But Kirchburg and all the rest of them have conveniently forgotten the history of the last century. They got an old-fashioned ass-whipping *twice,* and they've been bit players shunted to this godforsaken corner of the world stage ever since. What's this Kraut really after anyway? To be top dog in this dead science out here in the boondocks?

As Lee stares across the table at Kirchburg's florid scowl, he figures, *What the hell, give the rope one last jerk.* Raising the can of Coke, he says, "I understand how hard-got your situation is. You've got to choose between saving the Aegean Association and keeping your directorship." He shakes his head, smiles, and tilts the can in an ironic salute. "You're between a rock and a hard place."

Kirchburg leans forward and clenches his hands, his boney fingers going white with tension. A vein pulses in his right temple. "I am the Aegean Association."

Lee finishes the Coke. The rocks over the Kraut's shoulder are shaped like sharks' teeth but are the color of a wetback's ass. "Not any more."

Kirchburg's fingernails dig into the back of his left hand. "Ich bin…" he begins.

"Leopold…," Lee interrupts. It's time to change the subject. "I have news about your Ms. Altay."

Thin lines of blood appear under the nails of Kirchburg's right index and middle fingers.

"She has," Lee continues, "made contact with Allison Wade. Something is about to happen with the documents. The bones, too." It's all conjecture, but Kirchburg doesn't need to know that.

Kirchburg flattens his palms on the table. The thin cuts where he has just gouged the back of his hand look like runes of an ancient script that, ironically, only he could read. "What? Sophia and that BBC reporter? Where?"

"I'll know in an hour." Lee wonders, not for the first time, at the fact that these high-minded academic eegits are so easy to string up *because* they've got poles up their asses. "I do believe," he adds, "that Ms. Altay giving those computer files to Joe Travers is what's caused all this trouble."

Kirchburg's eyes narrow. His breath wheezes. He still hasn't noticed that he's gouged his own hand.

If that don't beat all, Lee thinks. His work is often hard, but then there are days like this. Despite what Joe Travers said, it helps, of course, to have God on your side.

⚗ 67

The burly guard grabs Abrahim by his arm, yanks him to his feet, and pushes him toward the holding cell's door. Abrahim is both terrified and relieved. The cell reeks of piss and fear. The old man with the wild white beard has been alternating between vociferous prayers praising Allah and scatological diatribes against the human race. Worse, the Kurd with tattoos slithering down his neck and arms has been eyeing Abrahim in a way he knows all too well. When Abrahim was first dumped in the cell, a small man with a bruised forehead and animosity in his eyes stared at him, licking his lips and tapping the top button of his fly. When that man was removed from the cell, he laughed in Abrahim's face and said in truculent German, "Sie warden krieger, mein Lieber."

After Abrahim stumbles through the doorway into the gray hall, the guard's grip becomes a vise on his biceps. Abrahim is wearing the white T-shirt, pants, and socks he was issued when he was processed. The police did not beat him then, but they were irate because a European camera crew caught them jouncing him into the station.

Being released from that cell is a blessing, but he's choked by the sense that he is being led to hell. His chest heaves, and small high-pitched squeaks he cannot stop escape his throat. He tries to pray, but words do not come.

The walls of the yellow-gray room he's shoved into moan of past pain. The guard shuts the door, leaving Abrahim standing in front of a gray steel table. A man with short hair and a scarred face sits on the other side of the table and glares at him. The smoke from the man's cigarette hangs whispering in the air. A brown folder and a black metal ashtray half filled with butts lay on the table murmuring of sin. A second, larger man, bald with a thick mustache, stands with his back to the wall. The smudges on the wall hiss of torment, but the standing man is utterly silent, the smoke from his cigarette mute.

"Sit down." The scarred man's words are a command not an offer.

Abrahim pulls back the steel chair and does as he is told. His hands flutter in his lap like baby birds unable to fly. The man's nose is sharp and veined but not scarred like the rest of his face. His nails are bitten deep, as though he has his own demons he tries to tear out through his fingers.

"We know who you are and what you did, Abrahim," the scarred man growls. His Turkish is from the East, near Mount Ararat where Abrahim was born. His front teeth are crooked and stained yellow from cigarettes. Dark bags sag below his eyes.

Abrahim has a coughing fit, and his shoulders shake even after he stops. He thinks, *God in His infinite wisdom knows, but how do they?* He looks down at his jittering hands and then over at the stocky man inhaling his cigarette, the tip a flash of hellfire. The air is acrid from the smoke, the odor of the two men, and his own foul stench.

The seated man stubs out his cigarette. "Tell us about the murder!" The demon speaking through the man is hideous. "Tell us, Abrahim!"

Abrahim recoils against the chair's back. His soul leaps away from this vile creature but cannot escape the room. There was no *murder.* And, talking about what happened might abate the anguish, might lighten the horrific burden. Words begin to rise from the void in Abrahim's stomach, but fear constricts them in his throat.

"Abrahim," the man says, leaning forward, his hands splayed on the table, those bright bitten nails crossing the folder. "Tell us." The fiendish voice vanishes for a moment and then reappears. "We know everything anyway."

Only God knows everything. Abrahim looks at the man's flat eyes. The man knows not God—only demons. He knows nothing that matters. Abrahim bows his head, calls back his fleeing soul, retreats into it, and says, "Confiteor Deo omnipotenti…"

The man slams his palms on the folder. The ashtray jumps. The table rings—more knell than call to prayer. As Abrahim looks up, the man is rising, lunging across the table. Another demon's voice shouts, "You pissant faggot!"

Abrahim smells onion seasoned with sulfur.

The man bares his stained teeth. "You will die in that cell! A Kurdish pedophile will disembowel you through your asshole!" This is yet another demon's voice, the most fiendish of all. "I'll send you back to that cell right now. Is that what you want, you fucking fairy?"

Despite the blazing words, the man's eyes remain dull. He would do it. His demons would coerce him. But the man himself would take little pleasure in knowing it was done.

"Confiteor Deo…," Abrahim begins again.

"Shut up!" The man cuffs Abrahim's left ear.

Abrahim sprawls from the chair onto the floor, his ear ringing—an alarm he has heard before. When he opens his eyes to the thorns pricking the side of his head, the standing man's shoes are so highly polished that he can see his own blurred reflection. But the left shoe is also scuffed along the sole near the tip. And a shred of cigarette ash lies on the left shoelace. The smell of the ash is different from that of the scarred man's cigarette, but still somehow familiar. The right shoe cocks as though it will kick Abrahim in the face. He knots himself, throws his arms around his head, and squirms away.

"Get up!" It is the swarm of demons within the man at the table. The stocky man has still said nothing.

Abrahim obeys a second time, but his legs are yogurt.

"Sit!"

He slouches into the chair and clenches his hands, trying in vain to regain control. His breath comes in short, sucking gasps like those that occurred after his fits as a child.

"What happened to your fucking eye, Abrahim?" The man fingers the edge of the folder. "Why did the Austrian hit you?"

Abrahim covers his mouth to stop yipping. His lips are dry, but his eyes are watering, stinging more from the shame than the blow. When he licks his lips, he tastes salt and iron.

The man rises from the table, grabs Abrahim by the back of his t-shirt, and twists the collar so that it cinches his neck, burning like rope. Abrahim begins to gag. The man yanks the back of his shirt over Abrahim's head so that the heat of his fear, trapped beneath the shirt, chokes him. The man's fingers, the nubs of his nails, rake his back. "What is this welt?" the demons screech. "How did you get this?"

Abrahim's soul, caught in his constricted throat, wails silently at the memory. When the cave was empty, when Doctor Altay was not there as she had promised, the man hit him in the face, blackened his eye, then made him kneel. And the man clawed his back just before that climactic, always debasing, moment—and just before Abrahim bit down *hard*. But how could the interrogator's demons know all this?

When the scarred man lets go of the shirt, Abrahim lurches forward, striking his head on the table. Still gagging, he raises his face and pulls down his shirt to cover his back. His soul nests in his chest. He cannot look into the man's eyes, but he must face these demons. The shame of what he did is hell, but he did it only to save someone he loves—and he *murdered* no one.

The man picks up the folder and waves it at Abrahim. "Confess." It is the man's voice, not a demon's. "It is the only way you can be saved." Or another demon with a less diabolic tone. "The only way." The man slides the folder across the table. When he pulls a cigarette from his pack, his hand trembles.

Watching the man's hand quaver as he strikes a match and lights his cigarette, Abrahim thinks, *My Lord and my God*. The man's demons are strong and sinister, but they are not the power in the room. They bow to the silent man. He, that large bald man with the polished shoes and the rich tobacco, holds sway over life and death. He alone is capable of immolating Abrahim whenever he wishes.

"Open the folder!" The ghoulish voice returns. "See what you've done!"

The silent man drops his cigarette and grinds it into the linoleum. Abrahim's soul tries to take flight again, but the wailing walls snare it. He can't make his hand stop shaking enough to open the folder.

"Look at what you've done, you fucking fairy!"

Abrahim feels the warm wetness and degradation flowing down his leg.

The man's hands explode across the table and wrench the folder open.

The close-up color photograph of the dead man knocks Abrahim back. He gasps, squeezes his eyes shut for a moment, and then gapes at the rolled eyes and twisted neck. Abrahim gags hot sourness, swallows hard, and scratches at his left eye.

"Look at what you did!"

The wetness pools on the metal seat.

The scarred man swats Abrahim's hands away. "Look at these, you piece of shit!" He spills horrendous photos across the table.

Abrahim can't look. It's too hellacious. He cringes in the wetness. The air is aflame, searing his breath.

The second man, the Power, steps away from the wall. "Who else was in that cave?" he asks. His voice, though not diabolic, is deep and despotic. "We know someone else was there."

Abrahim ignites from the inside out as he realizes that the Power already knows. His chest and forehead are already burning.

The bald man fires a cigarette with a shining lighter. The smoke is stronger but not as acrid, the odor redolent. "Who did it with you?"

Abrahim's hands and feet blaze.

The polished shoes clap across the linoleum. The Power's massive fist strikes the table. "Was it the American, Joseph Travers?"

"No. Not him! No!" The voice is not Abrahim's but his soul's. He himself is incapable of speech. His body is engulfed in flame. "I was trying to save So…Soph…Joseph was leading the bad man to…" He remembers being yanked away after the biting and choking and spitting, a tyrannical voice ordering him to run or die, and his body being heaved from the cave.

The cigarette darts so close to his eye that he can feel its hellfire despite his own conflagration. "Was it Doctor Altay?"

Abrahim leaps to his scalding feet and faces the Power's piercing eyes. "No!" he shouts. "No! No! I was protecting her! Saving her!"

"Tell the truth!" the Power roars. "Tell us what happened in that cave!"

"I…I was…" Abrahim combusts. "I can't remember…" Fires rage in his extremities. "I don't know!"

The Power steps back. His dark eyes widen. He looks from Abrahim's face to his chest.

"She was *never* there…" Abrahim stammers. He becomes Saint Elmo's Fire, crackling, utterly aflame. "I…"

The scarred interrogator lunges *away* from Abrahim.

Sophia must still be saved. Abrahim's chest erupts. The flames turn to lava. "I was alone!" he blurts. "All alone!"

The scarred interrogator's demons shriek. His pulsing fingers point at Abrahim's chest.

Molten heat flows from Abrahim's forehead. "Soph…Sophia must be saved!" His soul's voice reverberates around the room, silencing the walls and even the photographs strewn on the table.

The demons reel from his soul, and even the Power slams back against the wall.

Abrahim stretches his arms out to the sides. Blood spills from his wrists and hands, spotting the floor. His socks turn red. He looks down toward his thundering heart. The crimson stigmata spreads across the white T-shirt.

⚕ 68

The distant hammering barely reaches Joseph Travers in the dimly lit cavern where he studies the text etched into the walls. The words are English, but the syntax keeps shifting. Whenever he is about to grasp meaning, the words transpose and their sense eludes him. Even chanting them aloud is doing him no good. He is neither lost nor back among the bone piles, but meaning escapes him no matter how hard he tries to comprehend the message cut in stone. When Nihat Monuglu's Hulks dropped him back at the Alfina Hotel in Ürgüp, he took off his shoes and dirty clothes, brushed his teeth, and washed his face and arm. He then lay down on his bed for just a moment and found himself scanning the juxtaposing text.

The hammering stops, only to be replaced by a coarse voice that echoes around the cavern, clanging against stone. Light flashes everywhere. When Travers' shoulder shakes, the cavern's walls crumble into dust and his headache thunders back. He opens his eyes to Monuglu's face peering down at him. He doesn't understand Monuglu's expression any better than he understood the message engraved in the dream's wall. The frown is customary, but there's concern as well as irritation in the Turk's eyes—and his eyebrows are arched as though he has just asked a question. The hotel room's overhead light glows behind him.

Dizzy and sweating, Travers rises on his good elbow. He doesn't know how long he has been asleep, but it can't have been long. He's wearing only his boxer shorts so that his mashed toe, singed calf, and stitched thigh are wavering before him. The room's three-drawer dresser and straight-back chair are swaying. Behind Monuglu, the Hulks swerve as though they are the aftershocks of some disaster. They've come for him again, but he has no idea why.

"Get up, Joseph," Monuglu says. His white shirt is wrinkled, and his breath smells like an ashtray.

Feeling bile rise, Travers swallows hard. If he's going to make it to vertical at all, he'll have to move slowly. He shakes his head and says, "Nihat, you've got to stop…"

"Get up, now!" Monuglu shouts in his face.

Travers' head flops back on the pillow. His headache explodes, and light bursts behind his eyes.

His voice lower, Monuglu says, "Joseph, you must talk to someone."

Travers sits up and swings his feet over onto the floor. "I thought," he says, "that talking with me is bad for people."

"Joking with me," Monuglu says, "has not worked good for you before." The usual threat is there, but just as with his eyes, there's something troubled in his voice—concern, misgiving, something. "It's the boy. Abrahim."

Travers sucks in his breath. There's nothing to steady him. "What about him?" he asks.

"The Göreme police found him this afternoon." Monuglu scratches his mustache. "He is in custody."

Travers wonders if Altay knows.

"The boy is bleeding." Monuglu takes his cigarette case from his pocket and then shoves it back in. "Maybe dying."

"What?" The bile's back in Travers' throat. The carpet is about to lurch up and slap him. "They…assaulted him?"

"No!" Monuglu holds out his hands. "He bleeds." He rubs the middle finger of his right hand against the heel of his left. "His hands and feet." He taps his chest. "And his ribs."

"What?" Travers repeats. He can't make the room settle. "Sweating blood?" It takes him a moment to find the word. "Stigmata?"

"Yes," Monuglu says. He wipes his mustache with nicotine-stained fingers. "That's the word the physician used. *Stigmata.*" He waves to Travers. "You must come."

⚕ 69

Sophia Altay sits cross-legged on her prayer rug, unraveling the thick braid in her black hair. Evening's last light slips through the sheered oval above the stone altar, muting the red and gold saints on the wall. She has just pushed the blocking stone into place; the air in the cave, though still, is cool, at least relative to the day. She runs her fingers through her hair. Even though she kept her head covered at all times when she was out, her hair holds a fine grit. Rubbing her palms together, she feels more grit. She is becoming, she muses, a tufa spire, a fairy chimney.

Untangling her hair, like shoveling dirt and chopping vegetables, helps her think. Though she feels safe here, nothing has gone right. The fraudulent documents, especially the digital versions, are already spreading virulently, making her need to authenticate the originals that much more pressing. And Joe missed the rendezvous call at 19:00. The back-up time is still an hour away.

She straightens her spine and inhales, bringing her breath deep into her belly. Given the day's treachery and her understanding of what must have happened to the flash drive she had entrusted to Joe, she has to produce the scrolls immediately. She glances up at the smaller angel hovering at the shoulder of the red-robed saints. There is no clear path, no easy way, even if Joe is all right.

She takes the plastic water bottle from her woven bag lying next to her on the rug. Swirling the water, she thinks about her lack of options. She drinks deeply and then pours thirty milliliters into her cupped hand. When she wipes the grit from her face, her damp hands and face tingle in the dry air. After setting the bottle on the rug, she leans forward, slides her knees under herself, and stretches like a cat.

She pulls the phone from her bag. Although the boy who sold it to her assured her the phone had no global-positioning chip, she still has been very careful. She keeps the ringer off at all times. Even when she is far from the town center of Göreme, she never speaks on the phone for more than a minute. And Joe is the only one who knows the number. When she tried to contact her mentor in Cambridge and the call rang through to voicemail, she left neither message nor number. She last checked for messages after she camouflaged the Puegot but before she began her furtive hike to her cave church. When she flips the phone open, she sees that there is a text message. Reception is nil this far up the escarpment so it must have come in during her trek.

The words knock her back on her haunches. Her breath catches in her throat as she again reads, *Abrahim arrested. Going with Mister Monuglu to see him.* That's it, all of it. She strikes the keys frantically, but there is nothing else.

Taking slow, deliberate breaths, she reads the text a third and fourth time. And then a fifth. If Joe is using the word *mister* without irony, he must also be in Nihat Monuglu's custody. Allowed one message, isn't that the American way? And, Abrahim? *Abrahim arrested.* They will brutalize him, the prisoners if not the police. She still cannot believe that he would kill another human being. He might, if he felt attacked, strike back—but he would never deliberately murder anyone. Whatever he did or did not do, he will never survive in prison. He will never even make it to trial.

Her eyes well. Although she knows she's wholly out of range, she taps out Joe's number and then grimaces at the phone when the call does not go through. She flips it shut and hurls it down on her bag, where it bounces onto the prayer rug. Raking the fingers of both hands through her hair, she glares at the red-robed figures gone blurry on the wall.

☦ 70

As Nihat Monuglu walks briskly past the nurse's station, Joseph Travers limps along at his shoulder. The medical clinic's hallway smells of disinfectant. The nurse's aide at the desk shuffles folders and avoids eye contact. The dark floor tiles are worn, and the walls are green gone to bile.

Monuglu led Travers out of the hotel room without another word, and he has said nothing to Travers since. During the ride in the Mercedes, Monuglu let him text Sophia Altay and did not demand the phone number. Travers looked out the car's window at the vast, spired countryside, the chimneys and ridges and ranges fading into darkness. He thought that Monuglu had been right earlier—he, Travers, had not known what he was saying after the news conference.

He's aware that he has been mistaken about some, probably much, of what has happened. Though the digital translations certainly stirred a media storm, they only aided those trying to discredit Altay. He has been wrongheaded about other things, too—the shadows, the mugging in Selçuk, even Kenan's death. But a sense of what he must do between sundown and dawn emerges through his confusion.

Monuglu pushes the stairwell door open and strides up the stairs. The back of his white shirt is wrinkled, and the heel of his right shoe is scuffed. Travers hobbles after him but can't keep up.

Sweat breaks on the back of Travers' neck by the time he reaches Monuglu in the second-story doorway. "Sorry, my friend," he says, "but I'm not as quick on my feet as I once was." The sweat isn't only from the physical exertion; he's afraid of what he'll see in the next few moments.

"I will enter the room with you," Monuglu says, "but then I will leave you alone with him."

Travers nods. "Nihat," he says, *"why* are you doing this?"

Monuglu scratches his mustache. "The boy has information," he says. "Knowledge useful to the people of Turkey that will otherwise be lost."

Travers looks into Monuglu's dark, tired eyes. "That's not it," he says. "Or not all of it."

"He is a Turk, and only a boy." Monuglu looks away. "We each have sons, my friend."

Travers continues to examine Monuglu's face—the dark stubble from his not having shaved, the flecks of gray in his mustache, and the bags under his eyes. This might be the most deeply honest statement the Turk has ever made to him. "But Abrahim is a murder suspect," Travers says, his voice soft.

Monuglu returns Travers' gaze. "I believe that he is too...weak to have killed the Austrian. He did not cause the death. And, the evidence tells me there was another person in that cave when the Austrian died."

A gaunt orderly pushes a steel and canvas cart carrying soiled bed sheets past them.

Travers thinks about Monuglu's choice of words. "Nihat," he says, "I want to apologize for what I said to the reporters about your altering the documents. Even if you wanted to, you would not have had the time..."

Flames spark in Monuglu's eyes, but he banks the anger. "You jumped to conclusions, my friend," he says. "You Americans do that."

"Yeah," Travers says. "Sometimes we do."

"And that ossuary and its contents belong to the Turkish people."

"Yes, but to the world, too."

"I have read the documents," Monuglu says, "the Turkish versions on the memory stick you gave me."

"They are no threat to the Republic of Turkey."

Monuglu's harsh laughter erupts in three short bursts. "Perhaps not literally. We are, whatever may be said, a *secular* nation." He combs his fingers slowly through his mustache before adding, "But you are naïve. Those in power everywhere will feel threatened by the anti-government rhetoric. And those false documents...they are already being used *politically* by Zionists, Islamists, and Christian fanatics."

Travers takes a deep breath and exhales. "The real letters, *taken together,* aren't a threat to...."

Monuglu snorts again. "Tell that to those who followed you here to Cappadocia. The documents will stir up extremists everywhere. And those in power will retaliate.... Arabs and Israelis. Europeans and Americans..." The bags under his eyes look like bruises. "They are barbarians, all of them. And they are here because of that bone box." Pointing down the corridor, he adds, "Come."

Travers reaches out and touches Monuglu's thick forearm. "I have questions about...about *both* deaths—Kenan's and Günter's. Things I need to know before I see Abrahim. I don't want to jump to conclusions."

Monuglu scowls. "We do not have time."

"Kenan," Travers asks, "he had money on him?"

"Two thousand euros." Monuglu's frown softens to inquisitiveness.

Travers leans his shoulder against the wall. "Weren't there fingerprints on the bills?"

Monuglu's smile is crooked. "Yes. Sirhan's."

"Just his? No one else's?"

"No. No other prints at all."

"And he'd been drinking?"

Monuglu's eyes narrow. "High alcohol content in his blood. And raki in his stomach."

Travers nods. "And Abrahim?" he asks. "You said you do not think he killed Schmidt?"

"The boy," Monuglu says, "he was servicing the Austrian to protect Doctor Altay...and you. To keep him from following you to Altay. He bit the Austrian's schwanz, and the Austrian hit him. Began to beat him."

Travers frowns. "But I had no idea where Sophia was," he says. "I went for a walk because I needed to."

"W...no one, not even the boy, knew that. Americans are not the only ones who jump to conclusions." Monuglu shrugs. "In any case, I have suspicions that the boy was not even in that cave when the Austrian died."

"Then, who killed Günter Schmidt?"

"That is not clear to the police. The evidence at the scene is contradictory."

"What really happened?"

"There's no way to be certain, my friend." Monuglu shrugs again. "Not even the boy knows. But perhaps Herr Schmidt became irrational. In the pain and anger of that moment, perhaps he attacked someone he shouldn't have." He turns and lumbers along the hallway.

Yes…, Travers thinks, *somebody who reacts intensely. Somebody strong enough to overpower a trained boxer. Somebody protective enough of Abrahim to keep Schmidt from further hurting—or even killing—the boy for what he had just done. And somebody smart enough to leave contradictory evidence in that cave.* Lost in thought, Travers waits another moment before following Monuglu. When he rounds the hallway's corner, he sees Monuglu approach Leopold Kirchburg who's pacing at the other end of the corridor. Two uniformed men armed with automatic rifles stand at attention in front of the last doorway.

Travers slows as Kirchburg stomps over toward Monuglu, shouting, "I demand to see Abrahim. He is my employee."

Monuglu tilts his head. "*Was* your employee," he says, his voice even but with, for the first time in his dealings with Kirchburg, the overtone of a superior officer. "You are in no position to demand anything."

Kirchburg's eyes flash. His cheeks, already red, darken further. "I must speak to the boy. Now."

Monuglu pulls his shoulders back and steps closer to Kirchburg. "The boy is in custody. My custody. Only those I permit will see him." He clears his throat. "And you, Herr Doktor, will not."

The two guards stare straight ahead, unblinking.

Kirchburg shakes his long boney finger at Monuglu. "I will have your… I will have you…"

Monuglu cocks his head. "Do not threaten me, Herr Doktor. It is not healthy." He turns to Travers. "Isn't that true, Joseph?"

"Du bist…" Kirchburg rolls his hand and begins to raise it. Then, glancing at Travers, he opens his hand and claws at his beard.

"It's true, Leopold," Travers says. "Definitely. I've finally come to understand that."

"Him?" Kirchburg asks. "You are allowing *him* to see Abrahim?"

Monuglu glowers at Kirchburg. "I have ordered him to. Now get out of my way, Herr Doktor."

Kirchburg's fingers twitch as he turns to Travers. "Find out…," he says. "You will answer to me when you are finished."

Travers shakes his head. "I don't think so, Leopold."

Kirchburg grabs Travers' shoulder.

Monuglu sweeps his arm up, snatches Kirchburg's wrist, and twists.

Kirchburg's hand jerks free from Travers. His torso contorts, and his eyes bug.

"If you touch my friend again," Monuglu whispers to Kirchburg, "I will tear your balls off." He wrenches Kirchburg's arm and shoves him hard.

His eyes wide, Kirchburg stumbles backward past Travers.

Pointing over his shoulder at Kirchburg, Monuglu barks Turkish at the guards. "Come," he then says to Travers. "You must talk to the boy."

⚕ 71

When Travers enters the windowless room, his chest clinches and his heart pounds. The room is stark except for the hospital bed, two monitors, and an IV tree. The air closing in on him smells of antiseptic. Abrahim, lying on his back in a pale-green hospital gown, looks far too much like Jason in the morgue.

"Oh, God," Travers murmurs. "Oh, God!"

White restraining straps cross Abrahim's chest, arms, and legs. Gauze and surgical tape bandage his wrists. The IV shunt runs whole blood from a plastic pouch into the vein in his arm. His head is turned a little to the side. His good left eye and battered right eye are closed; his long lashes and tousled hair make him look seraphic. His dark skin has faded to gray—and it's in this pallor that he is Jason. It is this look of death in a young man that crushes Travers.

Travers clutches the bed's raised metal railing with both hands. Abrahim retreats, diminishing before his eyes. Jason lies unbreathing, lost. Travers wavers. The sweat on his neck chills again. His spine is ice so brittle that he might splinter onto the floor.

Monuglu lays his hand on Travers' shoulder and, his voice low, says, "Seeing me is not healthy for him. I will be outside. You will have the time you need."

When the door shuts, the boy's eyes flutter open, the left more quickly than the swollen right.

Travers does not know what to say, even if he could make his voice work.

The boy's eyes close. His breathing softens, and then his eyes re-open. "Sophia?" he asks, his voice in some distant place.

Travers swallows hard. The boy is at once Abrahim and Jason, alive and dead.

Abrahim's left eye is rheumy and his right bloodshot, as though he has been crying somewhere deep inside himself. There is no fear in his eyes, though, only an immense sadness and loneliness.

Travers knows he will lie to keep the boy alive, but he still can't quite form the words. He reaches out with his right hand and holds it, shaking, just above the boy's left temple. He clears his throat and says, "I know…everyone knows that you did not kill Günter Schmidt. He hurt you…your eye."

Abrahim looks up at the ceiling. "And you," he whispers. "He hurt you."

"And me," Travers says. "But we both know that Saint John was right. Vengeance is empty. It harms *us.*"

Abrahim continues to stare at the ceiling.

"Doctor Altay…Sophia is safe," Travers says. "She sends her love."

The boy's eyes focus on Travers' face, reading the lie. But when he turns his head away, his forehead touches Travers' hand. He doesn't flinch but instead shuts his eyes and presses his head to Travers' palm.

"Abrahim," Travers says, "Sophia is safe for now." He lets his hand settle on the boy's head. "But, yes, there is still danger." As he begins to stroke the boy's hair, his eyes fill. "She needs you." This is both truth and falsehood layered inward farther than he can fathom. He really can't be sure what value, ultimately, Altay will put on her discovery.

Abrahim's eyes open for just a moment before he sighs, his forehead resting once more against Travers' hand.

Travers glances at the monitor screens. Their green lines go on spiking peaks and settling plateaus, but he feels like the boy is being borne away. Not at all sure of what he's doing, he gently turns Abrahim's head, leans over the bed, and cups both hands over the boy's ears. He feels heat in his fingers and palms coming not from Abrahim or himself but from the contact between them. Not knowing what to say, he closes his eyes, lets his mind empty, and surrenders first Abrahim and then, as tremors run through him, Jason. He leans hard on the railing, his life flowing into and through his hands.

The dark room with its sharp odor peels away, and the world, life itself, furls through him. He is on Ayasuluk Hill immersed in birdsong, in the morgue gazing at the discolored corpse of his younger son, by an Arizona creek with hot air clapping all around him. All of it is here and now, not in his hands or in Abrahim's head but within the juncture. His hands no longer shake or tremble. When he opens his eyes, Abrahim is looking up at him.

"Glorificamus Dei," Abrahim whispers.

"Sophia loves you," Travers says. He used the word often with Tom and Jason when they were young, but only intermittently in recent years as things fell apart. And, obviously, in Jason's case, not enough. He had always meant it, but he had no idea what the anguish would be like when he could no longer say it at all. He has not said the word aloud to anyone in months.

Abrahim neither moves nor says anything. His eyes continue to look into Travers' face, not searching but dwelling there.

"Sophia will come to you," Travers says. "Tonight." His—their— plan will have to change yet again, but, whatever else happens, he will ensure that Sophia and Abrahim are reunited. He lifts his hands, which tingle as though they are wet and a breeze is blowing through the still room. He straightens, leans back away from the railing, and takes a deep breath. "Sophia will come," he repeats, "Not right away. But in a few hours." Yes, the plan *must* be altered once more. "She will... She will take you home."

Nodding, the boy says, "Dominus vobiscum."

"Et cum spiritu tuo," Travers answers.

"Ossa," Abrahim whispers. "Sanctus servator ossa."

"Yes," Travers says. "Rest, Abrahim." He glances around the room, knowing that he won't detect whatever electronic bugs Monuglu has planted. "Don't say anything more. I will send Sophia."

⊢⊙⊣ 72

In the clinic's hallway, Nihat Monuglu takes Travers by the elbow and leads him past Leopold Kirchburg. Separated by one of the guards, Kirchburg glares at Travers. His face is florid, and his shoulders are rounded forward as though he's going to implode. Sneering, he says, "Du bist ein toter Mann."

Abrahim's last words still running through his mind, Travers ignores the Austrian. He knows something that not even Sophia Altay does. He also understands what Monuglu admitted to him on the way into the clinic. Everything from the moment he arrived in Istanbul is fitting together—all one event with voices, human words, flowing through it, words both near and far in time and space. The first follower wasn't really the first—only the first Travers noticed. From the carpet peddler at the Blue Mosque to this clinic's technology, it has all been a single moment. He needs to confirm a couple of his hunches, but he already has heard what he needs to hear and possesses what he needs to possess. His strength is that he has no vested interest, that in his isolation, his emptiness, Christ's voice and John's words have spoken to him beyond the bounds of pursuit and profession, creed and country.

Outside the clinic, night has fallen. As Monuglu pushes open the front door, he growls, "Did you learn anything I should know, my friend?"

Travers stops on the clinic's cement stoop. "Yes," he answers. He assumes that Monuglu or one of his operatives heard every word, though probably no one comprehended Abrahim's Latin. "We need to talk."

"True," Monuglu says.

"Abrahim will tell you whatever you want to know if you bring Sophia Altay to him unharmed."

"Doctor Altay is a Turkish citizen," Monuglu says, turning on the sidewalk so that he faces Travers. He raises his palms as though he has been a mere bystander, an objective observer, the last week. "My job is to protect her as well as the antiquities." He scratches his mustache. "As you know, I take my responsibilities seriously."

"Is…was saving Abrahim a responsibility you took seriously, my friend?" Travers asks.

"Yes," Monuglu says. "Absolutely."

Travers smiles at Monuglu, steps from the stoop, and limps along the sidewalk past him toward the parking lot where the Hulks are leaning on the Mercedes and smoking. Stars are spreading overhead, glinting like those of his childhood mountains. Travers' smashed toe sparks with each step, his burn throbs, his stitches itch, his elbow stings, and his head aches, but each breath pulls his sense of being alive through the pain.

As Travers crosses the parking lot, Monuglu takes hold of his shoulder. "Whatever happens, do not," he says, "speak about any of this on television. I…"

"I have no desire," Travers interrupts, "to speak publicly to the media again. Not now…"

"Not even when this is over."

"Not ever." Travers shakes his head slowly. "Nihat, you are my friend. One of the few I have right now. The bones and the documents may cause… But you know that I pose no threat to you or your country or your religion."

"That is true."

Travers reaches over and touches Monuglu's shoulder. "The bones will tell their own story, whatever it is. Just as the letters do." He pats

Monuglu's shoulder gently, almost affectionately. "And *you* will protect and then make public not only the bones but both those letters, too—the original, authentic versions. This, my friend, you'll do."

ⵣ 73

Sitting alone in the backseat of the Mercedes, Travers drinks from the bottle of water Hulk Minor gave him. As the car heads up the narrow cobblestone street toward the Sarihan Cave Hotel, the staccato thrum of its tires over the cobblestones drums pain into his bones. The amphoras in the garden remind him of his debacle at the news conference, but his mind is clear. He has made his phone calls and sent his text messages—and now he is ready to meet Charles Lee in the hotel's lobby. When the Mercedes stops at the hotel's main entrance, Travers leans forward so that his head is between the two Hulks. "Thanks for the ride," he says as he raises the bottle. "And this."

As he hobbles out the car's door, stars gleam above the escarpment the Sarihan is carved into. The air is calm—still hot but no longer oppressive. Voices fall from the terrace, an incomprehensible potpourri of languages. And the smell of roasting lamb reminds him of how little he has eaten.

Lee, standing at the opposite end of the pale stone and wood-paneled lobby, talks with the handsome, square-jawed CNN reporter. Lee turns the moment he sees Travers, stops speaking mid-sentence, and meets him by the front desk. "It's about time y'all got here," he says as he pulls a cell phone—a smart new Samsung model—from his pressed blue jeans' left front pocket.

Travers nods but doesn't say anything.

The desk clerk, another dark-eyed beauty, lowers her head and shuffles papers.

"You've seen the Turkish kid?" Lee asks.

"Hello, Charlie," Travers says. "Abrahim? Yes, as my text said, I have. And Leopold."

"And Altay," Lee says. "What about her?" He rotates the cell phone counterclockwise between his thumb and fingers.

Travers scans the lobby, pausing for a moment to make eye contact with the CNN reporter.

"What about Altay, Joe?" Lee repeats. He squeezes the phone as though it's a hand exerciser.

"I haven't seen her today," Travers says. As always, he'll speak only truth to Lee. "Or even talked with her."

Lee grabs Travers' arm with his free hand. "What in the hell are y...?" He glances at the reporter, tightens his grip, and pulls Travers across the lobby toward a potted palm.

Travers looks into Lee's eyes. "Let go of me," he says quietly.

Lee loosens his grip but continues to stand close to Travers. "But you know where the bones and the letters are?"

"The bones. Yes, I do. The Turkish kid told me."

"They're here?"

"No. Back..." Travers takes a deep breath. "The Turks think the kid might be a goner. And not even Sophia knows the bones' location. I'm the only one." He tilts his head toward Lee. "And that changes things."

Lee leans back and eyes Travers. "It surely does."

Travers lowers his voice. "I'm thinking of making a trade."

"What?"

"You heard me. That Turkish kid, Leopold, all those reporters—everybody wants those bones. The holy relics of the Christ."

Lee squeezes the phone again.

"But like you said in Selçuk," Travers adds, "hell will freeze over before the bones are ever actually authenticated."

Lee nods. "There's no way to prove *whose* bones they are. Not beyond doubt, anyway."

Travers touches Lee's elbow. "But Sophia's scrolls," he says, "the originals, *can be* authenticated."

Lee cocks his head.

"Their value…"

"*If* they're real!" Lee interrupts.

"Oh, they're real, all right, Charlie." Travers glances again at the CNN reporter, who is still standing at the other end of the lobby, feet set apart and hands clasped behind him, staring at Lee and Travers. "And when they're authenticated, they'll be beyond value."

Lee glances from Travers to the reporter and back. "You're not going on TV again!" His whisper is fierce.

Travers scratches his chin. "I didn't come to Turkey to cash in. You know that. But the opportunity…"

Lee waves his index finger in front of Travers' face. "You've got to…"

Travers brushes Lee's hand away. "I know what I'm going to do," he says. "And I know the risks. Leopold already threatened to kill me. In front of Nihat Monuglu."

Though Lee raises his finger again, his voice softens as he says, "You can't do this alone."

"We'll see."

"I can make arrangements."

"I don't want your help." An edge comes into Travers' voice.

"I've got assets."

"No, Charlie. I'm doing what's best for me."

"I get that." Lee glances down at the Samsung he's holding. "But make sure you talk to me. We're on the same side."

Travers smiles. "You've said that before."

"We're in this together."

"You've been telling me that practically since I got to Turkey. And I understand now. Completely. But I'm doing what *I* have to do."

"You've still got to stay in touch." Lee holds out the phone.

Travers looks again into Lee's eyes.

"Here." Lee proffers the phone. "Take it."

Travers shakes his head as he gazes at the phone.

"You need somebody at your back."

"Probably," Travers says, still staring at the phone. "But, no thanks." He reaches into his pocket and takes out his old Amish, which is turned off. "I've got a phone."

Lee rubs his eye with his free hand. "It's a piece of shit. And you never even have it on."

"Yeah. That's a fact." Travers smiles again. "Most of the time I don't even carry it." He nods at the Samsung. "But I'm not taking your phone."

As Lee raises the Samsung, he pats his bulging right front pocket with his other hand. "It's my backup. I always carry a backup." He shrugs. "Y'all know the old slogan: *Be prepared.*"

"I was never a Scout, Charlie." Travers turns, beginning to step away.

Lee thrusts the phone in front of him. "I..." His voice remains controlled, but the tendons in his neck look taut. "You've got to..."

Travers stops and stares at the Samsung.

"Just take the damned phone."

Travers smiles at Lee, the levels of irony in this moment, in Lee's offer and in the phone itself, dancing before him. "Yeah, Charlie," he says. "You're right. Again." He takes the phone and slips it into his pocket. "I promise I'll put it to good use."

⊹ 74

At Ürgüp's outskirts, Travers passes the crumbling wall in which he hid the flash drives. The stones glow in the light of the rising crescent moon. He has made his final calls, and he has left everything but Charles Lee's phone in his Alfina Hotel cave room— his clothes, his belongings, even his wallet and passport. When he reaches a dirt road, he turns and walks from the town's last ambient light into the buzzing night filled with dark tufa spires rising into sky.

Stark, muted beauty spreads ahead of him. The air smells fresh and dry. He is not being followed because, as he understands, there is no longer a need for shadows.

On the dusty trail, shadows of another sort, memories of people, rise about him like apparitions dissipating in the Cappadocian breeze. Thoughts of Jason are twined with those of Tom, of Mary and Christine, of his mother and father and sister, of friends from school and work, and of Sophia and Abrahim, who will, if Travers has finally gotten it right, reunite in a couple of hours. He looks at the moon framed between two fairy chimneys. The moon and stars may be wheeling as always through the heavens, but at this moment they appear still—stuck in the inevitability of their course. *The killing must end,* he thinks. *In the morning. At first light.*

Time swirls and wisps as he walks. Though he is physically exhausted, his breathing is steady; the pain, though persistent, finds a rhythm. Finally, a lone willow looms ahead like a cascade of deeper darkness. As he approaches along the dirt track, something flaps in the branches. Something else scratches against stone nearby. Scant light carves outlines of bushes and sharp rock cliffs. An engine purrs far in the distance.

The figure that emerges from the shadows is small, covered, a woman moving gracefully toward him. "Joe," she says as she touches his forearm.

"Sophia," he answers, and he follows her through the brush, up an incline, and along a sandy path between jutting rocks. As the sinuous trail rises and the land falls away, they climb over boulders and across the face of the escarpment. The trail narrows to the width of his shoulders, vertical rock on his left and vast emptiness on his right. His breathing quickens, and dizziness hovers at the edges of his mind. A long way up, they pause by the low mouth of a cave just before the trail seems to jut into stars.

"Here," she says, touching his arm again. She has not used her customary stealth to ensure that no mark has been left on the trail.

He nods, reaches into his pocket, and ducks into total darkness. When he emerges, he glimpses light in her eyes. She takes his hand as they round the hairpin bend, their faces close to the tufa so that he doesn't have to gaze into the void. He holds tightly to her small, rough hand. He could not have made it this far alone, and no one unfamiliar with the terrain could follow them farther, at least not in the dark.

⊹ 75

Charles Lee and Leopold Kirchburg stand in the unlit parking lot behind a motorbike rental shop. Lee has led the Kraut here to this empty back alley five blocks from either of their hotels because this meeting has to be absolutely private. No rooftop patios this time. In fact, the meeting will have never occurred at all. "That's why I'm making this work," he says.

Though Kirchburg glowers at him, it fizzles in the darkness. "What's in it for you?"

"Nothing." He's got the Kraut by the short hairs again. "I'm giving y'all a shot at the Christ's bones *and* Ms. Altay."

Kirchburg scratches his beard. "There's always *something* in it for you Americans."

Lee ignores the insult—there's too much riding on all this. When he steps out of the shadow of the shop's overhanging roof, moonshine glints on the rim of the Coca-Cola can he holds. "Y'all can save the Aegean Association." He doesn't add, *...and your own skinny ass, too.* "I'm offering you your *only* chance to recover the bones that were in that ossuary. Take it or leave it."

"But you are going to remain here?" The Kraut's words are more an accusation than a question.

"Till morning." Lee nods. "I've got some unfinished business with Joe Travers."

"Where is he?"

"I met him at the Sarihan, but he went back to his hotel in Ürgüp."
The Kraut's academic reasoning skills are about to leap up and bite
him in his Teutonic ass.

Kirchburg studies Lee's face. "Is he…still involved with So…?"

"He's in deep shit, is what he is." Lee swigs his Coke. "Once he
went on TV, he became a target for any lunatic or fringe group. Fact
is, he told me *you* threatened to kill him."

"I did not…"

"Yeah, Leopold, he told me you did." Lee shakes his head. "In front
of Monuglu."

"I…we are all in danger."

"Yes, we surely are," Lee says. "And that's why your Ms. Altay is
running like a scalded dog back to Selçuk for the bones. If you leave
ASAP, you can beat her to Saint John's. The helicopter's waiting." He's
been given an unrestricted budget to ship the Kraut's carcass the hell
out of town so that the Eagle Consortium's business here in Cappadocia can be finished. "You'll get the bones. And Altay will have to
come to you…," he can't help but add, "…on her knees."

Something, maybe a nocturnal lizard, skitters across Kirchburg's
shoe, and he does a quick two-step. "So you are certain," he asks, "that
Soph…that Fräulein Altay is going to Selçuk?"

"Sure as Scheiss." Lee stifles a grin. He's been counting on Kirchburg's obsession with Altay as well as the bones to keep him from
showing a lick of sense. "Earlier, right there in the Sarihan's lobby,
Travers told me that he was going to reveal the bones' whereabouts
in the morning. And he let slip that the bones aren't here. And God
knows there's nothing in this mudhead country between here and
there."

Kirchburg's boney index fingers form a crooked steeple that he
taps against his lips. "And you are sure she…"

"What would y'all do in her shoes?"

Kirchburg's fingers knit, and he curls his lips. "Sophia must…"

"Leopold," Lee interrupts, "you know the truth of what I'm saying here…"

"Die Schlampe…" Kirchburg's voice cracks.

Lee covers his smirk with the empty Coke can. "And what's the only reason why anybody would be heading like a bat out of hell for Selçuk?"

"Die Knocken."

"*Jawohl!*" Lee scratches the side of his nose with the can's rim. "Like I said, I've already arranged the transport. I can get you to Selçuk first. And you can be waiting at the cathedral's gate for your Ms. Altay."

⚷ 76

Sophia Altay climbs on top of her cave church's altar, turns, reaches up through the sheared oval, and hoists herself. She wriggles, dangling for a moment against the night sky, swings her leg up, and disappears. In the cave's sparse light, the embracing saints and hovering angel on the arched ceiling say nothing to Joseph Travers about Altay's abrupt ascent. Her backpack, dark computer, and supplies are all mute. He crosses the cave, kneels on the altar, twists, and looks into the sky. He can hear scratching above him but can't see her on the spire ascending into the darkness. The sky above, the rock all around, and the land far below begin to wheel. When grainy bits of tufa rain on him, he ducks back inside and sits on the altar. Brushing grit from his hair, he waits for the dizziness to subside.

When the scratching and the tufa shower increase, he rises and moves to the center of the cave. Altay's boot appears in the oval, her leg swings down, and she drops onto the altar. A leather strap crosses her khaki blouse. Her eyes are radiant even in the twilight. "I never get used to the rookeries," she says. "There's *nothing* between you and sky." She pulls the strap over her head and lifts the narrow aluminum cylinder from her back. "Now, Joe," she says, "there are two people who know where the letters are." She hands him the tube.

The aluminum is smooth and cool in his hand. He raises his eyes to hers. "Are you ready?" he asks, taking hold of the strap.

Her smile is troubled as she looks down at the tube swaying by his side. "Are you?" When he doesn't answer immediately, she goes over to her supply cache and pulls out a bottle of water and bread wrapped in white paper. As she returns, she says, "We don't have to do it this way."

"Yes, we do," he says. He goes over to the altar and lays the aluminum tube on it. "I do."

As he returns, she twists the cap off the water bottle and drinks deeply. She then gives him the bottle, unwraps the pide bread, takes a round flat piece with sesame seeds, and offers it to him.

"Thanks," he says, "but I'm not hungry." He raises the bottle and gulps the water.

She looks at the pide for a moment, takes a bite, and chews it. After she swallows, she says, "I'm not hungry either," and hands him the bread. "Eat. Please."

He takes the bread with one hand and returns the bottle with the other. The pide tastes of butter and sesame. When they've shared three pieces and finished the water, he asks, "You're good with the plan?"

"It's what we have."

"And the bones, they're worth the risk?"

"You're the one taking the risk!"

He nods, aware that she didn't answer his question.

"We have to see it through," she says. "*All* of it." She stows the bottle and the remaining bread and then roots through her supplies. "I understand," she adds over her shoulder, "that we'll never be able to prove that the relics are Christ's. But people want *something* to believe in. And those beliefs will prove stronger than any scientific evidence."

He sits on the altar below the sheared oval of night sky. But the bones, he thinks, don't say who Christ and his disciples really were. Their words do. It's human thought, preserved in words, that has influenced people down through the millennia—from *Hammurabi's Code* to the *Upanishads* and the gospels and the *Koran* and all the religious and political declarations and manifestos that have followed. "Our words," he says, "mark us as deeply as our bones do. More deeply."

She pulls out the woven red and gold bag she carried when they first had dinner on the rooftop in Istanbul. She places the bag on the altar next to him and takes from it brown paper and twine, materials that remind him of his mother sending packages from Prescott to her family back East. "Maybe they do," she says, but her attention is focused on the task at hand. Without turning from her work, she adds, "Maybe some day, despite all the damage that's been done, the letters will…" She stops unraveling the twine and shakes her head. "I still don't trust him, Joe."

"We have to," he says to her shoulder. Trust has been the issue all along.

She finally gazes into his eyes. "I know," she says. "I know." She shakes her head again and then looks away from him at the faint images on the roof.

He reaches over, barely touching her arm. His eyes are burning, mostly from the tufa dust and lack of sleep. He can't find any light words so he says simply, "Abrahim is waiting. And you've got a long way to go."

She nods without turning again. As she finishes her work, he limps across the cave. He rubs his eyes but can't stop the burning. He has to push hard to roll the blocking stone away from the entrance. Pain throbs yet again. When he's finished, he gazes up at the saints clinging to each other. The hovering angel stares quizzically down at him, as though only a fool would *remove* a blocking stone.

Abrahim shines the flashlight on the sarcophagus, but his hand is shaking and the beam wavers across the carved circle, six-pointed star, and equal-armed cross on the tomb's lid. Unlike those carved on the ossuary he discovered, these symbols appear in a line rather than lie one within the others. The underground crypt at Saint John's Basilica smells more of dust than of decay. The carved stone sarcophagus, about five times the size of a bone box, stands in the center of the eight-by-eleven-meter cruciform area. The ceiling is low, and the walls are eroded brown brick. A shaft of faint early morning light crosses the sarcophagus from the crypt's entrance, but shadows fill the four alcoves where the other, smaller tombs stand. A layer of powdery grit, more tan than red, covers the stone floor.

Herr Kirchburg stands to Abrahim's left. The ubermeister bows slightly, but only because the top of his head would otherwise scrape the crypt's ceiling. He is sweating profusely; his breath makes quick coughing sounds that unnerve Abrahim.

Sophia Altay stands on Abrahim's right. Her head is covered with the blue scarf she wore when she appeared in the infirmary and rescued him just as Joseph prophesized. The bleeding stopped just after, or perhaps even during, Joseph's visit. And then the demonic voices ebbed, the terrifying Power retreated, and time itself whisked away. He floated within a dream, a vision that became a miracle when Sophia, her face covered in blue limned with gold, stood at his bedside. One by one, she released the restraining straps. She stood him, wobbling, and helped him dress in new white pants and a shirt and shoes. The shoulder she lent held his balance. The room's chant was soft, Gregorian, an almost inaudible humming. It was all wondrous, a redemptive moment, but one for a saint, not a sinner like himself.

She held his bandaged hand as they rode through the darkness in a long black car driven by a hairy giant, a bear of a man who smelled like the Power's smoke in the interrogation room…and before. He wept rapturously as the small, droning airplane carried them among the stars above a world dotted with minute lights. His body and spirit borne aloft, he flew beyond thought until they began their descent into İzmir. He then remembered clutching the sacred scrolls he had stolen, huddling through the night in the alley doorway, and quaking with fear—and his tremors returned as the airplane bumped down twice before settling onto the tarmac.

The giant was gentle with both of them and extremely respectful with Sophia as they crossed to an even longer black car parked in the shadows farthest from the terminal. The Aegean whispered rhythmically, but he could not understand her. His tremors increased as he became more acutely aware of where they were headed and why.

At the first light of false dawn, Herr Kirchburg, the ubermeister himself, stood waiting for them at Saint John's Gate of Persecution. Though he was alone, without any of his hellhounds, his presence perturbed Sophia. Their loathing boiled over, and they hurled spite and invective at each other until the giant stepped between them. And then, the three of them—all of them—deferred to him, Abrahim.

He led them through the ruins to the sealed crypt, Saint John's famously empty grave. The giant opened the vault, but, upon Doctor Altay's request, remained above ground to guard against any intruders. And so he, Abrahim, took the flashlight and descended ahead of Sophia and Herr Kirchburg to the resting place he had chosen for these most sanctified and treasured and alarming relics.

Now, Sophia's hands are folded in front of her, and her fingers are laced. Her breathing appears measured, but her face is crushed with ire and her squinting eyes fire contempt at the ubermeister who has, yet again, eclipsed her moment of discovery.

"Achtung!" Herr Kirchburg shouts as he thrusts the black steel pry bar at Abrahim. "Beeil dich!" As always, he is demanding that another do the work under his dictums.

Shivering, Abrahim takes the bar. When he passes the flashlight to Sophia, their eyes meet. Her eyes open to him and gleam, offering permission rather than demanding obedience.

"Geh!" Herr Kirchburg commands. Though the crypt is cool, sweat runs down his temples.

aises the light so that it shines steadily on the tomb's lid,
im jimmies the bar so that the lid begins to slide to the
ting a dark slash between it and the tomb. Herr Kirchburg
s face; his grinding jaws cause his beard to twitch. As Abrahim
the lid another five centimeters, Sophia purses her lips. Then,
enly, Herr Kirchburg is clawing at the lid, yanking it to the side.
Nein, Herr Direktor!" Abrahim yells.

When the ubermeister shoves him out of the way, the pry bar
clangs to the floor, causing a cloud of dust to swirl up toward Sophia's
light.

"Leopold!" she shouts, looking over her light at Abrahim's arrange-
ment of the bones: the broken femurs form a cross within a six-pointed
star, and the skull lies in the center.

"Halt die Schnauze!" Herr Kirchburg screams at her. His eyes are
maniacal. Clasping the side of the sarcophagus, he grins and then
lowers his gangly arms into the tomb.

Abrahim steps forward and raises his hand to his mouth in a silent
scream.

Herr Kirchburg's hands cup the skull, and, as he lifts it, his smile
shows fixation without elation, obsession without joy. The smooth,
rounded bone looks bleached in the light. The mandible and teeth
are missing, and the eye sockets are dark holes. His eyes gleaming, he
stares at the skull as though Altay and Abrahim do not exist. He continues to smirk, his upper lip wet. His voice rasping from the dust, he
murmurs, "Mein Gott," as he struts around the sarcophagus toward
the crypt's entrance.

Sophia steps over and blocks his way. She takes a deep breath and
squares her shoulders.

Abrahim's scream becomes vocal, high-pitched, piercing. He stoops
and scrabbles for the pry bar.

Herr Kitchburg lowers the skull so that its back is in Doctor Altay's
face. "Hau ab, Schlampe," he sneers.

"Fils de pute!" she hisses. She raises her hand until her fingertips
touch the back of the skull. "It belongs here, Leopold." Her hand
trembles. "Give it to me!"

Abrahim rises with the pry bar.

Herr Kirchburg scowls at Sophia, clears his throat, and snarls, "Das ist mein, Schlampe!"

Her jaw set, she stares up past the skull into his eyes.

"Sophia!" Kirchburg yells, his voice a curse. He flicks his hand, striking her cheek with his studded gold university ring.

Doctor Altay's head snaps back. She drops the light and staggers against the wall.

Howling, Abrahim swings the bar fast and hard across Herr Kirchburg's temple and ear. The ubermeister jerks sideways, stutter steps, and begins to slump. His mouth opens, but only a guttural rattle escapes. In the narrow shaft of light from the crypt's stairwell, the ancient skull rolls slowly, as if stuck in time, from Herr Kirchburg's fingers and seems to hang there for a second before plunging to the stone floor and shattering in the dust.

Herr Kirchburg's head and shoulders strike the wall before he crumples onto the floor. Blood is already seaping from the gash above his ear. Sophia stumbles back toward the entrance and braces herself in the doorway as the giant rumbles down the steps behind her. Abrahim falls to his knees, the pry bar clanking in front of him. Still screaming, he looks up at Sophia, then down at the smashed skull, then across to the bleeding man, and finally back to the fragments of bone. His eyes are wide with what he has wrought.

⛭ 78

Though the valley is dark, the tufa spires glow. The wind is rising with the sun, sweeping along the high, narrow trail and ruffling the back of Joseph Travers' collar. Even though he takes quick careful steps, pebbles underfoot tumble down and away toward the valley. The aluminum tube is slung by its leather strap over his shoulder and behind his back. Although he is carrying nothing else and heading mostly downslope, his breathing is short and shallow. His stomach is unsettled, and his eyes are dry and burning. The day is quiet except for the murmuring breeze, the cooing of pigeons in rooks on the cliffside, and his own ragged breathing.

As he rounds a sharp bend, one hand brushing along the tufa to stave off vertigo, he hears scrabbling. Twenty yards ahead, Charles Lee crawls from the low mouth of a cave onto a cramped ledge, pulls himself to standing, and, leaning back against the rock, slaps dust from his jeans with one hand. His other hand holds the cell phone he gave Travers. His Dallas Cowboys cap is grimy, and his brown cotton shirt is stained with sweat and tufa. Dust forms epaulets on the shirt's shoulders. He lifts the phone, glares at it, and then smashes it against the rock.

Stopping ten yards from Lee, Travers says, "I see you found your gift."

Lee flinches, then stares up at Travers, looking first at his face and then at the aluminum tube. He throws the phone off the cliff where it clatters down into silence.

Travers slides the tube around in front of his chest.

Glancing again at the tube, Lee pulls a handheld global-positioning system from his pocket. "Y'all should've known I'd come for that," he says, sneering, his teeth bright even in the day's early light.

"I did," Travers says. "And you really should've figured that I'd know that a phone with a GPS chip is the only sort of gift you'd give me."

Lee looks over Travers' shoulder up the trail toward the bend and the light washing the spires to the east. "You're alone?"

"Yeah. All alone."

"Altay hotfooted it back to Selçuk?"

"I don't know where she is." Once more, Travers will speak only truth to Lee. "She went to see Abrahim." More truth. "And Monuglu was waiting for her." All truth.

"You turned her in?" Lee laughs. He pockets the portable GPS. "If that don't beat all." His face is flushed and sweat beads above his eyebrows, but his eyes hold a hardened certainty.

Travers lifts the aluminum case and waves it so that light glints from it. "I needed this," he says. "And she no longer served a purpose here. That's something you understand, I think."

Lee grins. "I do believe," he says, "you've made the right move, for once."

"Yeah, I have."

In the distance, there's a whooshing like fire rushing through pine trees. Travers glances over his shoulder, where a green-and-gold-striped hot air balloon, vibrant against the pale morning sky, hoves into view five hundred yards away and two hundred feet above the cliff on which the two men stand.

Raising his right hand, Lee curls his forefinger. "Hand it over, Bubba."

Travers grasps the strap loosely. "So that you can destroy the letters?" he asks. His breathing is slowing, becoming less shallow. "I don't think so."

Lee reaches behind his back and pulls a black handgun from his belt.

Travers freezes, his breath catching again. He knew he was headed into harm's way, but he didn't expect a gun. "Charlie," he says, "You don't need that." Pulling the strap over his head and shoulder, he takes a step back.

Lee flicks off the safety and raises the gun so that its barrel points at Travers' face.

A shiver runs through Travers, and sweat forms on the back of his neck and along his spine. He lifts his left hand, dangling the tube over the edge of the cliff. "If you shoot me, this'll go sailing safely down into the valley." His voice sounds more steady than he feels. "And you'll have come all this way for nothing."

The balloon's burner fires again, the noise bouncing down into the valley. "What the fuck!" Lee says as he looks at the balloon drifting toward them. He then waves the gun at the aluminum tube. "Give me that, goddamn it!"

"I will." Travers nods at the gun. "I get that you'll kill me if you need to."

"You've got that right." Lee takes a step toward Travers.

Travers nods. "Your mission gives you license."

Lee's eyes narrow, but he doesn't say anything.

Travers takes another deep breath.

Lee's hand tightens on the gun's grip. Sweat snakes down his cheeks to his chin.

"The Eagle Consortium can't have documents like these come to light." Travers lets the strap slip in his hand so that the case again dangles beyond the cliffside. *"Your superiors…"* He lets the phrase hang there for a moment. "…couldn't have been happy when you screwed up the mission."

Lee's finger dances on the gun's trigger guard. He takes another step forward.

Travers inches farther out and glances up at the tufa spire ascending into the sky. A wave of dizziness breaks over him, and he doesn't dare look down. "Your Eagles need to stop hiring incompetents."

The hardness in Lee's eyes cracks, and the deep blue starts to spark. With the back of his arm, he wipes sweat from his forehead.

"You bribed Kenan to betray Sophia. I saw it eating at him the whole time I was in Selçuk."

Fire erupting in Lee's eyes, he takes three steps toward Travers. "That goddamn drunken bug eater didn't do the job I…"

"Still, murdering him was a critical mistake," Travers interrupts. *"You* screwed things up from the get-go." He shifts his weight so that he's still farther out on the path's periphery. "Was he going to give back the money and tell Sophia about the payoffs for spying on her? And the big payoff for stealing Abrahim's discovery?"

Lee blows out his breath. His eyes harden once more, and the veins in his neck bulge. "Give me the goddamn case!"

"I am." Travers holds up his hand, palm out, almost in a gesture of surrender.

Lee rolls his wrist, the gun's barrel inscribing a circle in the air. Taking another step toward Travers, he raises his left hand to brace his wrist and steady his aim.

As Travers looks down the gun's barrel, the approaching balloon's burner fires a third time.

"Those fuckin' rugheads!" Lee moves another couple of steps closer.

Travers plants his feet. "Actually, they're Brits. Allison Wade and her BBC crew. Shooting us live. And if you pull that trigger, the whole world will see you do it."

Lee looks up into the blinding brightness, starts to raise the gun, and stops himself. His eyes narrow again, but the barrel of the gun, pointing once more at Travers, wavers. "Those letters'll fuck everything up. Everything, goddammit!"

"Did you invoke God's name when you pushed Kenan off that curtain wall? Did you, Charlie?"

Brandishing the gun, Lee shouts, "Yeah, I did. And you're gonna meet that bug eater in hell!" He fires over Travers' head.

Travers cringes as the shot echoes among the tufa spires. He takes half a step back, but there's nowhere to go. "It doesn't have to go down like this," he says, though he can barely hear himself over the ringing. His breath is coming in short strokes that form a sort of chant.

"Like hell, it doesn't!" Lee cocks his head.

"Nihat Monuglu is waiting out at the road. For me. For us."

"That fuckin' mudhead! I'll never let those letters fall into the wrong hands!"

The wrong hands! "There's no way out," Travers says. "Except for both of us... Together..."

Lee's face darkens, and he spits into the dust at their feet. His eyes are sharp slits the color of the Prescott sky.

"All right. Okay." Travers takes a deep breath, loops the strap around his wrist, and raises the aluminum tube, which rotates in front of him like a chrome baton. When he glances over his shoulder, the bottom of the balloon's basket is a brown rectangle within the balloon's bright curve and the infinity of sky. Ravi is leaning out over the rail, aiming his minicam at the two men. Wade, standing at Ravi's shoulder, is waving, crossing and uncrossing her arms above her head. When Travers gazes beyond them into the vast sea of sky, he becomes lightheaded.

Lee points the gun at Travers' face. The tip of the barrel, only six feet away, shines darkly. His finger is on the trigger, but he doesn't squeeze it again. He steps forward and reaches for the aluminum tube with his left hand.

Travers raises the tube so that Lee firmly grasps the other end. As Travers pulls back, his left foot slips on the trail's loose stones. With his right hand, he slaps at the rock wall. His head swims, and his fingers scratch the flaking tufa.

When Lee jerks hard, Travers loses his grip on the tube—but the strap looped around his wrist tightens. If he flicked his wrist and let go, just let go, he would be free and Lee would stumble backward down the trail and step into sky.

The strap burns Travers' wrist as he yanks the tube from Lee.

"Goddamn eegit!" Lee mutters. He wipes the back of his hand across his mouth. When he reaches for the tube a second time, animosity contorts his face.

Travers unloops the strap, raises the tube, looks Lee in the eye, and lets him take the tube.

When Lee takes a step back, his right foot slips on the scree. As the gun fires into the sky, Lee just catches himself on the edge of the precipice. His Dallas Cowboy cap flips off his head and falls toward the valley. He teeters for another moment before regaining his balance.

The balloon continues to close in on the two men. Gasping for air, Travers holds Lee's gaze until the balloon's shadow crosses them. Lee glares at Travers and then turns his face from the encroaching camera's lens. Travers closes his eyes and presses his spine against the rock wall. The inside of his eyelids are a vivid, pulsing yellow and orange bordered with red. The air feels thin in his lungs and fragile around him, as though it might shatter. He takes a series of breaths but can't stop the world from wheeling.

When he finally opens his eyes, Lee is gone. Time unfurls in air blasted with light. This rock wall he is braced against is not the curtain wall at Saint John's, not Hagia Sophia or the Blue Mosque, not a morgue in Chicago, not a quarry in the National Forest outside Prescott. It is simply one of many tufa spires in Cappadocia, a rock rising into sky, as holy or unholy as any other. But he is here, planted, his eyes wide open. The balloon is coasting away, Ravi's camera pointing down the trail. The air eddies, creating troughs and crests.

His hand trembling, Travers takes from his pocket the small digital recorder Monuglu gave him and shuts it off with his thumb. "It's empty," he says. "The case is empty, Charlie." He's standing alone, his body shivering and the tufa scratching his back. He can't yet control his breathing, but he can finally surrender, completely and absolutely, to the present moment.

At first, he doesn't remember the words, but they form gradually like glyphs scrawled across the sky. His breath still comes only in short strokes. "Each…morning…is…my…prayer," he says, his voice staccato. "Every…day… is…blessed." The sun is fully risen. The sky is luminous, the spires across the valley bright. He coughs, takes a breath, and, exhaling, becomes, if only for a moment, the still point between rock and sky.

⌖ 79

The guard in the dark uniform and white helmet, gloves, and spats ushers Travers into the spacious office. Nihat Monuglu sits in a wooden armchair behind a massive hand-carved desk. Behind him, a large window looks out onto Ankara's Museum of Anatolian Civilization's lush garden. Monuglu's blue suit is freshly pressed; his white shirt and red tie are immaculate. He has shaved, but his eyes are bleary, as though he hasn't slept in days.

Without smiling, Monuglu stands and extends his hand to Travers. "It's good to see you, my friend," Monuglu says.

As Travers shakes his hand, he says, "It's good to be here, Nihat." He stands on the plush chamomile and indigo wool carpet for a moment until Monuglu gestures to one of the two matching straight-back chairs at the front of the desk. When Travers is seated, he gazes at the bronze bowl and small bronze lion set on pedestals against the wall to his left. On his right stands a stone relief of a sphinx. He wonders what Monuglu's real office must look like, in what ministry building it's actually located, and if anyone, Turk or infidel, is ever allowed in it. The desk here is clean except for a new brown leather briefcase set far to one side.

"Your accommodations are satisfactory?" Monuglu asks, still with no acknowledgement of what the two men have experienced.

"Of course," Travers answers. The previous morning, he was whisked from Ürgüp in a silver Mercedes driven by Hulk Minor to the Kayseri airport where he was flown in a private jet to Ankara. The driver who met him there, a lean young man in a khaki uniform without insignias, took him directly to the Sheraton Hotel, gave him a keycard, and informed him that he should stay in his room and rest. His suitcase and clothes were already there. Room service was provided, but neither the television nor the internet was working. A somber, elderly doctor performed a perfunctory physical exam and pronounced Travers well and healthy despite his injuries. He was not allowed to leave his room, even for a walk to the hotel's posh lobby.

"Excellent," Monuglu says. "I am glad that you have finally found a place that suits you." This time, Travers catches a touch of mirth in Monuglu's eyes. "And I am pleased that you did not take any of your hikes." He reaches into his suitcoat pocket and removes Travers' passport, wallet, and cell phone. As he lays them on the table in front of Travers, he adds, "You will have some decisions to make in the next few minutes, my friend, but I assure you that you are free to do whatever you choose." He nods to the briefcase just in case Travers hasn't already concluded that the conversation is being recorded. "Your business here in Turkey is, I believe, almost finished."

Travers nods. "Thank you," he says. "I appreciate your hospitality." He slips the passport, wallet, and phone into his pants pockets. "I do, though, need to find out what…" As the office door opens, he looks over his shoulder.

Sophia Altay hesitates for a moment before striding toward the desk. Her pale green dress swishes as she walks, and her green headscarf accentuates her eyes. She sits in the second chair, places her red and gold cloth bag on the floor in front of her, removes her scarf, and shakes out her hair. Only then does she look Monuglu in the eye.

He nods deferentially and folds his hands on the table in front of him. "Welcome, Doctor Altay," he says, but he doesn't smile. "Thank you for joining Mister Travers and me."

"Mister Monuglu," she says. Turning toward Travers, she adds, "I'm happy to see you in one piece, Joe." A small scab mars the swollen cheek below her left eye.

Travers smiles at her. "Intact," he says. "No shards."

"That's good." As she turns again to Monuglu, her eyes flash. "I must know what you have done with Abrahim."

Travers starts, then looks from Monuglu to Altay and back.

Monuglu lifts his hands, waves them as though telling her to slow down, and says, "I assure you, Doctor Altay, the young man is safe."

"I need more than your assurances."

He slides his hands along the top of the desk and then refolds them. "I understand. But first, I must congratulate you on your discovery of the first century ossuary and its contents." He looks at her but does not quite meet her eyes. "And on behalf of the Ministry of Culture, I would like to thank you for your donation of the artifacts to the Museum of Anatolian Civilization. They are quite safe here."

"What have you done with Abrahim?" Altay does not raise her voice, but her eyes are firing.

Monuglu smiles at her and turns toward Travers. "While you were hiking in Cappadocia yesterday morning," he says, "an incident occurred at the archeological site at the Basilica of Saint John in Selçuk."

Travers glances at Altay, but she is still glaring at Monuglu. "An *incident?*" he asks.

"An altercation." Monuglu takes his cigarette case from his pocket but doesn't open it. "I was here in Ankara yesterday, but I have read the various reports." Turning the case in his hand, he finally looks into Altay's eyes. "But the doctor was present. Perhaps she would…"

Altay's eyes are fierce as she shakes her head.

"So far, Joseph," Monuglu says, "the details of the altercation have not reached the attention of the media. But the Director of the Aegean Association, Herr Doktor Leopold Kirchburg, who you have met, was injured severely by one of his employees. The young man Doctor Altay has mentioned. Herr Kirchburg will eventually recover, but…" He turns toward Altay, places the cigarette case on the desk, and meets her gaze. "All of the consequences of the incident are not yet clear." He cocks his head. "It is probable that any charges against the young man will be dropped, but Herr Kirchburg is yet to be convinced that it is in his best interest not to pursue the matter." His smile is genuine. "And, Herr Kirchburg is, as you know, a single-minded man." He shakes his head. "It will take some time, but I assure you that he will *not* press charges."

Altay sits back in her chair, exhales, and looks at Travers.

"Is Abrahim in jail?" Travers asks.

"In custody, yes." Monuglu spins the cigarette case on the desk and then looks up at Altay. "But not in jail. No. There are concerns about his health. The issue now is finding the most suitable situation for him while the matter is resolved. He must be kept out of the public eye but not himself be in any further danger. Something acceptable may be worked out regarding the boy even as we speak." He continues to gaze at Altay as he adds, "But there is also, Doctor Altay, the issue of Charles Lee. His arrest in Göreme."

"*He's in jail?*" Her tone is scornful.

"Yes," Monuglu answers. "He has very powerful friends, but they will not keep him out of a Turkish prison." He glances at Travers and then spins the cigarette case again. "You've seen the video, Doctor Altay?"

"Of course," she says, gazing at Travers. "It's all over the television and internet." She looks again at Monuglu. "And it completely exonerates Joe, despite that Fox News merde about Charles Lee, devout Christian and patriotic American, trying to recover the documents from the madman who stole them." She gazes again at Travers. "In fact, many of the reporters, especially that BBC woman, are turning you into something of a hero, except, of course, that you've disappeared." Her smile is ironic. "Or, *because* you've vanished."

Travers sits back, looking from Altay to Monuglu.

Folding his hands over his cigarette case as though he is hiding playing cards, Monuglu says to her, "It seems Joseph shuns attention. A good idea for everyone involved. Still, he has been...*associated*... with two deaths here in Turkey. But he is not responsible for either... What is the English phrase? *Correlation, not causation.* I have already informed him that he is free to do whatever he chooses. And, Doctor Altay, he has decided not to speak with anyone in the media."

Altay sits up straighter. "Where," she asks, her voice tight, "is Abrahim? I traded the letters for his freedom."

His hands still folded, Monuglu cocks his head, gazes at Altay, and says, "In point of fact, you offered those documents freely to the Ministry of Culture for their safekeeping and authentification. Did you not?"

"I did, Mister Monuglu," she answers, practically spitting the words across the table.

"And are the museum's experts already verifying that *your* versions released to the media are the authentic documents?" Monuglu's tone is conciliatory, but his eyes have hardened.

"Where is Abrahim?" Altay hisses.

Monuglu waves his hand vehemently at her. "Answer my question, please, Doctor Altay."

Altay swipes the right side of her face with her hand. "Yes," she snaps. "Yes. Yes."

"And did not the boy then attack Herr Doktor Kirchburg at Saint John's archeological site? Injure him severely?"

"Only to protect..." Altay stops speaking. Her eyes blaze. "Pharisee! You...!" She curls as though she is going to leap across the table.

Travers puts his hand on her shoulder, but she shakes it off.

Her eyes unblinking, Altay turns on Travers. "Joe, I..." She chokes on her anger. "I trusted you."

Travers gapes at Monuglu, who squeezes his cigarette case. The vast frozen emptiness that has too often suffused his life spreads, crackling, from his chest. "No, Nihat," he says. His voice is brittle. "Don't do this."

Monuglu opens his hands, palms upward, but not apologetically. "Something must be done about the boy," he says as he balls his hands into fists.

For a moment, Travers doesn't breathe. A cold sweat breaks along his back and neck. "Nihat, you… I… We agreed."

Monuglu waves a thick hand to silence him. "Doctor Altay," he says, his voice low, "you must still trust Joseph. Much is at stake here."

Altay stands and throws her bag over her shoulder. "Merde," she mutters, shaking her head and glowering at Monuglu. "Merde!"

Monuglu stands, too, and presses his hands on the desk as though he will spring across it. "Doctor Altay, you misunderstand."

Travers steps between them and lays his arm over Altay's shoulder, feeling her ferocious energy. As she tries to pull away, he grasps her more firmly. Outside the window behind Monuglu, midday sunlight dapples the garden.

"Joseph," Monuglu says, still looking at Altay rather than at him. "I am your friend."

"Merde!" Altay shouts. She reaches up and yanks Travers' arm from her shoulder.

Monuglu doesn't respond to her. The three of them stand there for a moment, a trinity fixed and unwavering.

"Joseph," Monuglu says again, "do you remember the promise you made to me about your actions when these events were finished?"

"Yes."

Altay continues to stand stiffly.

"And you will ensure that your friends honor that pledge, too?"

Travers glances at Altay who is glaring at Monuglu.

"You take responsibility?" Monuglu's eyes have not left Altay's face.

Travers gazes at Altay's feline eyes, her thin nose, and her tapering face. At her hair tumbling over her scarf. "For not speaking about what's happened, yes, Nihat," he says softly to Altay.

"In Göreme *and* Selçuk?" Monuglu asks.

Travers looks at Altay's shimmering agitation. "Yes," he says, "as long as we can talk openly about the artifacts, the bone box and its contents."

"Acik!" Monuglu shouts at the closed door across the room.

Altay turns toward Travers. The tension in her body doesn't slacken, but her gaze is more quizzical than irate.

"This meeting is over," Monuglu says more loudly than necessary. He nods to Travers and Altay and then at the door. "You are both free to go." He then adds under his breath, "Do *not* say another word. Nothing."

The office door is opened by the uniformed guard who escorted Travers from the museum's entrance. Abrahim stands next to him. His shirt and pants are pale, clean, and a little too large for him. He looks into the room until his eyes meet Altay's, but he doesn't step across the threshold.

"Go," Monuglu says. "Both of you."

As though he has been forbidden to do so, Abrahim still does not enter the room. His feet take small steps without moving forward; his hands flutter. His mouth opens but emits only a low murmuring. Tears stream down his face.

Altay bumps the chair as she turns away from Travers and hurries toward the door.

Travers looks at Monuglu, whose expression is impassive. "Thank you, my friend," he says.

Monuglu's nod is barely perceptible.

Altay's dress rustles, and then, for a moment, there is no other sound but Abrahim's murmuring. Monuglu leans forward, his hands rooted on the desk, watching the woman gather the boy in her arms. Travers nods to Monuglu and then follows Altay. He pauses ten feet from the door when Abrahim raises his head and lifts his eyes to the ceiling. The boy's glistening face catches light from the garden window.

Jay Amberg is the author of eleven books. He has taught high school and college students since 1972. Contact him at jayamberg.com.

FICTION AMBERG

Amberg, Jay.
Bone box

SOUTHEAST
Atlanta-Fulton Public Library

26 August 2015